P9-CEX-649

Death in Paris

Death in Paris

EMILIA BERNHARD

NEW YORK

This is a work of fiction. All of the names, characters, organizations, places, and events portrayed in this novel are either products of the author's imagination or are used fictitiously. Any resemblance to real or actual events, locales, or persons, living or dead, is entirely coincidental.

Published in the United States by Crooked Lane Books, an imprint of The Quick Brown Fox & Company LLC.

Crooked Lane Books and its logo are trademarks of The Quick Brown Fox & Company LLC.

Library of Congress Catalog-in-Publication data available upon request.

ISBN (hardcover): 978-1-68331-768-5
ISBN (ePub): 978-1-68331-769-2
ISBN (ePDF): 978-1-68331-770-8

Cover design by Lori Palmer
Book design by Jennifer Canzone
Map by Wikimedia Commons / Public Domain
Floor plan image by Emily Bernhard Jackson

Printed in the United States.

www.crookedlanebooks.com

Crooked Lane Books
34 West 27th St., 10th Floor
New York, NY 10001

First Edition: October 2018

10 9 8 7 6 5 4 3 2 1

For Jennifer Piddington

she may not know who I am, but she knows what I do.

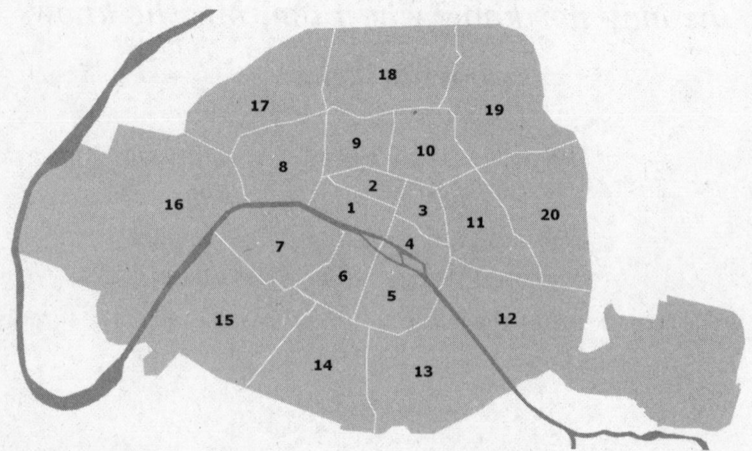

The *arrondissements* of Paris

Chapter One

"Edgar Bowen died in his soup," Rachel Levis said to her husband, looking up from her newspaper. They were just finishing breakfast, and the table was crowded with jams and mugs and the bag that had held the morning's croissants, now flattened in the center with some buttery crumbs still resting on it.

"His sleep, you mean." Alan tapped something on his tablet, frowning. The morning light of Paris made an aureole around his dark head.

"No, his soup. It says here in the *nécrologie*." Rachel rattled the pages of *Le Monde* at him across the table, then read aloud, "'Monsieur Bowen died, dining alone at home yesterday, after falling facedown into his soup.'"

"Oh, dear," said Alan absently. He shaded his tablet with one hand.

"'Oh, dear'? That's all you say?"

He lifted his eyes from the screen. "Oh, dear! Someone we don't know well and only hear of because he's also an expat has died in a laugh-worthy way! The world is a poorer place!" Alan made an "ooh" face, then licked an index finger and used it to pick up some crumbs. "Now, can I worry about the fact that the dollar is up?"

Rachel returned to the paper, hoping her face expressed disdainful hauteur. She would tell her best friend Magda when they met later. Magda would grasp the significance of the news.

* * *

"Edgar Bowen died in his soup," Rachel said to Magda as they sat in Rachel's kitchen later that day. The sun still streamed through the windows, belying the January cold outside.

"His sleep, you mean," Magda said.

"No, his soup. It was in the paper this morning. He had a heart attack, fainted face-first, and drowned."

"Oh, dear."

"Exactly." The two women's eyes met. Rachel had known Magda would understand. They had been friends for some twenty years, once girls alone in Paris who had each been grateful for a like-minded soul; now middle-aged women who were in the rare position of having witnessed all of each other's adult lives. Among other things, this meant that Magda knew Rachel had once been Edgar Bowen's girlfriend—knew that, in fact, Rachel considered her two years with him her first grown-up relationship. She thought for a minute, then said, "He was a good man."

"Yes." Rachel made the word definitive. "He was."

"He gave you that money to lend me right away that time, remember? And he never asked what it was for."

"I remember." Rachel half-smiled. "Just as well, when you consider . . ."

Magda gave a soft snort. "We were so young." Her voice was rueful. "Did we know we were that young?"

"No." Rachel shook her head. "You always seem old to yourself, no matter how young you are. Insight only comes in retrospect."

Magda put her hand over Rachel's on the table for a second. Then the past faded, and she took a sip from her mug. "What did Alan say?" she asked carefully.

"'Oh, dear.'"

"That bad?"

"No, that's what he said. He said, 'Oh, dear.' He didn't seem even to remember Edgar, never mind knowing who he was."

"Oh." Magda considered. "Well, in a way that's good." Long ago, Rachel had explained to her that Alan was a man tortured by overwhelming jealousy. He'd once become wildly angry at the mention of an early boyfriend, and Rachel had never dared to mention another. In light of that, it was probably fortunate that Edgar Bowen's significance had escaped him.

But even the thought of Alan's fortunate ignorance couldn't distract from the *un*fortunate manner of Edgar's death. "What a way to go." Magda shook her head ruefully. "You have to ask yourself which is worse: the fact of the death or the form it took?"

"For him or for us?" asked Rachel.

"Either, I guess. Or both."

Rachel thought about it for a minute. "For us, the death, surely. But for him, the form."

Magda looked puzzled. "How do you work that out?"

"Well, he's dead, and that's a loss for us, but he doesn't know about it, since he's dead. But now whenever somebody hears about it, they're going to say, 'In his sleep, you mean,' or, 'In his *soup*?'" She shook her head. "And that's a terrible way to be memorialized. Now he's forever The Soup Man." Her tone capitalized the last three words.

"Oh, I don't know," Magda countered. "He was kind; he was thoughtful. I remember him as gracious. I think he'll be remembered as more than The Soup Man."

Rachel thought of Edgar's tenderness with his son, David—the care and seriousness with which he had listened to a four-year-old's monologues and answered his questions. She thought of his patience with his ex-wife Mathilde, with whom he'd managed to carve out an equable relationship despite her being, as Rachel remembered, one of those French women who looked down her long nose at lesser mortals. Yes, he had been kind; he had been thoughtful. Maybe he would be remembered for more than soup.

"Well," she said, "I'll be able to let you know how his reputation stands—at the moment, at least—because I'm going to go to the funeral on Thursday."

Magda reached for a madeleine, nibbling at its golden cakiness with relish. "I'll go with you." She wasn't one to miss out on a bit of excitement.

Chapter Two

The outer arrondissements of Paris are crowded with *funérariums,* French funeral homes. They are all small, formal places, nondescript outside, stuffed with oppressively comfortable furniture inside. Edgar Bowen's funeral took place at one in the fourteenth arrondissement, in a room that Rachel was willing to bet the promotional pamphlets described as *soigné*—dignified—but which was, in fact, soulless. She supposed this was appropriate, considering its function. Spaced along its taupe walls were dark urns holding arrangements of inoffensive flowers; cushioned taupe chairs stood in rows on taupe carpet. The whole effect was that of a particularly sober conference center—but again, that wasn't altogether inappropriate.

She craned her neck to see better from her seat beside Magda in the back of the room. Edgar's son, David, sat in the front row, his mother on the chair next to his. Rachel hadn't seen either of them for twenty years, and she was surprised to find that the sight of Mathilde instantly called up a memory: a sunny morning early in her relationship with Edgar, when, eating a croissant in the kitchen in her hot-weather uniform of cutoff shorts and a man's sleeveless undershirt, she had been surprised by an as-yet-unknown Mathilde, cool in a linen sheath and high-heeled sandals. She remembered the way Mathilde had looked at her as she leaned on the countertop, the croissant flakes falling on the tiles beneath, the way she had passed through to the *séjour* and said to Edgar in English just loud enough to be overheard, "Your new cleaner is very young, isn't she?" Watching Mathilde now in her navy suit and topaz scarf, her nose tilted to indicate her superiority, Rachel knew that although David might have, astoundingly, evolved from a chubby four-year-old into a skinny young man, his mother hadn't changed one bit.

The funeral was decorous, with discreetly regretful eulogies delivered by the head of the bank at which Edgar had worked and by his oldest colleague at the same place. Everyone stood while the glossy coffin slid between the curtains that hid the crematory. When David walked up the aisle and out the door afterward, his eyes and nose were very red, but he had not been crying. Edgar Bowen hadn't been a man for lavish displays of feeling, and his funeral and son seemed determined to reflect that.

After the service there was a reception. Edgar had known many people—in fact, Magda commented to Rachel later, if you spoke just in terms of the haute bourgeoisie of Paris, Edgar had known everyone. The room was crowded with men in expensive sober suits and women in equally expensive sober dresses, the French distinguishable from the other nationalities only by the fact that their clothes were better cut. Rachel couldn't bring herself to go offer condolences to David, imagining the awkwardness of reintroducing herself to him and making stilted small talk. And she certainly didn't want to deal with

Mathilde. Instead, she moved from group to group, her head down and a camouflaging glass of wine in her hand, trying to hover discreetly. Since she and Magda knew none of the other attendees (Alan had been right about their lack of connection to Edgar's world), there wasn't much else to do. It wasn't that she wanted to eavesdrop; she just felt acutely her distance from Edgar and his life after her, and she thought that discreet listening was the easiest way to bring her closer.

Currently, though, discreet listening was only bringing her closer to people exclaiming in French or English, "In his *soup*?" She completed her circuit of the room, knowing nothing more about Edgar than that those who attended his funeral found his way of dying as ridiculous as her husband did. Pausing for a second, she stood beside a cluster of impeccably dressed women. Their hair was the curious shade of streaky ash blonde so loved by middle-aged French women, and each wore a muted scarf carefully draped over a black or navy sheath.

"Dans sa soupe*?"* one with a gray scarf asked, in French this time.

"Yes." Her companion, wearing a pale pink scarf and navy dress, looked grave. There was a pause to show proper respect; then a woman with a pastel, patterned scarf spoke up.

"What sort of soup?"

"A *vichyssoise*." The woman in the navy dress leaned forward slightly. "Made that afternoon."

The others clucked, shaking their heads. A good soup spoiled by a bad death.

One asked, "Is it true he fell face forward into it?" She smoothed her neutral-color chignon as if protecting it from imagined splashing.

"Mais oui!" The second woman nodded. In every group, Rachel had noticed before, there was always one member more in the know than the others, mysteriously granted extra knowledge to dole out with a lowered voice and significant glances. Navy Dress was clearly that member here. "They say he had a heart attack and fainted. It was his *maître d'hôtel*'s night off, so there was no one to revive him. Still, they say if it hadn't been for the soup, he might still be alive. I was told he was found facedown in the bowl." She shook her head. "His hand was only a centimeter or two from knocking over his bottle of rosé."

Rachel gasped involuntarily, then covered her mouth and looked studiedly away, hoping the women hadn't noticed. She searched the room for Magda. Spotting her at last, standing in a corner talking to a dark-haired man in a navy suit, she wove her way through the throng and grabbed her elbow. "We have to go."

"What?" Magda turned away from the man.

"We have to go," Rachel hissed. "We have to go *now*." She smiled apologetically at the man.

"Excusez-moi." Magda also smiled at him, but awkwardly. "My friend feels sick, and we need to leave. *Pardon*."

The man raised his eyebrows slightly over his sharp nose. Still, he gave an obliging half bow as Rachel hustled Magda toward the door.

"God, what are you doing? What are you doing?" Magda struggled to free her arm. "Ow! What's the hurry?"

"I heard something."

"What do you mean, you heard something?"

"Wait." Rachel handed their tokens to the coat-check girl.

She didn't speak again until they were out on the sidewalk, a few yards from the funérarium. Then she stopped and faced Magda. "I'm sorry. But I didn't want to say anything until we were a safe distance away."

"Away from what? What is it?"

"It's just . . . well, I was listening to some people on the other side of the room from you, and a woman said Edgar had been drinking rosé with the vichyssoise he drowned in."

"Rosé with vichyssoise?" Magda's tone made it plain that she had no idea what was going on. "Well, it wouldn't be my choice, but I don't see why it's alarming."

"No!" Rachel spoke through gritted teeth. "You don't understand. Edgar never drank rosé."

"Oh come on. Never?"

Rachel shook her head.

"He wouldn't even have settled for it if there was nothing better in the house?"

"He always had something better in the house." Rachel's tone was explanatory. "He hated rosé. He said it was a good white spoiled."

Magda snorted. "Not bad. It's a play on Mark Twain, you know. He said golf was a good walk spoiled."

"I know what it is. That's irrelevant. The point is, something is wrong here."

"Where?" Magda was lost.

"*Here.* With Edgar's death."

"Okay." Magda held up a hand. "Calm down. What's wrong?"

Rachel thought for a long minute. "I don't know." She thought again. "I don't know." Then her voice firmed. "But something is. Something feels strange."

Magda sighed. "'Something feels strange'? That's like saying a thing is off. It's not much to go on."

"But I don't have much to go on! And a thing *is* off."

Magda looked at her. Rachel was usually the calmer of the two, but now her face was a picture of confusion and disquiet. "I'll tell you what." Magda settled her coat around herself. "Why don't we try having coffee and talking about it? Let's see what happens if we sit down and focus."

In Paris you are never more than ten yards from a café—good, bad, or simply open. They turned into the nearest one, grateful for its warmth, and slid into a table next to the plate glass front windows. In the summer, Rachel knew, these would be pulled back so that customers could sit on a *terrasse*, chattering and smoking in the warm air, but in January the glass offered the best of both worlds: a full view of the outside with the warm climate control of inside.

When a waiter deigned to come and take their order, Rachel asked for her usual hot chocolate and a coffee for Magda. As he headed off, she sighed with pleasure, looking around at the gleaming wood and pushing her feet against the springy carpet. What country besides France so understood the necessity of comfort when taking leisure? Indeed, what country besides France so understood the necessity of leisure itself?

"All right." Magda too gave a small settling sigh. "Tell me what you think is going on with Edgar. More than just 'something strange.'"

Rachel bit her thumbnail. What she'd experienced was a lightning bolt, a sudden knowledge that what people believed had happened not only wasn't what had happened but couldn't be. It was hard to unlock the unconscious logic behind such instant certainty, but Magda was right: if she wanted her feeling to be anything more than an interesting intuition, she needed to be able to explain how she could be so certain.

"Well," she started carefully, "first there's the rosé. Edgar didn't just have a mild dislike of it; he had a real, determined antipathy. He wouldn't allow it on his table."

"Okay, that does make its presence weird," Magda said. "But it doesn't obviously suggest anything more."

"Then there's also the fact that . . ." Rachel scowled in concentration. "I know the way he died is amusing, but it's only amusing because it's so freakish. This has been bothering me since I read his obituary. How often do people have heart attacks and drown in soup? The fact that it's so bizarre indicates that it's out of the ordinary, not the norm. But what if it's not the norm because it's not *normal*? What if something abnormal happened to cause his death? Do you see what I mean?"

Magda nodded and frowned at the same time. "Yes, *I* see it. But again, it's not obvious. Do you have anything else? Anything more concrete?"

Rachel began groping for a train of reasoning. "Edgar was in very good shape when I knew him."

Magda smirked.

"No, I don't mean that. I mean, he ate well, but he ate carefully. And he went to the gym—and that was before there were any gyms here."

For a moment the two women reflected on the Paris of twenty years before, gymless and untouched by fat-free food.

"Yes," Rachel went on, "he'd gotten a bit thicker with age. Who hasn't?" She glanced down at her just-arrived hot chocolate. "But I did see him at parties every now and again over the years, and he never looked heavy or out of shape. And the obituary didn't say he'd had any previous health problems. And I know, I do know that people have freak heart attacks"—she took a continuing breath—"but like I said, they're rare. And the heart attack from nowhere, the soup, the rosé—the details just don't fit."

For a long time Magda said nothing. Rachel looked out the window, watching the street. People walked past, their chins buried in their collars and scarves as they tried to avoid the cold, but one woman clicked by in a mini-skirt and three-inch Christian Louboutins—Rachel could just see the red soles. The woman wasn't wearing any pantyhose. How could she bear it? The winter winds of Paris were cuttingly cold, and even when the air was still, it could still be icy. Yet women like these were all over the city, exposing their perfect knees (Parisian women had wonderful knees) to the frost. She felt her own thick black tights insulating her shins and once more gave thanks for good old American level-headedness.

At last Magda took a breath. "Okay," she said. "Okay." She exhaled fully. "You know, F. Scott Fitzgerald died of a heart attack."

"F. Scott Fitzgerald was a drunk." Rachel stopped looking outside. "Edgar wasn't a drunk. That's my point: a drunk is the sort of person you'd expect to have a heart attack."

"No, that's not what I'm saying."

"Then what are you saying?" Rachel snapped. She was in no mood for literary discussion.

Magda filled her voice with patience. "I'm saying that everyone thinks Fitzgerald died from being a drunk, but he actually died of a heart attack. Given his habits, alcoholism was the logical conclusion, but they did tests and determined it was a heart attack. A myocardial infarction." She lingered pleasurably over the words, then drew another breath. "I'm saying they didn't stop at the obvious conclusion."

Whatever line of reasoning Magda was following, it was lost on Rachel. "So what?"

"So, it's only been two days since Edgar died. There hasn't been time for an investigation, which suggests the police did stop at the obvious conclusion. But *you're* not stopping there. And your points might seem irrelevant, but they're valid. If he *was* in good shape, how did he have a heart attack? If he hated rosé, why was it on his table? I'm saying that when you look at it your way, it does sound like something more than a farcical freak accident. I'm saying . . ." She drummed her fingers on the table. "I'm saying something feels strange."

Rachel relaxed. She knew from long and sometimes painful experience that Magda wasn't one to soothe out of politeness: if she said Rachel's reasoning seemed plausible, it seemed plausible. "Well what should we do?" She leaned in, pitched her voice low. "Should we go to the police?"

Magda shook her head. "No."

"No? Why not? This is the kind of thing they're meant for."

Magda sighed. "Yes, but just picture it. You go in, and you say, 'Excuse me, Mister Policeman—' "

"*Monsieur* Policeman."

" 'Excuse me, Monsieur Policeman. My former friend supposedly drowned in his soup near a bottle of rosé after a freak heart attack, but when I knew him twenty years ago, he hated rosé and was in excellent health. I haven't really spent any time with him since then, and I know people's tastes can change, and, no, I don't have any actual evidence, and the body has been cremated so we can't check, but—well, a thing is off.'" She looked at Rachel again, eyebrows raised.

Rachel pursed her lips. "I see your point."

They both sat thinking. Then Magda said, "But you know what we could do?" She held a breath, bit her lower lip. "We could investigate it ourselves. Oh my God!" A flush suffused her pale brown skin and her curls practically vibrated with excitement. "That would be so much fun! It would be like Holmes and Watson, or Commissario Brunetti and Vianello, or—or those other two—"

"Nick and Nora Charles," Rachel said.

"Nick and Nora, yes!"

"No." Rachel's voice was flat. Magda always became alarmingly eager when her interest was sparked, and after twenty-two years of friendship, Rachel knew it was best to defuse her as quickly as possible.

"No?" Magda looked crestfallen. "Why not?"

"Because Brunetti and Vianello are actual policemen, and Sherlock Holmes was a private detective, and Nick and Nora Charles were connected with the police. We fit none of those categories: we have no training or protection."

"But it would be fun!"

"Only until one of us was shot." Rachel took in her friend's disappointed face. "Seriously, I don't have any relationship here. As you pointed out, I'm just a former friend of the dead man. Even Nick and Nora Charles had some connection to the crimes they ended up detecting. Without any link, we have no way in and no way to investigate. And we don't even really know what we'd be investigating! So, no." She tried to mollify her: "Besides, as you said, there's probably nothing to investigate. Maybe he's just a man who'd come to like rosé and had a heart attack. Coincidence."

"Yes, okay." Magda sighed. "You're right. I just liked the vision of us detecting. Going around the city, looking for clues."

"Well, I'll tell you what." Rachel patted Magda's arm and spoke as if to a child, trying to get her to smile. "The very first suspected murder that one of us has a real, tangible connection to—we're on it. I promise."

"Well, if you promise." Magda's lips twitched, and Rachel wasn't sure who was patronizing whom. They slipped on their coats and headed out into the chill air.

"You know, *I* always thought F. Scott Fitzgerald died as a result of being an alcoholic," Rachel said as the door closed behind them.

"No." Magda shook her head. "Though that's what everyone thought in the moment too. The night before he died, he had some kind of precursor attack inside a movie theater and said to his girlfriend, 'They think I'm drunk, don't they?'"

"His girlfriend?"

Magda nodded. "Sheilah Graham. She wrote a book about it."

"How do you know these things?"

She shrugged. "I listened to a podcast."

They went down the steps into the Métro.

Chapter Three

Rachel's Métro car was warm with the heat of many bodies crowded together. Across the aisle, a young blonde woman perched on the edge of her seat, her open face and shining cleanliness instantly marking her out as American. The girl's wide eyes, the drowsy air, and the funeral service just passed combined to draw Rachel back to her own first experience of Paris, when she had been as wide-eyed as that girl, and as unable to believe that she—not Audrey Hepburn, not a girl in a Henry James novel, but ordinary, brown-haired, real-life Rachel Levis—was in Paris.

There were two sure ways to become an American expatriate in Paris, she thought to herself. The first was to arrive as a young adult—often the summer after college, usually on a temporary work or study visa—to fall in love with the city, and then to just stay: there were English language schools eager for teachers, or families who wanted au pairs, and various other ways to make a living (if not a luxurious one) for many years. This was how she had come. Fresh from graduation, she had been on a two-month, total-immersion, French-language summer course. She wanted to be a writer—Paris is full of Americans in their twenties who want to be writers—and, drunk on Hemingway and Colette, she wanted Parisian experiences to write about. She did all the things ingénues do in the City of Light: browsed cozily at Shakespeare and Co. and thought how a scene of a young girl browsing cozily at Shakespeare and Co. would be a wonderful opening for a novel; sailed in a *bateau mouche* on the Seine and thought how romantic it was to be in a bateau mouche on the Seine; and had an affair with a soft Parisian youth who, although he looked nothing like Jean-Paul Belmondo in *Breathless*, was foreign enough to make her feel sophisticated.

Now, twenty years wiser, she knew that such adherence to cliché usually leads to disillusionment when reality sets in. In her case, though, it had not. Somehow, while she had been experiencing the sights and sites of other people's fiction, the real Paris made its way into her bones. Riding the Métro from bookstore to cathedral to museum, she had become enchanted by the blinking light that counted off the stops on the maps in the Métro cars. Getting thoroughly lost while trying to wander the *rues* romantically in the rain, she had begun to enjoy the monochrome palette of soggy Paris: the gray sky over gray sidewalks facing gray streets came to seem not a sweep of dullness, but a worthwhile lesson in the possible shades of a single color. All those who choose Paris love the city more than any single thing about it, and this had become true of her. By the end of the summer, she rejoiced in Paris for what it was and found she couldn't bear the thought of leaving it.

She remembered the tiny room she'd rented on the top floor of an elevator-less building in the sixth arrondissement: freezing in winter and boiling hot in summer, but with a view of the tip of the Eiffel Tower. A cluster of low-paying jobs just kept her afloat, and late at night she sat at the small table stuffed into her small room and wrote the poetry she was just beginning to find central to her life. She was happy. So she stayed.

The man in the seat next to her shifted position, and his movement knocked her out of her reverie. The train slowed. The girl across the aisle must have recognized her stop, because she smiled and stood up. At the sight of the fanny pack clipped around her waist, Rachel thought of the second way to become an American expatriate in Paris: to be posted there by whatever wealthy institution you worked for—bank, legal firm, government entity—and be so successful that they never called you home. That was how Edgar had come. He'd arrived in Paris as a representative for a growing bank, and as it continued to grow he continued to ascend its ladder until he was head of the French international finance division. He bought a spacious *appartement* in the first arrondissement, married a Frenchwoman, had a son, then divorced with civility a few years later. He had the money to burnish his old interests with new acquisitions, and the sociability to cultivate new acquaintances until they became old friends. He was satisfied. So he stayed.

Rachel met him as this sophisticated, settled financier. She was a waitress and he a guest at a cocktail party, one of the few settings in which the struggling underbelly and the well-fed stomach of the diaspora met. The boy who wasn't Jean-Paul Belmondo was long gone by then, but even had he still been around, he wouldn't have been a match for Edgar Bowen. Fifteen years older than she, Edgar moved in worlds Rachel had only seen from behind a caterer's platter. Without ever patronizing her, he offered her opportunities to smooth and shape herself. He took her to galleries instead of museums, to unexpected restaurants he had discovered accidentally, like a true Parisian. Together they lingered in antiquarian bookstores, spending hours absorbed in their finds, then discussed them over dry white wine at a local bistro. She padded with naked feet through his appartement, luxuriating in its differences from her tiny room. Sitting now in the steamy Métro car, she could still see his face, respectful and serious, when she'd first read him some of her poetry, and remember the way he'd celebrated the publication of her first chapbook. Without him, she never would have had the courage to make poetry her profession. With him, she began to know Paris well enough to take it for granted, to love it with the well-worn love of the native. And although she was far from *une Parisienne* when their relationship ended two years later, she was becoming an adult.

Watching the blonde girl wander down the platform outside the window, Rachel knew she would never be that new, that unknowing, again. That long-lost ignorance had been what separated her and Edgar in the end: she had been just beginning while he had been beginning to settle down, and that separated them more than any list of grievances or raging argument could. After two years he had ended things with decency and as much grace as was possible in such a situation. Then, once they were no longer romantically involved, their lives had no reason to touch. Her pain at their break-up gradually reduced receded from a gouge to a pinprick; her time with him came to seem distant. After some years she met Alan, and because Alan was also an expatriate banker working for a large international bank, they would encounter Edgar occasionally at parties and events like the *Bal Rouge*, the financial community's February charity gala. They would smile at each other, brush cheeks, and make small talk, but the only way to avoid the vague awkwardness of ex-lovers was to pretend they were mere acquaintances.

And now he was dead. Now, Rachel thought as she got off the train at her own stop, they would never grow easy enough with each other to have a real conversation again. Now she had lost one of her few remaining links to the time when she had been less sure of herself but more sure about who she was. With that loss, her past selves became one bit less real, her present self one bit more her only self, and her complete self one bit less known. The truth of what Edgar Bowen's death meant to her suddenly came into focus. She stood silent on the platform for a moment, marking him.

Chapter Four

The difficulty with believing something is true, Rachel reflected the next morning, is that you don't know it's true. You know you believe it, but the knowledge that you believe it but don't *know* it undermines even your belief.

This complex fact irritated her all through breakfast. She knew Edgar's death was no accident but, looking at the situation rationally, if she had no evidence then her knowledge was nothing more than unfounded belief, which left her in the frustrating position of being certain of something and doubting it simultaneously. Finally she decided that the only way to put her mind to rest was to see just how plausible her doubts really were. True, she had been the one to say that they shouldn't investigate the hypothetical murder, but she'd said nothing about investigating her own beliefs. And after all, if it turned out those beliefs were wrong, that would prove that the desire to investigate was wrong too. That was her rationalization, and she was sticking to it.

Given that Edgar had supposedly died of a heart attack, the logical place to start was with his doctor.

"How do you find out the name of someone's doctor?" she asked Alan, keeping her voice casual.

He didn't look up from his tablet. "Just ask the person."

"But what if the person is dead?"

"Why would you want to contact a dead person's doctor?"

"It's just a hypothetical. Hypothetically, what if they were dead?"

Now he did look up, eyeing her before he answered. "I guess in that hypothetical case you'd ask one of their friends or relatives."

Oh. "Is there another way?"

He thought again. "I don't see one, short of calling every doctor they could possibly have seen, and asking. And even that wouldn't work because doctors aren't allowed to give out the names of their patients." He peered at her. "Why?"

"No reason." She made her voice casual.

His eyes searched her again. "Are you sure?"

"Yes. Just a passing thought."

Biting her thumbnail, she buried her head in her newspaper. She must be sure not to mention anything about the investigation to him in the future; she could do without his questions. But no way to find the doctor meant no way to find out about the heart. What about a gym? She could try to find his gym and ask about him. Except that gyms probably refused to give out the names of their members, like doctors—God, health nuts had such a high opinion of themselves. So, no doctor, no gym.

What about the wine? After all, that was what had first drawn her attention. And she bet that *cavistes* didn't have any irritating codes of ethics. Of course, trying to find a particular wine shop in France was like trying to find a needle in a pile of needles. *But,* her inner detective whispered, *isn't the internet made for just such problems?*

She waited until Alan left, then woke her computer and typed "wine store first arrondissement" into the browser. She had no way of knowing if Edgar still lived in the same arrondissement, or if he still used the same store—or even if she'd recognize the name of the store if she saw it—but since she had nowhere else to begin, she thought she might as well start there.

Unsurprisingly, the internet offered her countless wine stores in the first arrondissement. She scrolled down, looking to see if any sounded familiar. Not Nicolas, not Le Garde Robe, not Cellier Saint Ivresse—something like Cellier, but not Cellier; some word that also began with "c" and was also for wine. Suddenly her mind flooded with every French word starting with "c" that she knew: *citron, citoyen, cahier, cave . . .* Cave! That was it. Cave something. She tried typing "wine store first arrondissement cave."

And suddenly there it was: Cave Bernard Magrez. She recognized the name as easily as if she and Edgar had just dropped in the previous week. Not so with the location—it was, in fact, in the second arrondissement—*but close enough,* she congratulated herself.

She picked up her *portable* and tapped in the number. Only when a voice answered, "Cave Bernard Magrez," did she realize that she'd been so focused on finding the place, and so excited to have found it, that she hadn't bothered to formulate a plan. She had no idea how to proceed, and now it was too late to come up with something.

"Bonjour." She played for time, trying to think on her feet. "Is this Cave Bernard Magrez?"

"Oui, madame."

"The Cave Bernard Magrez at which Edgar Bowen is a customer?" As if there could be more than one place named Cave Bernard Magrez.

She heard the click of computer keys, then the voice repeated, "Oui, madame. How may we help?"

"I am calling . . ." Why was she calling? She stalled once more, then continued, "I am calling to inform you that, sadly, Monsieur Bowen has passed away."

There was a gasp down the line. "Oh no! Such a shame." The caviste sounded genuinely upset. "Monsieur Bowen was a fine man—a valued customer. He will be missed. Our deepest condolences."

"Thank you." A sober pause. The wheels in her head whirred rapidly. "It was very sudden. He died of a heart attack."

"Terrible. Terrible."

"Yes." She took a deep breath; she'd come up with a rough plan. "I am Monsieur Bowen's secretary." Did Edgar have a secretary? What if he didn't have a secretary? But no rebuff came down the line, so she stumbled on. "Unfortunately, the suddenness of his passing has left us somewhat in disarray. It was so unexpected, and now of course we must settle his debts. But his accounts are unclear." She licked her lips, got to the point. "I wonder, would you be able to remind me of his last order so we can pay it and move settlement of the estate forward?"

To Rachel this all sounded obviously implausible, and even she didn't know what she meant by "move settlement of the estate forward." But the caviste merely said, "Of course, of course." Rachel heard computer keys clicking. "Two weeks ago Monsieur Bowen placed his usual monthly order."

Damn: usual monthly orders didn't require elaboration. "His usual monthly order." She tried to keep her tone neutral. Could she pretend she'd forgotten what was in the usual order? Could she say she needed absolute precision and thus persuade the caviste to read it out?

But once more fortune was on her side: like many people faced with even a hint of confusion, the caviste wanted to help. "Yes, the usual order. A mixed case of reds and whites; then three white, Coche-Dury, and three Merlot, Château Trotanoy, to cellar; then two Mas de Cadenet rosé, and a Fonseca Port, also to cellar."

"Rosé?" Rachel squeaked.

"Oui, madame, two bottles, as usual. And our total bill for this quarter was—"

But Rachel, distracted by her own disbelief, hung up. She sat back, trying to digest what she'd heard. Two bottles of rosé! Apparently Magda was right. Edgar had changed. But she remembered the firmness of his dislike, his insistence that rosé was like sugary vinegar. And there were only two bottles, compared to the nine each of red and white. That was also strange. Maybe he'd just bought the rosé as a gift or for a guest. But the man had said they were part of his *usual* order. Could he have had a regular guest? A regular guest who sat idly by as he plunged face-forward into his soup? A regular guest who had suddenly decided to *help* him plunge face-forward into his soup?

She shifted in her seat, trying to make what she'd learned

fit with what she knew of Edgar. In the middle of this effort, she reluctantly remembered Occam's razor from her college philosophy course: the simplest answer was most likely to be the right one. The simplest answer here was that Edgar was a man restocking his wine supplies every month to fit his taste. If she couldn't accept that, the simplest answer that worked with what she knew of Edgar was that he was a man restocking his wine supplies every month to suit himself and someone he regularly entertained who liked rosé. Neither of these suggested murder. And if the order was just for Edgar, well, that was an awful lot of wine for one person. The evidence, such as it was, spelled out an accidental, unfortunately comical, death: overindulgence caused a heart attack—a myocardial infarction—which caused a drowning. Maybe it was the comedy and her desire to spare Edgar the embarrassment of it that made her feel his death was murder.

But the strange circumstances, the implausibility of a healthy man suddenly having a heart attack, even the simple fact of the rosé's presence—those didn't pass the Occam's razor test either. If he had ordered the rosé for a guest, why had that guest left no evidence of his or her presence, and why had they vanished from the scene? Why hadn't they come forward afterward? As for the possibility that the wine was for Edgar himself—well, your palate altered as you grew up, but surely not between the ages of forty and sixty?

She found it impossible to reconcile the facts and her feelings, and she wasn't surprised to find a headache coming on. She took two aspirin, then did what she always did when she needed to reorder her thoughts: she went for a walk.

She and Alan lived on the fourth floor of a squat building

in the sixth arrondissement. The location had been at Rachel's request: after living in the sixth during her first years in Paris, she never wanted to live anywhere else. She loved the energy provided by the Sorbonne students, who spilled over into her neighborhood; she loved the quiet alleys that snaked up from the Seine unnoticed until they suddenly burst out onto the bustle of Boulevard Saint Germain and Boulevard Saint Michel. Most of all she loved the Jardin du Luxembourg, the park that lined the east side of the arrondissement. Rachel didn't have much interest in untamed nature, but she did like parks, and in her opinion the Jardin du Luxembourg—less full of itself than the better-known Jardin des Tuileries, less vast than the Jardin des Plantes, and in possession of a concession stand that sold cotton candy—was among the very best.

Now she aimlessly wandered the Jardin's wide paths, trying to put her thoughts in order. In mid-afternoon on a cold winter's day, the park was all but deserted. A few elderly men in coats and gloves played *boules*, as they would no matter the season; the occasional pair of young mothers walked briskly along, chatting in little puffs of frozen air while they steered strollers in which sat babies made spherical by layered clothing; a couple sat on one of the benches dotted amid the skeleton trees, kissing with a focused abandon that defied the weather—but twenty years in Paris had taught Rachel that no matter the temperature, no matter the weather, no matter the place, there would always be at least one couple kissing extravagantly in public. Maybe the Paris tourist board hired them specially.

She ambled along the paths with her chin in her scarf, listening to the gravel crunch underfoot and feeling the confusion caused by her telephone conversation begin to dissipate. People did die in strange ways, she knew. Someone in ancient Greece had died from having a tortoise dropped on his head; Mama Cass had choked on a ham sandwich. It was a mistake to think the oddities of life were significant. Most of life was made up of oddities and, yes, coincidences. After all, if she hadn't been called as a last-minute substitute server for a New Year's Eve party all those years ago, she and Magda would never have become friends.

That recollection made her want to hear Magda's voice. She reached into her pocket, groped around, then realized that she'd left her cell phone back at the apartment. She turned around to walk home.

* * *

The bolts on her front door made their usual sound as she turned the key. Still in a nostalgic mood, she remembered that when she and Alan had first moved in, she'd loved the way the deadbolt locked into the floor and ceiling rather than the wall. She had since discovered that this construction was quite common in Parisian apartments, but it never stopped delighting her with its very French combination of ingenuity and good sense. She still took enormous pleasure too in the strange sucking noise the rods made when they lifted, and their snap back into place when she closed the door. But this second noise she didn't have time to appreciate, for as she opened the door, the landline was ringing.

She crossed the room and picked up the handset. It couldn't be Magda; Magda only called her on her cell. *"'Allo?"*

"Good afternoon," a young woman's voice said. "Is Madame Levis available?"

"Speaking." Rachel tried to unwind her scarf from her neck, but it got looped on the phone cord.

"Madame Levis, I'm calling from *Cabinet* Martin Frères." A *cabinet*? What did a law office want with her?

As if in answer to her unspoken question, the woman said, "We are overseeing the estate of Edgar Bowen."

"Oh?" She was no less confused.

"Monsieur Bowen has made you a bequest in his will, and we are calling to ask if you would be able to attend the reading of that will at his appartement on Monday."

Oddities and coincidences, Rachel thought, *oddities and coincidences*. Into the receiver she said, "I wouldn't miss it."

Chapter Five

Edgar had moved to a larger appartement since their time together, Rachel discovered, but he hadn't changed *résidence.* Why would he? The first was Paris's most gracious and luxurious arrondissement, and the Quai d'Orfèvres one of its loveliest surprises. She was no more than twenty yards from the statue of Henry IV on the Pont Neuf and the streams of traffic and tourists that endlessly passed it, but this narrow street was quiet as a country village save for the occasional bus driving down it, and even they seemed to muffle their engines obligingly. The five stories of the building that stretched up in front of her had been there, white and unperturbed, since the mid-nineteenth century, and she suspected that through his front windows Edgar had been able to look out onto the Seine. Rachel wouldn't have moved to a different résidence either.

The first arrondissement was home to many such spaces, she knew. She thought of Galignani, the bookstore that stood at the end of the Rue de Rivoli, untouched by tourist foot and happily selling English books for more than a century; of the courtyard of the Louvre at night, empty of visitors but with the glass pyramid, lit from inside, shining like an oversized jewel box. If you couldn't live in the sixth, she supposed, the first made a good second. Grinning at her accidental joke, she punched the old door code into the security pad. To her surprise, it worked. She listened to the tap of her shoes on the marble floor as she crossed the foyer to the elevator.

In the ride from first to third floor, she became nervous again. Everything about the situation was unfamiliar to her. She hadn't even known what to wear. Only after consultation with Magda had she settled on a plain black dress and plain black shoes.

"It's a solemn event," Magda said sensibly. "It's death *related*, at least. You can't go wrong with black."

Rachel had hoped that the outfit would give her at least some confidence, but in the moment it just made her feel like a nervous woman in a black dress. She gripped her coat more tightly around her as she rang Edgar's doorbell.

The door swung open, revealing an upright, suited butler.

"Fulke?" Rachel was astonished.

The butler was not. "Madame Levis." He stood back to let her in. "Always good to see you, madame." He spoke as if she were a frequent visitor.

Fulke had been Edgar's butler—well, more household manager at that stage—when Edgar and Rachel had started seeing each other. Although she was taken aback to find him still in residence, after a few seconds' reflection she had to admit she wasn't exactly surprised. Fulke had appeared indomitable even twenty years before, and time had altered neither his height nor his impressive bulk. He gave off the sense that he was eternal, a family treasure made human, so it seemed somehow right that, having served Edgar for all his life in France, he should also be there to usher him out of it.

"A sad time, Fulke," she said. She saw the shadow of an emotion flicker across his face, but he was too much the stereotype of a loyal retainer to reveal anything. Instead, he only inclined his head, holding out his hands for her coat. After hanging it up, he gestured toward the recesses of the appartement. "Madame." He ushered her down the hall to the appropriate room.

Rachel and Alan were far from poor, but the apartment she walked through now made it plain that Edgar had been truly rich. She passed a long dining room with a walnut table flanked by what seemed like endless chairs. Through double doors on the other side of the hall, she glimpsed a *salon* carefully decorated in biscuit and gold, pale oils and vigorous etchings on the walls, the doors to a veranda just visible as she walked past. And this was no casual, inherited bounty. Nowhere was there the fraying fabric, the sense of tattered overstuffing that Rachel had seen in the (very few) homes of French *vieilles fortunes* she visited through Alan's work. Edgar had too much taste and sense of self to fit under the label of *nouveau riche*, but he also hadn't had time to accumulate the casual sense of comfort and assumption that came with established wealth; he couldn't rest on the knowledge that his chairs were frayed by three hundred years of use. Still, she thought as Fulke opened a door on her right, how lovely it all was! How ordered and how elegant. She stepped inside the room and stood appreciating its luxury, hearing the door click shut behind her.

Behind a desk at the back of the room was a neat man in a

gray suit, who half-rose at Rachel's entrance, then sat back down. "*Enfin*, Madame Levis," he said. Like all the French, he pronounced it "Lev*eess*," with the stress on the final syllable. Rachel had long since stopped explaining that it was actually "*Le*viss," so she just smiled and nodded. He nodded back. "I am Maître Bernard, a *notaire* in Monsieur Bowen's law firm."

Five chairs had been pulled up in front of the desk. Four of them were occupied, and as Rachel slid into the one remaining, she surreptitiously took in what she supposed were her fellow beneficiaries. It turned out you *could* go wrong with black, for she was the only person in the room wearing it—except David, who wore the black velvet jacket over jeans that was the winter uniform of the Parisian male. The three other people seated in front of the desk were all women, and none looked funereal. The first was Mathilde, her posture as ramrod perfect as it had been twenty years before. She wore a long-sleeved sheath of pale caramel, and looped over her shoulders was a perfectly folded crimson scarf. What was *was* it about certain middle-aged French women, Rachel wondered, that they could use their clothes as a reproach? Not that Mathilde needed to use clothing to make anyone feel inferior; recognizing Rachel, she now inclined her head a fraction, a queen acknowledging a humble underling. Rachel was twenty-four all over again, shabby and embarrassed in her cutoffs.

The woman in the chair next to Mathilde's was about Rachel's own age, maybe a few years younger, with dark hair cut into a boy crop. She wore slim navy trousers and a navy blazer belted at the waist, covering a cream wool turtleneck; her only apparent makeup was dark red lipstick. Rachel recognized this too as a very specific French look: competent urban woman on the go, comfortable enough to be casual, but Gallic enough to care about style.

Looking at the third woman, Rachel reflected that the group might have been designed as a triptych—say, three of the Four Ages of Woman. No more than in her early twenties, this girl had the cloud of long hair worn by so many young French women. In her case, it was honey-blonde. Her fresh face was slightly round, with a flush of pink across her unmade-up cheeks, and this plus the matching roundness of her eyes gave her the look of a sweet-faced doll. She wore jeans, boots, and a sweater; she'd pulled the sweater sleeves down over her hands.

Wearing a look to match his black blazer, David sat apart from the women. His legs were crossed, but he had moved down in the chair so that they stretched in front of him. He stared at his fingernails, and as Rachel settled herself in the remaining chair, he gave a sniffle.

At almost exactly the same moment, the man in the gray suit cleared his throat. "Now that we are all here, we may begin."

Rachel, who had two living parents and two living parents-in-law, had never attended a will reading. Drawing her ideas from a confusion of sources, she'd always imagined that they would be a cross between mystery clichés and the scene in *Middlemarch* where Mr. Featherstone's will is read. Without a young widow in black gloves and heavily veiled pinwheel hat or a row of vulgar, overeager relatives, she felt let down and somewhat at sea. Did testamentary revelations really take place in well-lit *bureaus* in front of five quite ordinary people? How disappointing. Then she noticed the gleam in the notaire's eye. He, at least, felt there was drama in the situation. He opened the folder on the desk in front of him, drew a pair of narrow glasses from his breast pocket, and settled them on the bridge of his slender nose.

"Alors." He paused. "This is Monsieur Edgar Bowen's last will, executed three months ago, witnessed by the required two witnesses, in this case Monsieur Bowen's butler and his cleaner. It is thus fully legal, and it supersedes all other wills made by Monsieur Bowen." The formalities over, he relaxed a fraction and went on. "First, excepting bequests to follow, Monsieur Bowen leaves his entire estate to Monsieur David Bowen." He gestured toward David as if he needed identifying. "This includes this appartement, which has no mortgage; Monsieur Bowen's savings and his life insurance; and his company and private retirement savings. Monsieur Bowen *père* has made very careful arrangements on both sides of the Atlantic, and we are ready to assist with the tax." Maître Bernard allowed himself a small professional smile in David's direction. "You need not worry, Monsieur Bowen."

David's eyes were still red-rimmed, and the announcement of his new wealth produced no alteration in his expression. Maybe that was just his resting face, or maybe it was a mask he'd assumed to hide his feelings. Or maybe, Rachel thought, he was still stunned by Edgar's death. After all, he was what—twenty-five now? At that age the death of a parent still seems improbable, or at least an occurrence for the distant future, and its early arrival would stun. He sniffed again, just an ordinary sniff, but it reminded Rachel of similar sniffs when he was a small boy, determined not to cry as she washed dirt off his skinned elbow or a put a Band-Aid on his bloodied knee. Her heart softened.

"And now, the smaller bequests." Maître Bernard cleared

his throat, leaving an impeccably executed pause. "First, Monsieur Bowen leaves five thousand euro to the Montmartre Home for Cats."

Cats? God, thought Rachel. *It really is true that you never know someone.* But then why would you know someone you hadn't actually known for twenty years? She had to admit, she was in no position to pronounce on the norms of Edgar's inner life. Still, cats in Montmartre? *Good on you, Edgar,* she thought. She was a pet lover.

"Madame Levis." The notaire peered at her over his glasses. Rachel straightened like an obedient schoolchild. "Monsieur Bowen makes a request of you." He paused again. "He asks that you take charge of organizing and cataloguing his library so that Monsieur David may decide its fate. For performing this task, he bequeaths you the book of your choice."

Rachel smiled. Not only a secret cat lover but a secret sentimentalist! How fortunate that Edgar's hidden depths turned out to be so endearing. He'd remembered those afternoons they spent together in bookstores, had continued to take pleasure in her pleasure. For just a second, her throat tightened. Then she felt the lawyer's sharp gaze upon her, and that second passed.

The notaire cleared his throat once again and took a breath. "To Catherine Nadeau." The red-lipped woman leaned forward. "He leaves seven thousand five hundred euro," he read from the page in front of him, "'in thanks for your love, and for our time together.'"

Rachel had already guessed that the woman was Edgar's current girlfriend, and she was pleased to be proved right. Her pleasure didn't distract her from watching the woman's reaction, though. Catherine Nadeau grinned broadly for a second; then the smile vanished, the face fell, and she began to cry. She picked up her bag from where it sat on the floor and began to rummage through it for something she could use to wipe her eyes. Before she could find anything, in one smooth gesture Maître Bernard extracted a handkerchief from a pocket, leaned over the desk, and handed it to her. *Of course he had a handkerchief ready,* Rachel thought as she watched Catherine Nadeau dab her cheeks; in his business he must need one all the time. Immediately, she felt shabby for thinking such a thought.

Catherine Nadeau had collected herself, and the notaire allowed the air to settle before he continued. "Now, Madame Bowen. To you he leaves ten thousand euro."

Mathilde's expression did not change, but even she couldn't control everything: for a bare microsecond—so fast that Rachel almost wasn't sure she'd seen it—she flinched. Then she nodded again, another tiny movement of the head.

Maître Bernard inhaled, then let his breath out. "And now, Mademoiselle des Troyes."

The blonde girl straightened, widening her eyes. She caught her lower lip in her top teeth. *You could,* Rachel thought, *actually have heard a pin drop.*

"Monsieur Bowen leaves for you . . ." He peered intently at the document inside the folder, as if for the first time. "Ah, yes, '*in* affection and gratitude . . .'"

Just get on with it! Rachel yelled internally.

"He leaves you twenty thousand euro."

In her first year in college, Rachel had been much given to using the word "extraordinary" in her papers: books were "extraordinary"; philosophers had "extraordinary" ideas. Then one of her professors had written in an essay margin "What word will you use when something truly is extraordinary?" and that had been the end of that. Now Rachel was glad she had retired the word for all the intervening years, because at the news of her bequest Elisabeth's face became, in the truest sense of the word, extraordinary. There passed over it in rapid succession the look of someone who has expected a treat; the look of someone who knows it's poor manners to show that she has expected a treat; and the look of someone who, having felt both of these, suddenly finds she has received a bigger treat than she could ever have expected. Not that Rachel articulated these changes to herself with such precision. She felt them, recognized them wordlessly, but if asked at that moment what she'd seen, she could only have said that the girl turned pale.

Mathilde spoke. "For what reason?" Her eyebrows rose a fraction. Her voice was absolutely level.

The notaire flicked his eyes toward her. "As I said, 'in affection and gratitude.'"

What does that mean? Rachel wanted to ask. What *precisely* does that mean? She couldn't be the only person longing to know, but they all sat silent: Mathilde so contained she might have been a statue; David jiggling a knee up and down; Catherine Nadeau watching Elisabeth des Troyes's white, and now confused, face; and she, Rachel, too much a stranger in the room to speak everyone's mind. As for the notaire, he closed his lips and kept his client's secrets.

Chapter Six

"Twenty *thousand* euros?" Magda stressed the second word, as if the notaire might have slipped up and added it by accident.

Rachel nodded. "Twenty thousand euros."

She had arranged to meet Magda right after telling Alan about the reading of the will; his reaction had been similar, but the telephone had reduced its drama. In person, Magda's response suffered no such reduction. She underscored her astonishment by widening her eyes as she repeated, "Twenty thousand euros!" Then she added, "Which is twice what he left anyone else."

"Well," Rachel qualified, "except David. David got the bulk of the estate, which I promise you is much more than twenty thousand euros."

"But still . . ." Magda pursed her lips. "Edgar left twenty thousand euros to a girl who . . . How was she connected to him?"

"I don't know." In fact, Rachel realized, she didn't. No one had ever explained who Mademoiselle des Troyes was, or how she had come to be included in Edgar's will.

"Well, when a man leaves a girl twenty thousand with—what

was it?—*in* affection and gratitude, it's pretty clear what space she filled in his life. Or what space he filled in her—sorry, in hers." Magda snickered.

Rachel pretended to have missed it; Magda had these moments. It had begun to rain shortly after they met up, and they'd decided to stay dry by treating themselves to a drink at their favorite restaurant, Bistrot Vivienne. Now, to avoid responding to Magda, she studied the mosaic floor on which she'd rested her dripping red umbrella. *How clever of of the bistro to set up a terrasse in the glass-roofed Galeries Vivienne.* You could hear the soothing sound of the pattering rain while sitting warm and dry below.

She returned to the conversation. "But the money wasn't even the most striking thing. The most striking thing was the way she reacted."

Magda's face said she didn't think there was much that could be more striking than an unexplained bequest of twenty thousand euros, but out of politeness she asked, "The way she reacted?"

"Yes. Her face. Her face was extraordinary."

"Uh-oh." Magda waggled an index finger. "Professor McNaughton wouldn't approve."

"No, no, that's just the thing! It really was extraordinary. It was so . . . out of the ordinary."

Magda sighed. "This is like your rationale for suspecting murder last week. Could you be a bit less vague?"

Rachel gnawed her lip, took a deep breath. "All right." She paused to think. "When the notaire said Edgar had left her something, and then announced the amount, she was taken aback. Absolutely. But at the same time, she seemed more taken aback than she actually was."

Magda still looked confused. Rachel didn't blame her. She tried again, closing her eyes, attempting to project herself back into the moment. The notaire had said the words; the girl's eyes had widened. Then the answer came: "You know what it was? My mother used to say, 'I'm shocked, but I'm not surprised.' That's exactly how this girl was. I don't think she was surprised to be in the will in the first place. I think she at least half-expected that. And she knew the reason why. But she was shocked by the size of the bequest. But she didn't want anyone else to know that she wasn't surprised to be included, so she covered it up by acting *too* surprised at the amount. She overacted, but she overacted something she really did feel. *That* was what was extraordinary: watching her go through the process of disguise and arriving at her final reaction." Rachel leaned back, exhausted but relieved. She'd managed it in the end.

Magda apparently didn't feel the same. "Well, again, it isn't really very much, is it? Genuine surprise that somehow also seems performed." She frowned. "How did the others respond to their good fortune?"

Rachel considered. "David didn't really respond at all. He sniffed, but then he sniffed a lot anyway. I think he had a cold. To be fair, his lack of reaction didn't seem strange. He could well have had an idea what was coming; anyone with the internet can read up on French inheritance law."

Magda jumped on this. "Why would he do that? Did he give any indication he'd done that?"

"I'm not saying he did. I just meant you could, and then

you'd have an idea of what a son might inherit, and that might be why he didn't react strongly. But it's more likely he was in shock. His father had just died."

But Magda had moved on. "And what about the other woman? Madame Nideau?"

"Nadeau," Rachel corrected. "Yes, now that I think of it, her reaction was interesting—her immediate reaction, I mean. When she heard her bequest, she smiled, really grinned, as if she'd won a prize."

Magda perked up. "That *is* interesting."

"Just for a second, though. Then she started to cry."

"Well . . ." It was Magda's turn to consider. "It could be that the realization of what had happened in order for the money to come to her sunk in. That is, Edgar's dying. Or"—she raised her eyebrows at a second possibility—"she could have realized how she *should* be acting and started crying to mask her guilt."

Perhaps it was Magda's eyebrows, or perhaps it was the reference to masks, but Rachel suddenly remembered something else. "And then—"

"And then what?"

"And then who *who*, actually. Mathilde." Mathilde needed no explanation; Magda had met her. "Remember, I told you it was a point of pride with her not to react to things."

Magda nodded.

"Well, when she heard about her bequest she . . . she flinched for a second. Or rather, she experienced a flinch. It wasn't voluntary; she couldn't stop it. And when she heard about Elisabeth's bequest, she raised her eyebrows."

Magda thought for a moment, then said, "Raised them

how? Like, raised them in pleasure?" She raised her own as an example. "Or raised them in rage?" She raised them again, infinitesimally differently.

"Oh, the second, no question."

"You're sure?"

"Absolutely." Again Rachel struggled to explain. "The look on her face when she raised them wasn't pleasure. In fact, it was displeasure. And when the notaire finished, she asked him to repeat Edgar's explanation for the bequest. She said"—Rachel tried to capture Mathilde's icy timbre—"'for what reason?' That was not a happy voice."

Magda didn't say anything. Rachel understood that she was trying to decide what to do with what she'd heard. She waited.

"Well, it's still not much. But . . ." Magda paused. "It's also not nothing. Three people behaving strangely at a will reading is strange. Suspicious."

"Suspect," Rachel corrected automatically. "People are *suspicious* of circumstances that are *suspect*."

"Okay, their behavior is *suspect*. Suspect enough to deserve further examination."

"I know what you're thinking." Rachel started gathering her coat. "You're thinking we should go to the police."

"No, I'm not."

"You're not?"

"No." Magda made it sound obvious. "What could we tell them now that's stronger than what we had before? All we can say is, 'Not only did someone I know allegedly drown in his soup near a bottle of rosé after a heart attack, despite the fact that when I knew him twenty years ago he hated rosé and was perfectly healthy, but also, when I went to the reading of his will, one beneficiary smiled, another flinched, and a third received a surprisingly large bequest.'" She shook her head. "They'd laugh us out of the *commissariat*."

Rachel saw her point.

"I'll tell you what we could do, though." Magda's eyes began to shine. "Remember, in the café how you said that the next murder either one of us had a connection to, we would investigate?"

Rachel nodded.

"Well . . ." She opened her hands, put her head on one side.

"Well what?"

"Well, here you are!"

"Oh no." Rachel shook her head.

"Oh yes. One person behaving strangely at a will reading is nothing special. Even two could be explained. But *three* people behaving strangely? And one of them behaving strangely after receiving a surprisingly large bequest? It wouldn't look like much to the police, but it's practically the beginning of an Agatha Christie novel!"

Magda grabbed Rachel's wrist. This was always a bad sign.

Rachel made a desperate attempt to impose reality. "But I have to write. And you have work."

"Oh, work," Magda said airily. She ran an online business selling French linens and other household goods to foreigners. "The site's been running smoothly for ages. These days all I really need to do is check that the supplier's sending the stuff out quickly, and I can do that with a couple of phone calls. And you said you'd been blocked lately." Her grip tightened.

"Come on. We can be private eyes together. Sleuths! Shami! Gumshoes!"

Not for the first time, Rachel wondered how she'd become best friends with someone who so clearly didn't share her sense that disaster waited in every future. At least this time she had some hard evidence that would put Magda off—although it was going to be unpleasant to reveal it, She inhaled. "I have to tell you something."

Magda, plainly still distracted by dreams of hidden documents and dramatic discoveries, wasn't much interested. "Mm?"

"I called Edgar's caviste."

"Who?"

"Edgar's caviste. Cave Bernard Magrez."

Magda made a polite noise. "Huh! How did you find it?"

"I searched on the internet, and when I saw the name, I remembered."

"Huh? . . . Wait." She saw Magda catch on. "You said we shouldn't investigate!"

"I said we shouldn't investigate Edgar's death." Rachel gave the explanation that had soothed her own conscience. "But I was investigating my suspicion about the rosé. That's different."

Apparently Magda was not as easily soothed. "You always do this! Always! It's just like the time when—"

"Could you please not bring that up again? It was fifteen years ago! Anyway"—she offered the ultimate distraction—"it turns out I was wrong."

Success. "You were wrong?"

"Yes. Apparently Edgar's monthly order always included

rosé, two bottles. So I was wrong about his not having any in the house. And you were right: his tastes had changed." She swallowed. "So there is concrete evidence that Edgar *did* drink rosé. Which means he could well have been alone when he died, which means it very probably wasn't murder."

"Hmm." This was a syllable Rachel knew well on Magda's lips, and it didn't mean acquiescence. "What else did he order?" Magda squinted one eye.

She cast her mind back again. "Okay, if you include what he ordered to cellar . . . port, bordeaux, burgundy, chardonnay, and merlot."

"How many of those?"

She thought again. "Of the port, one. Then nine bottles of white and nine of red."

"In comparison, two bottles of rosé isn't really very much."

"No."

"It's so little, in fact," Magda said slowly, "that it seems to suggest he wasn't buying it for himself, but for a guest. A regular guest."

"I thought that too!" Rachel smacked her arm lightly. "But then I thought, surely if someone else had been there, we would've heard about it, at the funeral or in the obituary."

"Unless"—Magda took on a crafty look—"no one knew about it. If the other person cleared their place and left without being noticed."

She seemed so pleased with this hypothesis that Rachel hated to burst her bubble. But she did. "And presumably also cleared themselves of the splashed soup they'd be covered in and managed to avoid any notice on the way out."

"It's possible." Magda never could let go of an idea.

"But it's very unlikely."

"'When you have eliminated the impossible,'" Magda said in the voice she used for quotations, "'whatever remains, however improbable, must be the truth.'"

"But we haven't eliminated the impossible," Rachel pointed out, thinking that in any case Sherlock Holmes's assertion was ridiculous. Many improbable solutions were unlikely to be true. Such as a soup-suffocating murderer tidying up and making a clean getaway, all while avoiding Fulke's watchful eye. "In fact, what you're envisioning seems impossible. Listen to what it means: we'd be looking for someone mild-seeming enough, and close enough, to be a regular guest, but who silently seethed with murderous rage and who brought along an unnoticed change of clothes on the day itself, changed into them, and then slipped away, all without being seen." She paused. "Pretty improbable, I think you'll agree."

But Magda did not agree. "Improbable, yes. But not impossible."

Rachel knew when to give up. "Fine. It wouldn't be impossible."

Placated, Magda moved on. "And the girl's response—what's her name, anyway?"

"Elisabeth. Elisabeth des Troyes."

"All right, Mademoiselle des Troyes's response is strange too. And so is Mathilde's behavior. You were right last week: some things are wrong, and they deserve examination." It was clear Magda had fallen in love with the idea of detecting. "And really"—her face became pious—"you owe it to Edgar. He put his trust in you, and it seems only right that you should repay it."

Rachel did not point out that Edgar had trusted her with

his library, not with the right to investigate those closest to him in connection with a potentially nonexistent crime. She thought of her reverie on the Métro the day before, her acknowledgment of Edgar's importance. Unintentionally, Magda had hit the right nerve: she did owe him. He had helped her to stop being young and start being interesting—and, even more important, to start being interest*ed*. He deserved something in return for that, even if all she could offer was postmortem interest in him. Because she felt sure there was something of interest going on here. Something *was* strange, some things *were* wrong, and people *had* behaved in suspect ways. And to look for proof, to find clues and turn up hard evidence . . . yes, she also liked the idea of detecting. Rachel Levis, Investigatrix, she thought. Was *investigatrix* a word? It was now.

"All right," she said finally.

The waiter brought fresh coffee for Magda and a new hot chocolate—this time without whipped cream—for Rachel. Magda lifted her cup from the top, sipping the coffee from the gap between her thumb and forefinger. The gesture said she was too busy to bother with the handle: it said she was all business.

"Well now." She put the cup on its saucer, drew a breath. "The first thing to do is list our possible suspects."

"Just a second there, Columbo." Rachel held up a hand. "Who put you in charge?"

Magda wriggled with irritation, but had to concede. "Fair point. You're the one who knew Edgar. You have more right to be in charge." But from the way she thinned her lips, Rachel could tell she felt bruised. "Where do you think we should start?" Magda asked.

"Where do I think we should start? I think . . ." She pondered for a long moment then said, "I think the first thing to do is list our possible suspects."

Magda smiled reluctantly, then less so. The air between them softened. "Okay."

Rachel continued, "But I also think we can't carry on the way we just were, all feelings and maybes, as if it were a cozy mystery novel. We need to treat this like a police inquiry."

Together and apart they had watched countless true crime programs, each charting the investigation of a suspicious death, each investigation leading to a successful arrest. *Magda might not be Columbo and I might not be Sherlock Holmes,* Rachel thought, *but after all those documentaries, we know our way around a murder.* "We need to be logical," she said. "We should have no preconceived notions, and we should consider all possible suspects."

"All right, let's do that." Magda inhaled deeply. She held up an index finger. "First, the main beneficiary: David. Who now has a lot of money."

"True." The smooth nap of David's velvet jacket flashed through Rachel's mind. "But I didn't get the impression he was doing badly before this. He looked comfortably off; he was well dressed. I'd even say well heeled. So I think he had plenty of money already."

"For some people, plenty isn't enough." Magda made it sound as if she'd spent her life on the mean streets. "For some people there's never enough."

"Maybe." Rachel made a face. "But outside of fiction, you have to be pretty cold to kill your own father."

"Not if you're on drugs." Once more, the knowing tone.

"Everybody knows wealthy fathers have dissolute sons. Maybe he needed Edgar's money to pay off a drug dealer."

"Again, maybe." Rachel exhaled in a rush. "But I didn't see any signs of drugs. He wasn't twitchy; he wasn't listless; he didn't seem out of it or too tightly wound. He was thin, but you see lots of boys like that these days."

Magda nodded: you did. Besides, he was only their first possible suspect.

"All right, let's let him go for the moment. But he did become very rich as a result of Edgar's death, so we can't rule him out completely. He'll go at the bottom of our list." She moved on. "Now, Fulke."

"Fulke?"

Magda shrugged. "You said we should consider all possible suspects. He's part of the household, so he's a possible suspect. And you also said"—she changed to her quoting voice—"we'd be looking for someone mild seeming and close, who silently seethed with murderous rage and who had access to a change of clothes. He fits the bill." She leaned back.

"No he doesn't," Rachel said. "I just saw him, and he didn't show any signs of rage. Plus, he's the only person left *worse* off by Edgar's death." She began to count on her fingers. "When Edgar was alive he had a job, a comfortable place to live, and a steady income. If Fulke killed him, he'd lose all of those." She considered. "In fact, I think he *has* lost them, unless David keeps him on." Then she refocused. "And he's intensely loyal. During the time I was with Edgar, I never knew Fulke to so much as hint at anything about him, not even by twitching a lip. And judging from his behavior when he let me in and out, nothing's changed."

"Edgar might have been planning to fire him."

"Sure, he might have been, but there's no evidence to suggest he was."

Magda looked mulish. "Maybe there was some precipitating event we don't know about."

"Now you're basing a speculation on a speculation." Rachel shook her head. "Okay, there could be something we don't know. But without knowing that, I'd say he doesn't really need to be on the list."

Magda stood her ground. "But we can't *know* what we don't know. I think we need to do a little more digging on him in case there is something we don't know."

"What kind of digging?"

"I don't know. Something like . . ." She thought. "You just said he was the only person who had anything to lose by Edgar's death. Well, there must be some way of finding out whether or not that's true. Finding out whether he's in a worse position now than he was when Edgar was alive. Like if he needs to find a new job or if David's about to kick him out?" Her tone betrayed her own uncertainty.

Equally unsure, Rachel said slowly, "Can we find out those kinds of things?" She thought for a moment. "I guess I can try. There must be some way."

"Well, look what you managed with the caviste."

Privately Rachel thought that was down to sheer good luck, but she wasn't going to turn down a compliment. She just asked, "Can I have a few days?"

"Oh sure!" Magda nodded. "Obviously it'll take time."

"And until we find out something that makes us think otherwise, can he please go at the bottom of our list?"

Magda sighed. "Fine. He goes at the bottom. But he's on the list."

"At the very bottom. *Below* David."

"Yes, below David." Magda spoke with put-upon exasperation, but Rachel could tell she was enjoying herself: all she needed was a small hardcover notebook like the ones the detectives carried on *Law and Order*, and she'd be in her element.

"Now," Magda said, taking a deep breath, "we come to our more obvious suspects. Let's do them in order of amount of bequest. Madame Nadeau?"

"For seventy-five hundred euros?" Rachel made a face.

"People have murdered for less," Magda said cheerily.

Rachel wanted to point out that this ran directly opposite to her "sometimes plenty isn't enough" theory, but she didn't. After all, people *had* murdered for less.

In any case, Magda quickly qualified her own remark. "Also, she didn't necessarily know how much he was leaving her. Or need to know. She could have been motivated just by the fact that he was leaving her *something*." She warmed to her theme. "It's not hard to imagine. He says, 'Don't worry, my darling! You'll be provided for after I'm gone.' She thinks 'after I'm gone' could take a very long time, and she'd rather have it sooner, thank you very much. So she kills him." She thought for a second. "Or maybe she knows the amount and needs it right away. So she kills him. *And*"—she threw the word down like a trump card—"you did say she grinned."

Rachel *had* said that. "Okay. But why did she need the money? If we don't know that, we're just making up a motive."

"We don't know that *yet*." Magda sounded faintly irritated, as if she couldn't believe she had to fill Rachel in on the elementary goals of investigation. "It's what we need to find out."

Rachel didn't care for the tone, but she had to agree. She dipped her head.

Magda rolled on. "Now, Mathilde.

"Now, Mathilde. She of the uncontrolled eyebrows."

"Yeees . . ." Rachel couldn't help her hesitation. Now that they weren't in the realm of speculation, now that they were cleaving to rationality and fact, she felt less certain about her earlier conclusions. "He did leave her ten thousand euros, and she did react strangely. But you can't condemn someone based on a twitch and a look in their eyes. If we're considering things logically, we have to bear in mind that she does have plenty of money of her own. *Old* money. And that makes ten thousand hardly worth killing for."

"But we've only been assuming Edgar was killed for money. People kill for other reasons too. I remember reading somewhere that there are four main motives for murder: theft, jealousy, fear—"

"Oh, oh, that's Alan Grant in *The Man in the Queue*! I read that too." Rachel cast her mind back, then chanted, "Theft, jealousy, fear, revenge."

"Well, I think we can rule out theft."

Rachel pursed her lips. "And I think fear too. Mathilde and Edgar were on good terms when I knew him."

"All right then, not fear." Looking back, Magda did feel Mathilde was more likely to inspire fear than experience it. "How about revenge? That seems much more her style."

"Yes, but revenge for what? I think she had nothing to

be vengeful about for the same reason she had nothing to be fearful about. After all," Rachel flipped the bequest from negative to positive, "he did leave her ten thousand euros."

"Unless," Magda countered, "he left her the ten thousand to make up for some wrong. Who knows what he might have done to her in the last two decades?"

Rachel found it hard to imagine Edgar doing anything to inspire a years-long grudge. It just didn't fit with what she knew of him.

"I think . . ." She hesitated. "I think he left her the money because of David. They did have some kind of residual parental relationship, at least when I knew him. She visited him, and he was always warm with her when she was there. I think it's more likely that those were the reasons for the bequest."

"Still," Magda pushed, "who knows how things might have changed?"

Rachel gave in. "All right. Given that she has her own money, the ten thousand could be an apology as well as an acknowledgment. So, maybe. Revenge for something we don't know about?"

Magda nodded. "And now the best one: jealousy."

"No." Rachel shook her head firmly. "She never seemed jealous when I knew her. She was a snob, but she never said or did anything that seemed like the result of jealousy."

"Really? I remember your telling me at the time that she was constantly coming over to Edgar's appartement. You weren't too pleased about it either."

Rachel was confused. "But that was for David. She visited so that they could both be with David, to give him a sense of stability."

Magda sighed at her friend's innocence. "Rachel, I love you, but you are so naïve about people."

Rachel reddened. "You've said that before."

"Because it's been true before! If a woman keeps visiting her ex-husband's home, and especially if she keeps visiting it when her husband's new young girlfriend is there, she's not visiting for the sake of her son. She's visiting her husband to keep an eye on him!"

Rachel shook her head even more vehemently. "I really don't think so. *She* was the one who divorced *him*."

"That wouldn't necessarily make a difference." Magda tightened her lips. "Just because you leave someone doesn't mean you want them to stop loving you. As anyone knows who's ever had an ex find someone new before they do."

Rachel couldn't argue with that. And anyway, hadn't she seen enough romantic foolishness over the years to know it was pointless to try to understand the human heart? "All right," she said with a sigh. "Jealousy is a possible motive. I guess."

"Plus, we agreed we don't know about slights in the past. So I think we can say jealousy or revenge."

Rachel nodded.

"So that's Mathilde." Magda made a tick mark in the air. "And now, the luckiest heir. The girl."

Rachel thought for a long moment before she said, "I don't know." She twisted her mouth. "She just . . . she was so innocent. She's not vampy. She's not a seductress. In fact, she's the very opposite of both those things. She isn't a woman a man would leave money to in thanks for 'services rendered.'" She made quotation marks in the air. "And maybe that's what it was; she really isn't a woman at all. She's just a girl." She took a sip from her cup. "That's what struck me most about her: that she's just a girl."

"But that's exactly the kind of mask a skilled manipulator would put on! And it's also exactly the kind of woman some men do find desirable." Magda looked carefully at her. "There were fifteen years between the two of you."

"That's totally different. Totally." Rachel gave a tight headshake. "He was forty—that's still relatively young. Now he's sixty. Well, he was sixty. And a fifteen-year age gap is totally different from a thirty-five-year age gap."

Magda rolled her eyes. "Okay, fine. She still inherited a lot of money. That's motive all on its own."

"Only if you knew it was coming," Rachel countered.

Magda sat back. "Look, what's going on? You were the one who originally thought Edgar had been murdered, but now that we might have some actual evidence, you don't want to see anyone as a suspect. Do you still believe this was a murder?"

"Yes." And she did. But . . . "It's just that I think it's silly to think of any of these people as suspects. None of them would do it. I know what they're like. I know them."

"You *knew* them." Magda's voice was gentle, but it was firm. "You yourself said after the funeral that you last knew them twenty years ago. You have no idea what's happened in the interim. And two of them you never knew at all. You can dismiss possibilities, and you can be dismissive, but if we're being *logical*," she stressed the word, "as your knowledge goes, all these people are viable suspects. Any one of them could be the killer."

Rachel felt her eyes burn. Magda was right. It was foolish to imagine she knew Edgar or his family anymore. And as for

Edgar had been a collector, but he hadn't been an orga-
er. She paused to consider the irony of his asking her, a
nan whose own shelves were testimony to her love of read-
but also her hatred of cleaning, to undertake such a task.
l, she had to acknowledge that whatever his reasoning, his
uest and his mess were going to be useful to her.

She spent the next few hours looking over the books and
ing a bit of tentative reordering. As she went along, she men-
ly noted the tools she needed but didn't have. A pad and
ncil for cataloguing. Something to help her deal with the
st. A plan for how to proceed. Suddenly the scale of the task
ertook her, and she had to sit down. Well, at least she could
op worrying that she wouldn't be here long enough to do any
vestigating.

When she heard the clock in the salon strike one, she deci-
ed she'd had enough for the day. She would go home, take a
hower, put a pad and some pencils in her bag, and try to make
plan. As if on cue, she sneezed. She exhaled through her nos-
rils, sneezed again, wiped her hands on her trousers, and opened
he library door.

Fulke must have had supersonic hearing, because when she
losed the door behind her, he was standing in the entry hall,
holding her coat.

"Bless you, madame," he said politely.

"Thank you." Rachel slid her arms into the sleeves. "Fulke,
do you think you could find me a dust rag for tomorrow?"

"A dust rag?" His expression didn't change, but he seemed slightly disconcerted. *Maybe at the idea that any household over which he presides could contain a rag,* Rachel thought.

the other two, how could she know why Catherine Nadeau had grinned or what Elisabeth des Troyes was capable of?

"Yes," she said in a small voice. "They're all viable suspects."

Like Rachel earlier, Magda offered something to soften the embarrassment. "You're right about one thing, though. When it comes to David and Fulke, we really don't have good evidence. But even so, we have at least two, and maybe three, plausible criminals." She looked at Rachel. "We agree that we should make the girl our prime suspect, yes? After all, she's the one who got the inexplicably huge bequest and who acted most weirdly in response."

Rachel concurred. "But I don't think we should write off Mathilde too quickly. For her, those gestures were like someone else standing up and screaming."

"All right." Magda pursed her lips. "She's certainly capable of it."

Rachel thought to herself that if she were left to her own devices, she would make Mathilde the prime suspect. Maybe she had no clear motive, but she had the appropriate personality. Rachel could see her killing to get something she wanted.

The difficulty, though, was that her bloodlessness made it seem unlikely she would murder someone out of rage. She had too much sangfroid to reach the level of anger needed to kill someone for revenge or out of jealousy. *Or would you* need *a lot of sangfroid to carry that off,* Rachel wondered. Did Mathilde's flinch suggest she wasn't bloodless enough? After all, it would take considerable iciness to kill someone you'd once loved—or if Magda was right, still loved—and the father of your child. Mathilde's inadvertent jerk might have been a sign that there was reason to suspect her, but it also might have been a sign that she couldn't carry out the act. Nothing was clear.

As if reading her mind Magda said, "The trouble is going to be getting anyone else to see what we see."

Even after all her friend's eagerness, Rachel's heart was warmed by that "us," that spoken proof that she wasn't alone in her conviction. "You know the significance of what you saw because you were there," Magda continued. "And I know the significance because I know you. *We* know it's a murder, but how do we persuade someone in a position of authority to agree?" She pushed her chin out as she thought, then finally answered herself. "We need more evidence."

"Yes." Rachel made the word a sigh. "But where do we start? And how?" The questions were almost rhetorical, but they were also legitimate. She'd said it before: they had no special knowledge or skills, no formal authorization. Even after this listing of motives and possible proofs, they didn't really have anything to build on except expressions and twitches. Where *did* they start?

"You start with the library." Magda made it sound obvious. "Edgar has given you permission to be there, in his house, in his world. You're simply going to do as he asked and organize the library. Just pay attention to the people you meet while you do it." She smiled. "And as for me . . ." She drummed her fingers on the table as she considered. "I'll start by finding out some more about Madame Nadeau. Something about her grin speaks to me." Her eyes gleamed. The game was afoot.

Chapter Sev

If Rachel had had any lingering doubts about
would be exploiting the library for her own ends,
have vanished when she opened its door the nex
was, she was merely dumbstruck.

The room had obviously started out as an organi
store and contemplate books. At some point, though,
spun out of control. There were shelves with books
orderly rows, certainly, but there were other books la
ardly on their sides and jammed in horizontal pi
shelves. The floor was covered with stacks of random
As if that clutter weren't enough, once she'd picked
across to the bookcases, she discovered that what had lo
order from across the room was merely ordered chaos
bound gold-tooled covers snuggled against pulp pap
Victorian authors fought for space with Shakespeare. T
what could nominally be called a section of antiquarian
but even there, eighteenth-century texts stood next to
editions that lay side by side with bound nineteenth-
journals, none protected or preserved in any way other t
being placed on a shelf out of the sunlight.

"Yes. It's very dusty in there, and I'd like to wipe down the books."

"Certainly." He gave a small bow, then another in response to her thanks. "But other than the dust, you have had a successful day?"

"Most successful, thank you." She tied the belt of her coat.

This brief exchange reminded Rachel of her promise to Magda. But how do you investigate a butler? To the best of her knowledge, Fulke had no parents, no family, no life outside Edgar's walls—for all she knew, he might have been born in a tiny suit and shirt, and end each day by zipping himself into a garment bag. He certainly looked that way. *But one is not born a butler,* she said to herself; *one becomes one.* Presumably they were trained. Was there such a thing as (what she supposed must be called) butlering school?

If there were such places, though, Fulke would be long out of one. She stepped to the side of the pavement and stopped to concentrate. *Not a school, then. And if not a school, then what? Then a . . . a . . . of course!* She snapped her fingers: an employment agency. Fulke had presumably been hired from some sort of agency, even if it had been twenty years before, and if he were now looking to leave Edgar's household, presumably he'd take the same route, finding his next job through a recruiter. And she was certain that recruiters, like cavistes, could be found online.

After an hour on the internet back at home, she had the names and phone numbers of five agencies. Evidence suggested that the more sober and restrained their web pages, the better the quality of the services on offer, so she went with ones so discreet that their “positions open” listings featured no mention of salary at all. These were the sorts of places Fulke would turn to, she was sure, and five should be enough to start with.

By the time she called the fourth agency, she had her routine down pat. “Bonjour,” she said to the young female voice that answered, trying to make her own tone round and ripe, full of money and its expectations. “I do hope you can help. My husband and I have been wanting to hire a butler, and the passing of one of our dear friends has, we think, left his *maître d’hotel* without a position.” The voice made an encouraging noise. “But of course one cannot simply ask, particularly so close to the loss.” The voice made a sympathetic noise. “So I am calling the very best agencies, in the hope of finding the one that represents him, to begin inquiries.”

The voice made an understanding noise. Then it asked, “What is the name?”

“The maître d’hotel’s name?” Rachel suddenly realized she didn’t know Fulke’s full name.

“No, no”—the voice gave a little laugh—“the employer’s name. The record will be under the employer’s name.”

Rachel chuckled richly in response, as if at her own foolishness, “Of course. The employer’s name was Bowen. Edgar Bowen.”

There followed the same clicking of keys that she had heard from the caviste, and then the voice said, “*Oui*, Monsieur Bowen is our client, but we have no notation that his maître d’hotel is in search of another posting. Or retiring from service.”

“I’m sorry?” The formulas of discretion were confusing. “Does that mean the butler isn’t leaving his job?”

"According to this record, he is not."

"He's still working for Monsieur Bowen?"

But in focusing on understanding the voice's code phrases, Rachel had forgotten to police herself: her own voice had gone back to its normal inflections. The other voice said nothing for a long moment, and when it spoke again it was clipped and suspicious. "Who is this speaking, please?"

Rachel and Magda had long ago agreed that everyone should have a pseudonym prepared in case of emergency. "Susan Vandervelt," Rachel said.

"Madame Vandervelt, may I take your contact information, so that we may telephone you back to discuss this further?"

Rachel and Magda had never considered the value of prepared contact information. Rachel felt silence beginning to stretch out in front of her and her own heart starting to beat faster in panic. *Stay calm,* she ordered herself. *Think like a detective. Act like a detective. Do what a detective would do.*

She hung up.

Two minutes later, she was on the phone with Magda, repeating the voice's words.

"What does that mean?" Magda snapped. "That he's not seeking a new posting or retiring from service?"

"I had trouble understanding that too. But judging by the last thing she said to me, it means he isn't leaving his job with Edgar. Or with David now, I suppose. So it means that David hasn't dismissed him. But also"—she took a breath—"it means he hasn't resigned. He isn't trying to leave."

"All right. But so what?"

Rachel laid out the connection. "If he isn't trying to leave, it means he doesn't see any reason to leave. He isn't worried that if he stays, someone will discover something or figure something out."

There was a silence. Then Magda said, "Or it could mean he thinks he's safe. Or that he's not taking any action until he's sure he *isn't* safe."

"No," Rachel said firmly. "I don't buy that. I don't care who you are; anyone who's just committed murder would want to get out of the range of suspicion as quickly as possible. Especially if you commit a murder like that, where there's plenty of mess that could get on you or your surroundings and mark you out."

"Maybe he's a seasoned murderer," Magda said. "Maybe he's practiced enough to be able to keep his cool and play the long game."

"He's been Edgar's butler for over twenty years." Rachel was no longer patient. "Where in that period do you see him gaining experience in murder? Or did he acquire his seasoning before he took his position with Edgar? From hired assassin to butler in one quick step?"

Again Magda fell silent. When she finally spoke, her tone was truculent. "Fine," she said. "The bottom of the list."

Chapter Eight

When Rachel opened the library door the next morning, she found a tray with tea and a small plate of cookies waiting for her—and the books polished to gleaming. A clean yellow dust cloth hung folded over the end of one shelf. She wondered, not for the first time, why she didn't have a butler.

But she was here to observe, not ponder the unfairness of life, and in any case no decent person can resist the lure of a library. Maybe because the books looked so much better without dust, she found herself warming to her task. How to approach the job? She spent a happy half hour considering whether to arrange, then catalogue; or catalogue as she arranged; or catalogue, then arrange by what she discovered when cataloguing, without coming to any decision. She decided to begin by listing the contents of the piles that surrounded her.

In the nearest stack, she found a complete first edition of the works of Lord Byron in French. Two stacks later, the entire pile was a first edition of the collected Dickens. There was a small first edition of Stevenson's *Strange Case of Doctor Jekyll and Mister Hyde*; there was the New York Edition of Henry James. The shelf of antiquarian books turned out to house early

French medical texts (*Librarie Jose Corti beside the Jardin du Luxembourg,* she thought: they had gone there often), first editions of Samuel Beckett, and—she leaned closer. Was that a complete set of the Paris Edition of the Gutenberg Bible? Even she knew that was fantastically rare.

Later that morning, she was writing down the last of the titles when there was a light knock on the door. It opened a few inches, and Mademoiselle des Troyes's blonde head appeared.

"Bonjour." She smiled tightly.

Rachel looked up from where she sat on an ottoman next to the tea tray, and smiled back. "Bonjour."

The girl stepped further into the room. "I wonder if I could just stay here and rest a little." She pushed a lock of hair behind an ear. "I'm trying to organize the papers in Edgar's bureau, and it's . . ." She didn't need to go on; her sorrowful face explained for her.

"Of course." Rachel gestured to a nearby chair. "It would be a pleasure."

The girl settled herself, saying nothing as Rachel began to look through the piles on the floor once again. Maybe she did only want refuge, for as well as not speaking, she scarcely moved, her hands clasped in her lap and her gaze focused on some invisible point ahead of her. Rachel could feel her own insides quivering, partly with tension and partly with overwhelming excitement at the good fortune that had fallen into her lap. Still, she knew enough to stay silent: people tell you things when they're ready.

Eventually, the girl sighed. "It's very quiet here without Edgar. I don't know how I'll get used to it."

Was it so loud when Edgar was alive?"

"No." She frowned as if considering an essential question. "But when he was here, one knew. He had great presence." Her eyes filled with tears.

Rachel felt a sudden flash of empathy. Even when she had known Edgar, the force of him had been more than his appearance suggested. When he was in a room, or, yes, even just in the same apartment, the air felt more alive. He didn't need to be near you: his mere presence in the vicinity made the atoms crackle. And the lack of that had been hard to adjust to. She remembered moments alone after their break-up, when she had suddenly realized that her loneliness wasn't for an expected remark or a specific incident, but for a vitality; it was a realization of how still the air was without Edgar. For a minute, she felt for Mademoiselle des Troyes as one young woman might feel for another. She patted her arm. "Yes. He was a vivid man. That loss is hard, I know, mademoiselle."

"Elisabeth, please." The girl blinked, gave a watery smile. "My mother named me after the princess killed during the Revolution." She said apologetically, "My mother is a bit . . . unusual."

Rachel rolled her eyes. "I think all mothers are a bit unusual."

Elisabeth laughed, an openhearted sound, surprisingly loud, and looked at Rachel with real pleasure. Trying to build on her luck, Rachel said carefully, "How long did you know Edgar, Elisabeth?"

"I've known him for about three years."

Rachel noticed the present tense. "You were his secretary?"

"No, no." She shook her thick hair, then pulled the sleeves of her carnation-colored sweater down over her hands, like a child trying to warm up. "I came first as his cleaner. I am at university, and I needed money, so I went to an agency, and they sent me here. After three or four weeks, he said I was no cleaner, but he knew I needed the money. He wanted to keep me on so he could pay me. So I became his *aide de bureau*." Rachel recognized the French phrase for Girl Friday. "I just"—Elisabeth waved her hand—"assisted him with his life."

"Life Assistant": another position going begging in her own case. But there was no time to dwell on this injustice; the girl was asking her a question.

"And you? How do you know Edgar?" She used the formal pronoun *vous*. *Are murderers that polite,* Rachel wondered. Then she sighed inwardly. In France, they probably were.

"Well . . ." She decided honesty was the best policy. "We met a long time ago. More than twenty years ago. And for about two years I was his *petite amie*."

Elisabeth's eyes widened. "*Ah bon!* Then you know! You know that Edgar was so kind!" She looked earnestly at Rachel, one devotee to another.

"Yes." Rachel nodded. She did know. "When we met, I was a catering waitress, and I was embarrassed to admit I wrote poetry in my spare time. But he said I should think of myself as a poet who just happened to be doing some catering. He believed in me. And he was the first person I ever read my poems to." She smiled as she shook her head. "He applauded." For a second she lingered over the memory. But duty called. "And you? In what ways was he kind to you?" She tried not to sound too probing as she probed.

"Oh, he was always thoughtful about my welfare, even

from the first day I arrived. Always there would be coffee or a cold drink while I worked."

Rachel thought this was more an example of Fulke's professionalism than of Edgar's care, but she said nothing.

"And he always asked how my studies were going," she continued, "if I was enjoying my life. I'm doing media studies at CELSA." She used the acronym for the Sorbonne's school of journalism just outside Paris, the Centre d'Études Littéraires et Scientifiques Appliquées. "I'm focusing on television structures and demographics. Once he knew that, he would ask me my opinions of certain programs or for my ideas about why a program worked or didn't work.

"Of course," she added hastily, as if she feared Rachel would think ill of her for this fraternization, "we didn't interact like that from the first. But if you take someone's suits to the *pressing*, if you help him answer his post, if you answer his phone, you become close. And then, after some months, he began to invite me to stay to dine some nights when Madame Nadeau wasn't here, and sometimes to watch and discuss a television program after. We began to talk, you know, as friends. Not as employer and employee." Like Rachel a few seconds before, she smiled in remembrance. "And he was so thoughtful! He would keep a bottle of my favorite rosé on hand, just in case I stayed to dinner."

Rachel jerked to attention. Had she really heard what she thought she'd heard? She just had time to shift position in an effort to hide her jump before Elisabeth began again. "He was good to me," she said sadly. "Very good. And so when he—" Then she stopped abruptly, her eyes widening.

Rachel caught her breath. First an inadvertent revelation and now a significant halt! She had hoped to find one small clue, but here was an embarrassment of riches. She didn't know which line to pursue first, but after a second she decided the wine could wait. Better to press on than circle back.

Damping down her excitement, she leaned forward gently, making her voice soft. "What?" She considered touching the girl's arm as encouragement, but held back. "He what?"

"I don't know." Elisabeth swallowed, looked at her hands once more. "I lost my train of thought."

"We were agreeing that Edgar was very kind. And you were telling me how he was kind to *you*." Rachel tried to keep frustration out of her voice. "And you were about to tell me something he did, or maybe asked?"

"No, no," Elisabeth's tone was a closing door. "He never asked anything. He was kind. He was kind in all ways. Always." She sat back, bringing one of her hands, no longer covered by a sleeve, to her mouth. Its knuckles were white, and Rachel knew she would get no more from her now.

Chapter Nine

"Which do you think she realized and regretted?" Magda said. "That she'd mentioned the rosé or that she'd started to reveal something else?"

"Or both?" Rachel added. They were having lunch at Le Chant des Voyelles near the Centre Pompidou, and the waiter had just put down their starters. She waited until he left, then said, "I don't know. But both make her look bad." Then she reconsidered. "Well, except that she has no way of knowing that we know about the rosé. So she must have regretted the start of some revelation. But what? And actually, she has no way of knowing that we don't know about the rosé either—after all, those women at the funeral knew. So maybe she *was* realizing her mistake, after the fact."

"So not very conclusive either way." Magda took a spoonful of her soup. "And you don't think she might have been about to reveal a change in their relationship?" Magda asked. "One way of reading what she said—all that 'he's warm, he's kind, we were closer than just employer and employee, I've said too much'—is code for 'we were lovers.'" Her tone made it plain she would choose that reading.

"No." Rachel shook her head. "No, I truly don't think so. In fact, after our conversation I'm more convinced that they weren't. I know it's ridiculous to say it in this day and age, but she's not that kind of girl."

Magda gave her a look.

"I know, but that's the best phrase. Honestly, I don't think the possibility of sex with Edgar would even occur to her."

"Fine." Magda shook her head. "She's not that kind of girl. But he could have been that kind of man. It could have occurred to him." She waited for a long minute, and when she spoke again, it was with many pauses and hesitations. "You don't think—well, that he might have, you know *coerced* her? And that the money was meant as an apology? Or an attempt to make it up to her?"

"No." Rachel was firm. "Just—no."

"All right." Magda looked carefully at her. "I'm sorry. But one of us had to say it."

"I know." Rachel nodded. She wasn't angry; the question had needed to be considered. "But there's no way. Edgar just wouldn't be interested in that kind of sex—he didn't have that in his character." She saw Magda's face: they both knew about plenty of women who said just those sorts of things about men who turned to have *precisely* that in their characters. "I know. But it's true. Besides, there just wasn't any sense of sexual involvement of any sort, in her body, in her tone. And she said Edgar was kind. She stressed that, and it didn't sound forced or false."

If not fully convinced, Magda was at least convinced enough to let it go. "All right. He's not that kind of man; she's not that kind of girl. But then we're left with the question, what kind of girl *is* she?"

Rachel took a bite of her *oeufs en cocotte* to buy herself time to think. She had discovered Le Chant des Voyelles many years before, as a Paris novice, and over twenty years she'd kept returning to it. If you asked her what made her come back, she would point to the restaurant's comfortable friendliness; to the way that on summer nights your dining experience might suddenly be interrupted by a chatty passing transvestite; to the fact that, just two hundred yards from Paris's most famous shrine to postmodernism, the restaurant faced out onto an ancient cobbled lane. But eventually she would have to admit that it was the *oeufs en cocotte.* She had tried these eggs covered in sauce and served in ramekins at restaurants all over Paris, but none could better the ones she found here. Closing her eyes, she let the egg slide over her tongue, its pale taste complicated by the sauce's buttery tang. Then she turned her attention back to the subject of Elisabeth.

"She's—I hate to use this word, but she's *nice.* It's the perfect word for her. She's simple; she's sweet. She doesn't seem to have much depth, that's true, but that means she doesn't have any slyness or duplicity either." She took another mouthful. "But . . ."

"Yes?" Magda, who had looked bored during the description of the niceness, perked up as she sensed a complication. "But what?"

"Well, she must have a bit of deceitfulness because she stopped talking. She determinedly and deliberately kept something from me. She didn't do a very good job of hiding it, but the fact that she cut herself off in the first place shows there's something she doesn't want me to know. She's being deceitful about something."

"So not entirely guileless." Magda tapped her spoon against the bottom of her soup bowl meditatively. "Well, there's no rule that says simple people can't connive or commit murder. In fact, I once read that most criminals—at least the ones who are caught—aren't very smart. That's why they're caught. So"—she smiled at the waiter as he removed their dishes—"smart enough to commit murder, but not quite smart enough or wary enough to keep her guard up fully afterward?"

"But what about the rosé?" Rachel was reconsidering again. "That's more serious than not remembering to keep your guard fully up. It wasn't a slight slip. If she's the murderer—murderess—that was a serious error. Even if she thinks no one knows about the rosé on the table, or knows that Edgar didn't like rosé, she can't guarantee that someone won't find out at some point. After all, we did. So if she did do it, you'd think she'd be very careful not to make that kind of slip. But if she's innocent," she continued, her voice became thoughtful, "there's no reason why she shouldn't mention the rosé. So that would suggest she's innocent—that she mentioned the rosé because it meant nothing to her."

Having no spoon anymore, Magda tapped an index finger on the table as she considered these points. "Unless . . . unless it's a double bluff. Unless she's just appearing simple and sweet, but, in fact, she *is* the murderer, and the supposedly accidental slip was meant to convince us she wasn't the murderer, because no murderer would be that foolish."

"Occam's razor," Rachel said.

"What?"

"The principle of Occam's razor."

Magda was lost. "Isn't that the one that says the simplest answer is always the right answer?"

Rachel nodded. "And that principle would decree that your scenario is too complicated to be right." Then she realized something. "But, in fact, it doesn't make any difference if she's double-bluffing, or single-bluffing, or not bluffing at all, because bluff or no bluff, she has something she wants to hide, and that makes her suspect all by itself. And from what she told me, she was a regular dinner guest, too. Which gives her both means and opportunity." Then she stopped. "But we still don't know if she had motive, because *we don't know what she's hiding.*" Inwardly, she ground her teeth. Should she have pushed the girl more? Could she have driven her to reveal something really significant? Or even into a confession?

"Well," Magda said, narrowing her eyes, "we might be able to gather some kind of clue from what she told you." She leaned forward. "Tell me exactly what you said to each other."

Rachel took a deep breath, concentrating. "Well, first she said Edgar was so kind."

"And she called him 'Edgar'? Not 'Monsieur Bowen'?"

"No." Rachel made a face, but then remembered that Elisabeth had called Catherine Nadeau "Madame Nadeau." Intrigued, she asked, "Why?"

At that moment the waiter appeared with the main course. Rachel looked enviously at Magda's wing of skate, thinking what a pity it was to have a hot dish cool while its intended consumer had to give a long explanation. Maybe Magda would be willing to . . . ?

Magda moved her plate closer to herself meaningfully. Not

looking at Rachel, she quickly picked up her knife and used it to cut the wing's tender flesh. "Well," she said, "the fact that she didn't call him 'Monsieur Bowen' shows that they did have an informal relationship. It suggests that she's telling the truth about that."

Rachel was impressed by Magda's reasoning powers, but Magda just popped a piece of fish in her mouth, chewed, then took a breath. "Okay, then what did you say to her?"

"I said yes, he was kind, but then I asked her in what ways he was kind to her. You know, sort of opening the way. And she said he asked about her studies, and they spent a lot of time together, chatted like friends, and came to know each other quite well. They watched television together. She said he was very good to her. And then she said, 'So when he—' and she stopped. I did try to push, but she said I'd heard wrong." Rachel poked at her salade Niçoise.

"Right." Magda chewed another mouthful, swallowed. "Well to start with, that 'So when he' *blank* suggests that whatever he did, he did it after they became close."

Rachel picked up the thread. "And *that* suggests that he needed to know her well before he *blank*. And she did make it sound as if he'd made an effort to get close to her before he did whatever it was."

"And *that* suggests"—Magda was quicker now—"that whatever he did or said or asked or gave or took or *whatever*, he knew she'd need to be friends with him before she'd consider it."

"Right." Rachel gathered herself, counted on her fingers. "So. He couldn't just ask her casually—she was clearly upset by whatever he did ask—and whatever he asked depended on, but was in contrast to, his kindness."

Magda nodded.

"Those suggest it wasn't something spontaneous and it wasn't something easy. And all of that suggests—"

"—it was something big," Magda finished.

They looked at each other, mutually surprised and proud of their abilities. Rachel stabbed her fork into a piece of lettuce; Magda scraped off a bit of skate and put it in her mouth.

Rachel said quietly, "And from the way she led up to it, I'd say whatever it was, she agreed to do it."

Magda swallowed. "So she gets a lot of money after Edgar's death for doing something that obviously made her ashamed when he was alive. That's two motives: money and fear."

"True." But Rachel still couldn't deny her doubts. "But you could not find anyone who looks and acts less like a killer. And let's not forget—she didn't expect such a large bequest, so she wouldn't have killed him for it."

"Well," Magda said, "it's early days yet. In fact, if you look at the conversation a different way, it's quite positive: you've only been there two days, and already you have a lead." She sighed, but her sigh held a hint of satisfaction. "As you say, the very fact that she so obviously didn't give something away gave something away. She's clearly done at least one thing involving Edgar that she wants to keep secret." She took another bite, gave another swallow. "And Mathilde? Anything there?"

Rachel shook her head. "Not a thing. Not even the shadow of a thing." She speared a caper bitterly. "What about you? How did your research go?"

"Ah, Madame Nadeau!" Magda leaned over, pulled a small

hardcover notebook from her bag, and flipped it open. "Catherine Nadeau owns a boutique that sells decorative housewares. For walk-in trade, I gather, which would be why our paths never crossed. The store is called Le Cindy." She held up a forestalling hand. "Don't ask. I don't know. But that's what it's called. It doesn't have much of an online presence—maybe why I'd never heard of it—but it's in the first, on Rue des Bordonnais."

That was probably how Edgar met her, Rachel guessed. His browsing tendencies and love of unusual words and phrases would have led him to go into this strangely named store close to home.

Magda was still talking. "And here's something very interesting. I found this in an online local business newsletter. The store will have a 'reopening' next week after being closed for two months." She sat back, satisfied with her bombshell, then saw Rachel's blank face and leaned forward again. "Okay, I can see how that might not mean anything if you don't know retail. Let me explain. If a store is willing to give up two months of sales, that means there's some kind of trouble. And if a store is willing to give up two months of sales during the Christmas season, that means it's serious trouble, because that's serious income loss. And in retail"—she pointed her knife at Rachel to emphasize her point—"the only serious trouble is money trouble. Which means Madame Nadeau needed money."

Now Rachel understood. "She's using Edgar's bequest, or the assurance of it, to reopen her store. The bequest made the difference between the store's failure and a chance for it to be a success."

Magda nodded. "And that means—"

Rachel chimed in, so they spoke together again, "—it was worth killing for."

They looked at each other.

"We need to follow up," Rachel said.

Magda nodded again, firmly. "Right." Then stopped. "But how?"

Rachel was surprised at how obvious the answer was. "We'll go to the store."

"We will?"

"Sure. I'll be in the area. I like a nice boutique—we'll drop in. It'll be perfectly natural. It's a reopening; people will be dropping in all the time."

Magda made the connection. "You'll be in the area. You'll be working in the library. Which is in Edgar's apartment, which is also in the first." She took a bite. "We could go on Monday."

"Perfect." Then Rachel remembered their initial subject and frowned. "And Elisabeth? What are we going to do there?"

"Oh, Elisabeth." Magda thought. "She doesn't look like a criminal."

Rachel nodded.

"And she doesn't act like a criminal."

Rachel nodded again.

"But," Magda said, her voice was wise, "not all criminals look or act like criminals." Another pause, and then she said brightly, "Well, you'll just have to watch her to see if she does."

The astuteness born of a thousand true crime documentaries had spoken. There was nothing else but to keep watching and waiting. Rachel lifted a hand to signal the waiter. Since she needed to keep her strength up for all the watching, waiting, and walking into stores, she'd have the chocolate terrine with mint sauce to finish.

Chapter Ten

When Rachel arrived at the appartement on Monday morning, Edgar's entrance hall was dotted with boxes. It was also, she discovered, no longer Edgar's entrance hall.

"Monsieur David is moving in," Fulke said.

That was fast, Rachel thought. But it would inconvenience no one but Fulke, and he didn't look inconvenienced in the least. She could hear noises in the back rooms that she supposed must be David settling in. Should she say hello to the new owner of the place where she was working? She couldn't really ignore him—an introduction could be dodged at a funeral where he was chief mourner and she only a fleeting presence, but basic politeness seemed to dictate that you should at least be introduced to someone whose house you were working in. She corrected herself: be *re*introduced.

In response to her request, Fulke led her into the salon, where David bent over a box. Unsure how to start, Rachel was thankful to find the tricky navigation taken out of her hands when Fulke said in a slightly raised voice, "Monsieur Bowen, Madame Levis is here."

David lifted his head. The morning light made his sallow

skin pale and the edges of his eyes pink, but the pinched look she'd seen at the funeral and the will reading was gone. Instead, he wore the usual expression of a man in the middle of relocation: confusion combined with a healthy dose of frustration. When he saw her, however, he broke into a surprisingly sweet smile.

"Madame Levis? No, not Madame Levis. Rachel!" He stepped forward. "Hello! I thought I recognized you from somewhere when we all met with Maître Bernard, but I didn't realize who you were until after you'd left." He took her hand. "Now I see you haven't changed at all. You're just as I vaguely remembered you." He smiled again at this weak joke, then kissed her on both cheeks. He sniffed as he pulled away and said apologetically, "Sorry. I'm recovering from a terrible cold. A real winter beast."

Rachel searched his face for remnants of the child she had known, but saw none. Maybe a trace lingered in the long eyelashes or the vague softness that lingered around his jaw, but no more. She could see Edgar in him, though, in the hazel eyes and the shape of the mouth. Mathilde too was easy to spot: he had her autocratic nose with its fine nostrils, currently embossed with a thin edging of red.

"You're working in the library?" David asked. She nodded. "My father was a strange man, asking you to do that. Well, I might come and visit you. Although God knows I have enough to do." He looked around ruefully. "I always thought I didn't own much."

"Everyone thinks that until they move." She smiled. "And any time you want to take a break and come see me, I would be delighted."

"I'd like that." He sniffled again. "*Pardon*. Why not today? I'll come as a reward for finishing this horror, and we can have a proper talk."

"Lovely." Rachel smiled again. "You know where I'll be." She held up a hand in farewell.

"It was very good to remeet you!" he called after her. *Still a delightful boy,* Rachel thought—*and such a charmer!* Then she felt a pang of melancholy at being old enough to think of a man his age as a boy. *Ah, well,* she thought, *age comes to us all. Or most of us,* she qualified. It hadn't come, or had only very recently come, to Edgar. What was going on with his death that she couldn't see?

"Enough," she said aloud. She needed to stop thinking; she would shake herself out of it by concentrating on the books. She closed the library door and sat determinedly on the ottoman, taking up her pad and pencil. For the next few hours nothing disturbed her but Fulke's discreet delivery of tea. When a knock at the door interrupted her focus, she was surprised to see from her watch that it was nearly one in the afternoon.

"Come in," she called.

The door opened to reveal David. He looked around the room and smiled. "So, the inner sanctum! May I enter?"

"Of course! It's your home."

He crossed the carpet and sat down. Almost immediately one of his knees began to jiggle. Rachel found herself touched by this demonstration of nerves as well as by the hesitant voice in which he began. "You know," he said, swallowing, "since the will reading, I've thought I remembered . . . Could it be that once you tied my shoelaces?"

Rachel gave a laugh. "Once? When you and I knew each other, that was my main job."

"Ah!" He raised his eyebrows, and the gesture, although not supercilious, was his mother's. "This must be why it was the first thing I associated with you. And I think I remember us going to the park."

She nodded. "The Jardin des Plantes. Your father loved to go there on the weekends, and he would let you run around while we walked. Only"—she smiled at the memory and called, in imitation of Edgar's long-ago voice, "'Not too far!' I can't count the times I had to hunt you down."

"Yes, that's right." The air between them suddenly felt awkward, and a pause stretched into a silence. At last he said inconsequentially, "So, the library." He swallowed again, sniffed. "Dad always gave the impression that the library was full of valuable things."

"Oh, it is!" Rachel's antennae pricked up at the inference that he didn't know the room's contents. For her, such a lack of bibliophilia was unacceptable. He had no idea what pleasures he had in his grasp! "Look." She rose from the ottoman and crossed to a shelf. "This is a complete Dickens, the first full edition published in England. Have you read any Dickens?"

David nodded. "*Great Expectations*, I think." He popped up from the chair, his long legs like springs, and came to stand beside her.

"Now you can read them all," she said. "And in the original! And here's a complete Henry James. Have you read anything by him?" He shook his head. She moved over, patted the spines of the Samuel Beckett books. "Beckett is much more French, so you might like him better. And these first editions will only go up and up in value." She lifted her hand to a higher shelf. "And this"—she pulled down the Gutenberg facsimile, snug in its slipcase—"is a reproduction of the first book printed in the West with moveable type. Look," she said, sliding the first volume out and opening it at random to the Song of Solomon, decorated with brilliant marginal illustrations. "Isn't it lovely? It's a facsimile of one of only something like forty surviving copies of the Gutenberg Bible. I read on the internet that it's worth thousands in its own right."

David put out a finger and traced the blue and red trailing vines on the page. "Beautiful." Then he gave a little shake. In his face Rachel could see the beginnings of an awareness she knew well. It was like the first time she had seen the Eiffel Tower up close: a thing that had seemed familiar, manageable, had revealed itself to be immensely complex, vastly more than she had ever envisioned. She could see the dawning realization of possibility on David's face as he took the volume from her, staring at it.

Just then there was a light knock on the door, and Fulke entered with fresh tea and cookies. He substituted the new tray for the old and withdrew. David put the Gutenberg volume back carefully and sat down again, pouring the tea. Again his leg began to jiggle. "So," he said. "So."

The spell was broken, Rachel realized. She had been mistaken in her belief that this would be a reintroduction. They were strangers, and beyond those long-ago shoelaces and the Jardin des Plantes, they had no point of connection. What did they have to say to each other besides remarks about the books or the past, really? Then she thought, *Well, we do have one other topic of conversation.* She cleared her throat.

"How have you been?"

She saw that he understood. "Oh, well." His shrug said he was managing. The knee kept going.

She tried again. "It must be difficult to be here."

"Not really." This time his shrug was French—*this is trivial*, it said. "This isn't where I grew up; it's more somewhere I used to come to visit Dad. And I'm only moving into a bit of it. Elisabeth is still working in the bureau, and the dining room is too big for me on my own, so I'm just using the salon and the bedroom. So moving here is like moving into a place that's been in the family, but isn't really your home."

"Oh." It was hard to know what to do with that. "You must"—she paused delicately, but nothing in the air made her feel she couldn't continue—"miss your father here, though. I mean," she retracted slightly, "you must feel his absence."

"Oh yes." He put up a hand and pinched his nostrils together, breathing in. This conversation was not going well either. Maybe she shouldn't have asked. But he continued. "We were close. Very close."

"Yes, you were, I remember." She smiled at the memory.

"Right from the start, after the divorce . . ." he trailed off, then restarted. "He was easy to be with. My mother—" He stopped.

Oh, please, let it not be like Elisabeth, Rachel thought. *Please let him go on*. She took a deep breath. "Your mother?"

He rose abruptly, crossed over to the window, and stood with his back to her as he spoke, drumming his fingers on the sill. Finally he said, "My mother is very focused on what matters to her. Maybe more on that than anything else." His tone made it clear that he did not come very high on Mathilde's list of what mattered.

Not knowing what to say, Rachel said nothing. David crossed the floor, settled back into his chair. "I don't mean she was an absent parent. Far from it." That knee again. "And it's not just that I lived with her. She was so often at Dad's apartment when I was too."

"Yes." One side of Rachel's mouth quirked. "I remember that."

"She still wanted to spend time with Dad after the divorce. I guess she wanted me to have a sense of family." David shrugged. "Although maybe they really were friends, because I think she even kept that up all these years. I found some rosé in the cave yesterday, and Dad hated rosé. So he must have kept it around for her."

"I'm sorry?" Rachel felt herself grow cold, then hot. "Your mother drinks rosé?"

"She loves it." David pursed his lips. "*Declassé*, yes?"

"You—" Her voice was high. She swallowed and tried again. "You don't drink it?"

He shook his head. "'The wine of the untutored palate,' Dad used to say. Well, I suppose people are complicated—even my mother. And Dad . . ." He started to smile, but then his face fell. "He never could say no. I remember, when I was thirteen, it turned out I was going to need—*les bagues*—braces. Oh, my teeth were a mess!" He grimaced at the memory. "And the dentist said that to fix them I should wear my—how do you say it in English?—my outside dental gear all the time."

"Headgear," Rachel supplied.

"Yes, that's right, headgear. He said I should wear my headgear all the time. He said I could think of it as a fashion statement." He rolled his eyes. "To a thirteen-year-old! Of course I was in despair. I would be a monster! No girl would ever kiss me! And my father"—his knee jiggled faster as his voice sped up—"he paid for me to have those braces that go inside the teeth, so no one would ever see them. They were a new thing then, and not cheap. But for me . . ." He smiled again, shook his head. "So of course he bought her the wine she liked!" His eyes were even redder than before.

Heartache at his sorrow battled with excitement at his revelations, leaving Rachel at a loss for a response. But before she could even try to formulate one, he popped out of the chair yet again. "Would you excuse me a moment?"

"Of course." She nodded and continued to sit after he was gone, trying to focus. When he returned, although he held a wad of tissues, he looked much more bright-eyed. She felt guilty for starting the conversation. He was, after all, a grieving child, not a therapy subject or a witness: what was information to her was family to him. She tried to think of something lighter to talk about.

But there was no chance to start over. "I'm sorry," David said. "I'm meant to be going out for lunch. I forgot. I'm meeting a friend." He sniffed again, swiped at his nose with the tissues. She stood up and made to move forward, but he held out a hand to stop her. "I won't kiss you—I don't want you to get my germs." He smiled his sweet smile.

She would have liked to hug him, both to comfort him and to make some sort of apology for causing him pain, but he was gone too quickly. She sighed and stared out the window herself for a second, following the choppy waves that lifted the gray surface of the Seine. Then she smiled and started to pack up her bag. Mathilde a rosé drinker! The plot thickened.

* * *

"The plot thickens," Magda said. She had listened to Rachel's report of the day's discoveries as they walked toward Catherine Nadeau's store.

"Of course," Rachel said, feeling she had to point it out, "Elisabeth made it plain she has something to hide, which still puts her at the top of our list."

Magda drew her collar more tightly around her throat to keep out the cold. "Unless David said anything else of significance. Did he?"

"Apparently Mathilde still visited the appartement a lot even after he grew up, spending time with Edgar."

Magda turned to look at her. "Was she there that night?"

"Well, obviously he doesn't know *that*."

Magda deflated a bit but shook it off. "All right, don't get cranky. And speaking of David, he moved in? Is there anything significant there, do you think? It seems quick."

"I thought so too. But neither he nor Fulke seemed to find it even worthy of comment." Rachel shrugged.

Whatever suggestion Magda would have put forward next remained unspoken, because they had arrived at their destination. "GRAND RELAUNCH!!!" said a loud banner strung across the store window. Beneath it was a somewhat calmer yellow smiley face with "Back at last!" written over the top. Rachel pushed the door open, and a bell tinkled.

She looked around. It didn't seem like Edgar's kind of

place. The store's shelves were crowded with whimsical decorative items. Pineapples featured heavily: as lamps, as bonbon jars, as the sort of candles that smell strongly when you shove your nose into them, but not at all when you light them. There were hearts complexly woven from wrought iron, and giant birdcages that would never house a real bird—*statement birdcages*, Rachel thought to herself. Artfully arranged tables held various household accessories designed to appeal to those who describe their own taste as "quirky": drawer pulls made to look like dachshunds, a neon pink lamp in the shape of a hippo. Paris was littered with boutiques likes this; most were there one month and gone the next.

Catherine Nadeau emerged from the back room. If at the will reading her outfit had been elegantly casual, today it was all business, entirely black. The red lipstick remained, though, decorating a smiling mouth.

"Bonjour!" she said, coming forward. "Bonjour et *bienvenue*!"

"Bonjour!" Rachel replied. Then her face became surprised (she had practiced in front of the mirror the previous evening). "Oh my goodness! I think I know you!"

Madame Nadeau looked at her closely, then nodded. *"Mais bien sûr!"* She smiled in welcome again. "You are the woman who arrived late to my Edgar's will reading."

Rachel suspected she wasn't going to like Madame Nadeau very much. Still, putting business before pleasure, she returned her smile. "Yes." She put her hand on her chest. "Rachel Levis. And this is my friend, Magda Stevens." Magda nodded.

"Catherine Nadeau." There was a flurry of cheek kissing.

"What a coincidence!" Rachel made herself sound happily

amazed. "Magda was just picking me up from my work in Edgar's library, and we noticed the store and thought we'd come in. Your stock is charming."

"So cute!" added Magda.

"Ah!" Catherine looked pleased. "That's exactly what I was going for."

"You succeeded." Rachel smiled again. "And you've just had it redecorated?" She gestured backward toward the banner.

"Redecor—?" Then Catherine understood. "Ah, no, no. We had to close for a short time. You know," she waved a hand airily, "this economy. It makes retail difficult. But now . . ." She cast a meaningful look at Rachel. "Well, I am able to open once more. Such a relief. Although also, of course," she added hurriedly, "so sad. I thought Edgar would be with us for many years more."

"Yes, well . . ." Given her beliefs about Edgar's death, Rachel felt this was a subject best avoided. "I'm sure he meant the bequest to be helpful. And it has been."

"Yes." Catherine's voice warmed as if at a private pleasure. "I don't expect further problems. So"—she opened her arms expansively—"please explore my store. I mean it to be homey!"

Rachel pretended to browse. The items weren't cheaply made or uniformly hideous. It was just that they were so determined to have personality that they ended up having none at all.

"How did you know Edgar?"

She jumped at hearing Catherine's voice so close to her.

"The same way you did, funnily. I was his girlfriend many years ago."

"Ah, yes. He seems to have had so many! But," Catherine

said, smiling conspiratorially, "you and I must be special; we are the only ones who were in his will." Suddenly she clasped her hands together. "Oh, I know! Because we are sisters in experience, you and your friend must have a drink with me to celebrate my little relaunch."

"Oh no, no, we couldn't," Rachel protested.

"I insist. You are my first customers since I reopened, and I have a lovely rosé in the *frigo* here."

Rachel said, "A rosé?" Instinctively, she looked for Magda.

"Yes, a little Mas de Cadenet. I adore rosé. It suits all occasions."

She retreated back into the depths of the store, and Rachel turned around to find Magda right behind her. "She adores rosé!"

"I heard." They stared at each other.

Catherine reemerged with three filled wine glasses on a tray, and they each took one.

Magda said cheerily, "To Le Cindy!"

"To Le Cindy," Rachel echoed. Catherine looked pleased, and she felt a twinge.

They chatted as they sipped the wine. Rachel learned that Catherine had met Edgar at a gallery opening two years before, and that they had been together ever since.

"He liked the idea of the store from the start," she confided. "I think he admired my business plan. You know, stores like this are very popular: one sees them everywhere."

"A secure venture." Magda's voice and face were serious.

"Oh yes!" She gave a tinkling laugh. "I think he recognized that. He even made several little investments here." Suddenly struck by a thought, she said, "I suppose I could see his bequest as his last investment." Again she sobered abruptly. "Not that I would do that, of course."

"Of course not." Magda sipped her wine, carefully not meeting Rachel's eye.

"So Edgar backed the store?" Rachel tried not to sound too interested.

"He helped a little." Catherine sipped her rosé. "I had a large amount of initial capital from my divorce settlement." Again she gave her high-pitched laugh. "Yes, I am a cliché! The Parisian divorcée who opens a little store after her husband walks out." She waved a hand. "Not that I'm complaining. I'm certainly better off without my husband, and he was generous in the settlement."

"And," Rachel said, gesturing around, "you put the money to good use."

Catherine nodded once, acknowledging the compliment. Then she made a face. "But one must be so mindful, so careful!" She clicked her tongue. "Let me tell you, the saying is true: if you want to open a shop, double your budget!" She took another sip. "Which is why Edgar's little contributions were so helpful."

"And apparently his final vote of confidence has done you a good turn, too." Magda said cheerfully. "You're up and running once more!" Then she dared a question. "And you don't anticipate further bumps in the road?"

Catherine waved a hand again. "Oh, I have a good plan for the future."

Seeing an opening, Rachel said quickly, "Well, you must allow us to contribute to your profits before we leave." She picked up a nearby pineapple candle. "I've been eyeing this the whole time we've been here. It's so fun. And"—she shoved her nose into it—"mmmm."

Catherine wrapped and bagged the candle. While handing over Rachel's change, she said, "You should give me your number. We could meet for an *apéro*."

Rachel hesitated but then remembered that she was on the job: this woman's information could be useful. They exchanged numbers.

"That store," Rachel said once she and Magda were some distance down the road, "Edgar put money into *that* store."

"Maybe it was love." Magda's voice was equally mystified. "Maybe love blinds you to tackiness."

Rachel stalked along, reflecting that she'd just paid fifteen euros for some of that tackiness. As if reading her mind, Magda said, "It was worth the candle, though. Look what we learned."

Rachel tried to separate her mind from her purse. What had they learned? "She really did need Edgar's money. In fact, it probably made all the difference to her business. I don't see that store lasting for another three months as it is, never mind without the injection of Edgar's bequest."

"And she drinks rosé!" Magda gave a little skip. "This is great! She had reason to do it, she could easily have done it, and there's strong evidence to link her to it."

"Yes, but Elisabeth and Mathilde drink rosé too," Rachel pointed out. "And we don't know if Catherine was at Edgar's place either. So it isn't as if we've closed the case."

"No, but we're further along." Magda was unwilling to let go of her elation now that they had an actual, legitimate suspect. "We're gathering evidence, getting all our ducks in a row."

Rachel felt that somehow those images didn't quite work together, but she let it pass.

Magda kept talking. "We could hardly expect the solution to fall into our laps after one week. That's never the way it happens. And better many suspects than none at all."

"Ugh." Rachel found both prospects equally disheartening.

"Cheer up." Magda picked up her pace. "After all, you get to have a drink with Madame Nadeau."

Chapter Eleven

As David unpacked over the next few days, he continued to visit the library occasionally, and despite his lingering cold he always seemed eager to talk. Rachel supposed it was natural that when faced with a figure from his past he should want to reminisce, and airing memories was part of his mourning process too. Whatever his reasons, she was happy to listen.

It was clear from what he said that Edgar had loved him very much. They'd spent a great deal of time together while David was growing up, and while that time had included plenty of sober guidance it had also included plenty of fun: afternoons browsing in the comic book stores so dear to French boys and men, ice cream at Berthillon's, ice-skating outside the Hotel de Ville, and once a ski vacation in Switzerland. When David described all this, his voice was warm with affection and past happiness.

His adult relationship with Edgar sounded equally strong and sympathetic. Whereas Mathilde had pushed him to take a prestigious major in college—architecture looked good on a résumé and in conversation—Edgar was the one who understood when his high grades had yielded no jobs. "He read the news; he worked in finance," David explained. "He told me, 'I know you did superbly well, but I also know there are no positions.'"

Certainly David's version of Edgar had liked money and the admiration it brought. David didn't say this directly, but it became clear from his stories of Edgar's bargaining skills and his excellent taste. Yes it seemed he had also been willing to be generous, at least to his son. "My mother," David said half-jokingly, "even with family, even with me, she holds onto her euros as if she's promised to look after each one personally. But Dad always had an open hand, and he was always willing to help me out when things were tough."

"Does he tell you anything useful, or is it all just glowing paternal memories?" Magda asked after one of Rachel's daily reports. Mathilde's fondness for rosé had come up since the initial conversation.

"You were the one who said I should pay attention to the people I met," Rachel pointed out, stung. "Besides, it depends what you think of as 'useful.' He tells me a lot about what Edgar was like, and what life with him was like, which is fleshing out our picture of Edgar."

In truth, David's stories soothed Rachel. She'd often wondered whether he'd flourished, whether Edgar had been as good a father to an adolescent as he had been to a child—but these weren't questions one could fit into small talk over canapés at a bank's cocktail party. The conversations with David might not give her many chances to ask hard-boiled questions or ferret out details, but what she learned made her feel better about the people she'd left behind all those years ago. And they did also offer her a clearer sense of what Edgar had become; that was no lie.

"We're building a picture, remember?" she said. Magda looked none too pleased at this reminder.

In fact, despite Magda's remark Rachel had focused on other aspects of life in the appartement. She now said, "Mathilde never comes over. Which suggests to me that if she did continue to visit Edgar after David was grown, it was for some reason other than David's welfare."

"Like jealousy, for example."

"Yes, like jealousy. I remember your favorite interpretation. But I also thought maybe she hoped that Edgar would continue to think of her fondly and leave her money, or maybe she was trying to get money out of him while he was still alive."

"Both plausible," Magda allowed. "Well, I'd say her absence does seem significant, but I'd also say we can't yet say why."

"Incisive," Rachel said, getting back at her for the remark about usefulness.

Magda looked at her closely, but Rachel's kept her expression bland. All Magda could do was say testily, "And what about Elisabeth? Remember her? Our *prime* suspect?"

"Ah." Rachel nodded. "Now there is something interesting. I don't really see her in the appartement, but I hear her, and she seems to be around every day. Edgar's bureau must be some sort of hoarder's paradise, because she arrives before me and leaves after, and we've both been there for two weeks. I think she's doing more than just organizing papers."

"It's taking you more than two weeks to organize the library," Magda pointed out.

"Yes, but it was in chaos when I arrived! This girl has been Edgar's aide de bureau for a year, and presumably she was keeping his documents in order all that time. I think—" She took a breath.

"You think what?" Magda waited, but Rachel, suddenly unsure, stayed silent. "I know," Magda said, leaning forward. "You think she's back there doing something related to whatever she stopped herself saying about Edgar."

Rachel nodded.

"What do you think that is?"

Rachel caught her upper lip between her teeth. "I don't know."

Magda closed her eyes in exasperation, but then opened them. "No, that's okay. We're still building a picture. And actually," she said, cocking her head, "we're not doing too bad a job of it. Mathilde's lack of presence is suspect; Elisabeth's constant presence is suspect. Two suspects."

"And don't forget Catherine," Rachel added. "Even if the cases against Elisabeth and Mathilde are growing stronger than just rosé and facial expressions, we still can't forget her very handy inheritance."

"No, indeed." Magda's eyes began to sparkle. She smiled at Rachel. "I'm sorry I was snippy. Even without David, I'd say we're doing very well."

Chapter Twelve

Catherine Nadeau phoned. Rachel had known she would. As they made opening small talk, she thought how little she wanted to spend time listening to her ex-lover's last lover's conversation. But Catherine was not going to be a new friend, she reminded herself again. She was a suspect. So she arranged to meet her the next afternoon for a drink.

* * *

Paris has many department stores, but only three that could be said to be at the pinnacle of luxury: Galeries Lafayette, Printemps, and Le Bon Marché. Ordinary people can afford many things at Galeries Lafayette, and they can afford a few things at Printemps. If they save carefully, they can afford a cup of coffee at Le Bon Marché. It is Paris's grandest department store and the shopping destination of Paris's grandest citizens. It was also where Catherine had arranged to meet Rachel.

The glass-roofed atrium of Le Bon Marché is a sensuous feast. Inhabited by a mass of upscale cosmetics companies, their counters peacock-bright with eye shadows and lipsticks, it shimmers with exotic promise. Years of repeated spritzes of various perfumes have given it an ingrained scent of sugar and musk—every breath makes you think simultaneously of warm cookie and powerful women. Rachel inhaled deeply as she crossed the atrium to reach the art deco escalators, and she felt melancholy as she watched the cosmetic counters, with their glamour and comfort, recede below her. *Farewell, pavilions of beauty!* she thought as she rose above the circle of glittering counters. *Farewell, glimpses of unaffordable womanhood!* Her line of vision moved up and up until she found herself looking at Catherine, seated at a table in the Rose Bakery.

"I've ordered you a Bellini," Catherine said after they exchanged cheek kisses. "It's the only drink one can have on a Friday afternoon."

Rachel did not say that she did not like Bellinis, or that she would have much preferred to make her own choice. Instead, she gave a broad smile. "You're a star!"

The waiter brought their drinks. Rachel waited until he left, then arranged her face into a concerned expression. "So, how are you?"

Catherine sighed. *"Ça va."* She took a sip of her drink. "I am busy with the store. And I am trying to understand my life after this big change. Trying to remember how to be a single woman, a single working woman." She looked mournful. "Who am I now?"

Inwardly, Rachel rolled her eyes. Catherine really couldn't remember who she'd been two years ago?

Indeed, as if recognizing her self-indulgence Catherine switched her attention to Rachel. "But how are you?"

"Me?" Rachel was surprised by the question. "I'm well. Busy."

"Still working on organizing Edgar's library?"

She nodded.

"And how is that going?"

"It's progressing. Slowly."

"But you must be able to focus well, alone in the apparte-ment. There are no interruptions." Catherine took another sip. "Or does the butler come to chat?"

"Fulke? No." Rachel shook her head. "But David comes to talk sometimes. He's already moved in," she explained.

"Of course." Catherine looked slightly bored.

"Of course?" Again Rachel was surprised. "Why of course?"

"He doesn't have anywhere else to live." Catherine said this as if it were common knowledge.

"I'm sorry?" Now Rachel was even more surprised, although she tried to hide it. "What do you mean?"

"As I say." Catherine shrugged. "He was evicted from his apartment. Edgar told me. I don't know why it happened. Edgar said something about nonpayment of rent, but I don't remember the exact circumstances. I do remember that he'd moved in with some friends; he was sleeping on their couch." She dabbed her napkin at her red lips, plainly not much inter-ested. "Is the household running well even though he's moved in? The staff hasn't made any complaints to you?"

What staff? What was the woman talking about? Were there other people she should know about, should be interviewing?

"Well," she said, "of course it's difficult. Everyone is upset, but they seem to be managing well." She left a space for Cath-erine about individuals and thus reveal the names of possible unknown staff, but when Catherine just took another sip of her Bellini, Rachel tried to bring the focus back to where she wanted it. "And you? How are *you* doing? After all, you lost the man you loved. And," she added hopefully, "all the money in the world can't make up for that."

"Yes." Catherine looked appropriately sad for a second. Then, "But I hadn't known him as long as David and Mathilde, or even as long as Fulke! They must all, even the servant, be nervous and uncertain."

How Fulke would burn to hear himself referred to as "the servant"! And although Catherine's tone was light, what she said was too pointed to be casual. Who was trying to get information from whom here? Rachel parried once more.

"David seems fine. And Fulke takes it as a point of professionalism, I think, to remain unruffled. About Mathilde I don't know." That was all true enough, as far as it went. Interesting that Catherine hadn't asked about Elisabeth, though.

"And the police have signed off on the death?"

"The police?" Rachel was surprised and puzzled. "I didn't know the police were involved." Did that mean they were beginning to realize what had happened? She wondered how Magda would react to that news. Would she want to share information with them now?

But Catherine was shaking her head. "Oh no, my mistake." She gave her glassy laugh. "I thought the police were called in to all deaths, but now I remember they don't have to sign off on deaths at home." She laughed again, as if at her own foolishness, but her eyes watched Rachel carefully, and for a second she looked disappointed. *A thrust deflected,* Rachel thought. Let her try again; perhaps the fourth time she would give away more than she sought to find out.

Catherine didn't try again, though. Maybe she had realized she would get nowhere with whatever she wanted, or maybe she had just got tired of trying; whatever the reason, she looked at her silver sliver of a watch and said, "I must go. I'm meeting a supplier to discuss some new products."

"Oh." Rachel looked around for the waiter. "Shall we get the bill?"

Once more Catherine smiled her red smile. "Oh, let me pay."

"Are you sure?" Rachel had her hand on her purse.

"Absolutely. It's no trouble at all. My pleasure."

* * *

"You hate Bellinis." Magda's voice was made fuzzy by speakerphone.

"Yes." Rachel was curt. "Alan pointed that out when I told him, too. Thank you both for the reminder."

"You told Alan you had a drink with Edgar Bowen's girlfriend?"

"I told him I'd been invited for a drink by one of the other beneficiaries, to reminisce. I didn't tell him what we talked about. Is that okay?" Then she collected herself: she didn't have to take her bad afternoon out on Magda. "Sorry." She opened the refrigerator door and took out the remains of the previous night's crème caramel.

"That's okay." Rachel could hear Magda take a sip of something. "And what was she like, in the end?"

Rachel cut a wobbly slice of custard. "I think we should move her up the list of suspects."

"What? Why?" Magda had been expecting a dismissal.

"Because she was there to sound me out too. She asked all sorts of leading questions. She was very concerned with whether

Edgar's death had caused any upheaval at the appartement. *Very* concerned. She asked me if the police had come around."

"What?"

Rachel nodded, then remembered Magda couldn't see her. "Yes. She tried to smooth it over, but she couldn't. I don't think she really knows how to deploy subtlety."

Magda's breath rasped into the phone as she inhaled. "Tell me exactly what you said to each other."

Rachel repeated the conversation. Remembering Magda's ideas about David at the start of their investigation, she held back the revelation about his inability to pay his rent. She knew Magda would say his lack of money was proof that he was on drugs, and demand they also move him up the suspect list—and because she hadn't heard the grown-up David talk about Edgar, she'd have no idea how ridiculous it was to imagine that he could kill his father. Better to just skip the exhausting argument and explanation and highlight the information from Catherine that actually mattered. She ended her recitation with Catherine's obviously false announcement that she had another appointment.

"God," Magda said when she'd finished, "she really doesn't know how to be subtle. Unless . . . unless she can't be subtle because she's desperate. Scared that someone knows what she did."

"But what *did* she do?" Rachel's voice was tight.

"That is the question." Magda was thoughtful, and somehow Rachel knew what she was going to say before she said it. "We'll just have to keep an eye on her."

Chapter Thirteen

Being an investigatrix is turning out to be very frustrating, Rachel thought as she walked across the Pont Neuf on Monday morning. Where was the sleuthing, the tracking, the ducking and diving? Where were all the capital-d Developments? Already two weeks had passed since Edgar's death, and all they had were conversations and theories. It really wasn't all it was cracked up to be in books and on TV.

But after an hour in the library, her strange meeting with Catherine and her frustrating conversation with Magda had left her mind. Arranging the books demanded focus, but not much thought, and in the semi-hypnotic state this induced, her mind became empty and her senses more alive. She found herself marking the time with sounds she hadn't even realized she'd noticed: the chink of the cup and saucer being brought on her coffee tray, the soft clicking of a door somewhere in the appartement at precisely eleven, then again at precisely eleven thirty. Now conscious of those clicks, she realized they must be the sounds of someone leaving and returning. Since Elisabeth arrived before she did and left after, and since David banged the door hard whenever he came or went (which in any case was

never before noon), by process of elimination she worked out that the clicks belonged to Fulke, going to and coming from his daily shopping. She would never tell Magda, but the fact that she had noticed these things subconsciously and then put them together swiftly made her feel she was a natural detective. She preened a bit.

* * *

The Friday morning of her fourth week in the library, the peace was broken by the sound of two voices. Fulke had told her when she'd arrived that David was not yet back from his night out, and the door had already clicked once, so she knew neither of the speakers could be the butler or the master of the house. In any case, both were too high-pitched to be male. She felt her heart beat faster; her natural detecting instincts were telling her that she should eavesdrop. She put down the eighteenth-century atlas she had been trying to shelve and moved softly to stand next to the door. Holding her breath, she all but pressed her ear to the wood.

"As I said, I am here to collect some items," snapped a voice she instantly recognized as Mathilde's.

The only response was an indistinguishable murmur.

"Trinkets!" Mathilde said. "Items of sentimental value."

More murmuring.

"I do not want you to fetch them for me. I wish to collect them myself. They have personal meaning."

Rachel still couldn't hear the other voice, but Mathilde's response conveyed the gist of what it said.

"Of course I'm allowed! I am his *wife*!"

Nothing, then yet more murmuring.

Mathilde exclaimed, “How do you *dare*! How can you? I must go into the bureau!” Her voice was outraged but also flinty: whatever she wanted, she would brook no objection.

“You are not allowed back there, madame!” The second voice suddenly spoke very loudly, the way timid people often do when they’ve geared themselves up to be brave. As Rachel had suspected it might, this quavering near-yell belonged to Elisabeth. When she spoke next, she was calmer. “As I just explained, Monsieur Bowen’s instructions were that no one else may enter the bureau until I have been through it and put Monsieur Bowen’s papers in order. Others may see them after that.”

“Others.” Mathilde managed to make the word sound like the worst of racial slurs. “I am not ‘others.’ I am a member of his family.”

“I’m sorry, madame.” Elisabeth’s voice shook. “I cannot contravene Monsieur Bowen’s instructions. They were in his will. Allowing you access to the bureau would be illegal.”

Elisabeth sounded determined, but she also sounded afraid. In fact, all in all, the conversation didn’t seem to be a battle of equals. Rachel knew from experience the way the determined could overpower the diffident, no matter how resolute the diffident resolved to be. She also knew she could learn more outside the library than in. And she also knew she couldn’t stand so still for much longer. She gave the door a hefty push, ensuring that it would open with a bang against the outside wall and announce her presence.

Mathilde and Elisabeth stood about ten yards away, at the entrance to the hall. Elisabeth’s arms were crossed over her chest as if to demonstrate that she intended to stand firm.

Mathilde, who still wore her camel hair outdoor coat, stood with her back to Rachel, but even so her stiff posture commanded the scene.

"I *thought* I heard voices!" Rachel filled her own with inoffensive cheer. "Mathilde, what a pleasure to find you here! We haven't seen each other for years, and now twice in a few weeks. What luck! You must come into the library and have a cup of tea." She stood back a bit, revealing the room's mess. "Or were you on your way out?"

Mathilde's smile was a crack in ice. "Bonjour, Rachel." She spoke normally, but Rachel saw strain in the corners of her eyes. Her glance took in the state of the library, and she turned her head with a disgusted shudder just small enough to seem instinctive, but just large enough to be intentional. "I was hoping to pick up a few *bibelots*, but it seems they are not where I thought they were. I will come back another time." She tightened the belt of her coat, turned on her heel—the first time Rachel had seen this action actually performed—and left.

Once the door closed behind Mathilde, Elisabeth let her arms fall to her sides. "Thank you."

"It was nothing." Rachel smiled at the girl. "She's a difficult woman. I know."

Elisabeth's lower lip began to quiver, and her eyes became wet. Judging it tactful, or at least wise, Rachel retreated to the library, once more picking up the atlas. Only later did she realize that Elisabeth's agitation had presented a perfect opportunity to extract some more information. Her detective instincts might be natural, she reflected, but they weren't honed. Yet.

* * *

"Oh my," Magda said. They had been looking at magazines at the Gibert Joseph bookstore, trying to get ideas for what Rachel could wear to the upcoming *Bal Rouge*, but now she closed her copy of *Vogue* and focused fully on Rachel. "Oh my," she repeated.

"I know, right?"

A man looking at skiing magazines in the next aisle swiveled his head.

"Keep your voice down!" Magda waited until he returned his full attention to his copy of *Skieur*. "Obviously there's something in that apartment that Mathilde wants."

"Wants a great deal," Rachel added.

"Evidence!" Magda's voice filled was filled with delight.

"Yes."

"Belongings? Photographs? Documents?"

"Presumably one of those."

"And Edgar wanted this something protected or hidden," said Magda. "But which? And from whom?"

"I don't know."

"And Elisabeth is supposed to get rid of it? Take it away but keep it?"

"I don't know."

"And why does Mathilde want it?"

Rachel sighed. "I don't know. We *can't* know. We can't even know what sort of thing it might be because we don't know what sort of thing matters to her—what sort of thing she might want to hide or take." Her whisper became a hiss. "Because *we don't know her*."

"We're *getting* to know her. We're building a picture."

"I know. It's just . . ." Rachel slumped a little. "I don't see how we're ever going to get to finish doing that. We're not the police; we're not trained investigators. How *can* we get more information on suspects? We don't know how to do this. How do people do this? How are we supposed to get anywhere? I just don't see us getting anywhere."

"That's a very negative way of looking at things." Magda sounded personally offended. "This is an *opportunity*. An opportunity to hone our investigative skills."

"Which assumes we have some."

"Don't be so silly." She put the magazine back in the rack and turned to face Rachel. "I can sense we're onto something. You're creative; you'll figure out an approach." She gathered her coat around her.

"You're going?" Rachel was outraged.

"I promised my mother I'd call her, and it's nine in Jamaica. You know what Jamaican mothers are like."

Rachel didn't know what Jamaican mothers were like, but she knew what Magda's Jamaican mother was like. If you said you were going to call on a certain day, Mrs. Stevens would expect the phone to be ringing at the earliest possible polite moment. She watched Magda go.

After she left, Rachel stood for a few minutes, paging through *Elle* without really paying attention. On television the police were always saying, "I'll talk to my snitches," and every literary sleuth seemed to have a network of carefully cultivated connections or village gossips to help them out. The difficulty with being an actual amateur detective was the lack of this inside information. No wonder none of the fictional representations ever featured a detective who was just starting out: without contacts you were nowhere.

Then suddenly she shook herself. How could she have forgotten? She did have a contact! Kiki Villeneuve. Kiki knew everyone who ought to be known in Paris, and if she didn't know them. she knew about them. She and Rachel had been friends for over a decade, but when Kiki's husband had died two years earlier, she had vanished, hiding herself away from everyone. She obviously wanted to be left alone, and Rachel, not wanting to intrude, hadn't contacted her. Now, though, she would get in touch with her. Kiki wasn't a village gossip—she never gossiped, she used to say. But she was an information hoarder and sometimes an information disseminator. Rachel would be delicate, and if Kiki were still mourning, she would back off. But she needed a contact—a stoolpigeon, a grass—and Kiki was the only person who qualified.

Chapter Fourteen

The French were not a friendly bunch, Rachel reflected as she settled into her Métro seat. *They're suave; they're impeccably polite; they're certainly elegant,* she thought, catching sight of a man in a perfectly tied scarf bracing himself against the side of the car. *But they're not by nature friendly.* Or maybe that was just Parisians, but since she lived in Paris, Paris *was* France to her. In any case, most of the French she'd met when she first arrived, with the exception of those who wanted to sleep with her, were not friendly.

The one notable exception was Kiki Villeneuve. When they first encountered each other, Rachel was part of a team catering a party for Kiki and her husband. Most of the Paris wives Rachel's team worked for were as thin and tense as violin strings, but not Madame Villeneuve (as they were told to call her). She was plump and rosy, and instead of telling them what to do and then vanishing, she helped load the trays, expressed fascination at the intricacies of laying out hors d'oeuvres, and opened a bottle of wine for them. As the evening wore on, she came back to the kitchen every now and then to check on them; she told them to call her Kiki, and she hugged each of them at the night's end. She was, in short, a warm blast after a long chill. Later she told Rachel that she thought her personality was the result of growing up in a tiny village, so small that no one was a stranger, but when Rachel met Kiki's husband, roly-poly Robert Villeneuve, who had grown up in Paris, he was just as friendly.

In fact, the Villeneuves were probably the best-suited couple Rachel had ever known, as kind and jolly to each other as they were to others, mutually supportive, delighted with and at each other. They were a matched pair in all senses. Robert's funeral was the first time Rachel had encountered Kiki alone or sad, and she knew the second was the result of the first. She didn't begrudge her these months of no contact.

Her cell phone pinged. She took it out of her pocket with dread. As she had suspected, the message was from Catherine:

How are things??? How is the library progressing?? Everyone well? xxx

The phone pinged again.

So enjoyed our chat!! Should have another soon!!! xxxx

She had been receiving these over-punctuated and and underpronoun-ed messages at regular intervals over the previous few days, all of them inquiring in not so subtle ways about the mood and occurrences at Edgar's appartement. *I don't want to get together with you again,* she thought as she stared at the phone, as if a tiny clairvoyant Catherine sat behind the screen:

I think you might be a murderer. And if you're not, you're some kind of ghoul. And if you're not that, at the very least you're deeply strange.

Tomorrow???? xx

Rachel put the phone on vibrate and stuffed it back in her pocket.

The Métro stopped at Chemin Vert and Rachel snapped the handle up and over, opening the door. Over the years she had visited Kiki's apartment so many times that now her feet seemed to take her of their own accord, mounting the station stairs and following the route as if it were signposted: down the Rue des Tournelles, with the synagogue that always cheered her, then across the Place des Vosges with its bleached winter walks and surrounding square of ancient brick buildings, down the Rue Francs Bourgeois until she reached the bright blue exterior of the Brasserie Royal Turenne, where Kiki and Robert used to take her for the mussels they loved, and at last to Kiki's résidence. Exactly as in the case of Edgar's résidence, she discovered, the old security code still worked. Of course, in this case only one year had gone by, not twenty. As she rode up in the elevator that still smelt of a thousand Gitanes cigarettes, she ran her fingers over the box of chocolates she'd brought and suddenly realized just how much she'd missed Kiki.

In her pocket, her phone vibrated.

When she rang Kiki's bell, she scarcely recognized the person who opened the door. Kiki had been as round and brown as a good French roll, but this woman was stringy, her skin yellowish and hanging in jowls from her face. For a moment Rachel thought she must have gotten off on the wrong floor. Then the woman smiled, and she saw the familiar warmth in her eyes, the good humor that still lingered at the corners of her mouth.

"Come in, come in!" Kiki gestured to her. "Yes, I've changed, I know. I'm used to it, but it must be strange to see."

Rachel nodded, unsure of the polite way to respond. "A . . . a little bit." She felt slightly off-balance, as if she were in the presence of a stranger. Still, this *was* Kiki, and when she walked into the open arms and was embraced with welcoming warmth, she knew it could be no one else. She was squeezed, kissed, and eventually released, reassured. When she brought out the box of chocolates, Kiki's eyes sparkled.

"Ah! Yes, that's exactly what I need. For medicinal purposes, of course. Just to put the flesh back on." She smiled again, sharing the joke with Rachel.

Tea was made, a tray was found, and the chocolates were arranged on a plate. At last they settled on the couch. Kiki took a bonbon, savoring it before she spoke.

"It was so good to hear from you. I'm sorry I was quiet all this time. It had nothing to do with you, I promise." She sighed. "You see, after Robert . . ." She looked out the salon window. "We had so long together. I don't . . . I couldn't really remember a life without him—and why would I want to?" A shrug. Rachel saw that her eyes were wet. "I couldn't see how to go on, or why. For a long time. To become used to silence, to being alone. Why live like that after—" She waved a hand in dismissive disgust. Then she smiled and sniffed. "Well. In the end, you outgrow even grief." She gave a small laugh. "You remember that you argued. That sometimes he drove you mad.

Time passes, and if you don't die, the world comes to be interesting once more. We're built that way, I think." She put her soft hand over Rachel's. "And now I'm so glad to hear from you! I find that in my absence many of my friends put something else in my niche."

"Oh no." Rachel shook her head. "I don't believe that!"

Kiki sighed. "Yes, it's true. Only Genette Maurois continues to telephone sometimes. And now there is you." She patted Rachel's hand. "But I suspect you came here for more than just the chance to give me candy. What can I do for you, my friend?"

On the way over, Rachel had considered how best to approach the situation. Because she still had no real concrete evidence, she didn't want to air her suspicions about Edgar's death—but she didn't want to lie to an old friend either. She had decided that the best way was just to ask for what she needed and explain why only if questioned. Still, she was tense. She didn't know what she would say if Kiki did question her, and in the last second before she began, she was suddenly, irrationally, convinced she would. Should she wait? Should she forego the whole thing? She took a breath, feeling as if she were plunging off a diving board, and said too abruptly, "I want you to tell me about the Bowens."

Kiki drew back slightly. "*Ah bon*? The Bowens?" She looked at Rachel for a few seconds, judging. Whatever she saw must have satisfied her, because she reached for another chocolate and said, "*Bien.* I am not an encyclopedia, and I never gossip. But just this once, because I am a lonely old woman and you are my only visitor," she smiled, "I'll tell you what I know, and I won't ask why."

Rachel rejoiced. She had a snitch. Her first snitch! She settled down to listen.

"About Edgar I know very little: he came as a banker; he prospered as a banker. But Mathilde, she's a Castel, you know." Kiki said this as if Rachel would understand what it meant. "On her mother's side, from Perpignan, near the border. They claim to be Spanish nobility. That's why they have those noses." She sketched a facsimile of Mathilde's long nose with her hand. "To look down. Anyway." She took a breath. "Like her mother, she's as proud as Lucifer, but in every other way she's her father's daughter." She grimaced. "A very unpleasant man. He loved only money. Perhaps he had a fondness for his wife and daughter, but if there had been a fire, he would have raced back into the house to rescue his wallet. And like so many who love money, he loved the spending of it most of all." She sat back. "In the end, Madame, Mathilde's mother, had to put her own money into a trust so he couldn't access it."

"So Mathilde married Edgar for his money?"

"Oh no. There was still money. A great deal of it by our standards; by hers, enough. Although I don't doubt she liked Edgar's money—as I said, she's her father's daughter. And of course even then it was clear Edgar would be worth much more in the future. So she had that too. But she married him for"—Kiki paused for a moment—"power."

"Power?" Again Rachel was confused. Edgar wasn't a politician or a magnate. If anything, Mathilde was the one with the power, social power.

"Not power as you might think of it," Kiki explained, "but there are different kinds. Among the *bien établis*, these old families, an unmarried woman has no power. She doesn't know anything of—of life. She is not yet mature. A married woman is established, has insight, understanding of the world. She is a force. With a child, even more so. And as she ages, becomes even more experienced, even more skilled socially, such a woman becomes *formidable*."

Well, Mathilde was certainly formidable. "But then why did she divorce him?"

"Oh, divorce loses such a woman nothing. In fact, it might be seen as bringing benefits. You have the wisdom of marriage and motherhood, and you have connections, but also the strength to flourish alone. So much the better!" She tossed her head, but then her tone changed. "As for the discarded husband going on with his life, however . . ." She clicked her tongue. "Mathilde wouldn't like that. An injury to the house of Castel—and of course to her personally." A deep breath. "That's why she couldn't stand all the ones after her: you, that Amandine, and so on."

Rachel made a disbelieving face. "Really? Even after so much time?"

"Some women are like that. They leave a man, but still he is supposed never to love another." Rachel remembered Magda saying something similar. Kiki added, "And the threat of this would not dissipate with the years. Quite the contrary. Elderly men, they like a warm bed." Her shrug said this was foolish, but also natural. "And perhaps Mathilde's fear was not unfounded, because Edgar did have new loves. The last I knew was a young woman with dark hair . . ." She lifted a hand to her own head as if in demonstration.

"Catherine Nadeau?"

"*Oui*, that's it. Catherine Nadeau. Of her people I know

nothing." Kiki smiled, "But perhaps she is related to Mathilde's father, because everyone said money just slipped through her hands. In any case, she was young. Although," she added, "to be fair, not grotesquely young, like some of these little girls one sees with men of Edgar's age."

Rachel thought of Elisabeth. Kiki must have seen some flicker of expression in her face, because she raised her eyebrows.

"Ah, this is what it is to be out of touch. Edgar got himself a *jeune fille*?"

"No, no." Rachel shook her head. "Or, yes, but not as a petite amie. Only a friend."

"And is she pretty, this young friend?"

"Yes."

Kiki pursed her lips. "That Mathilde would not care for. Did he make a bequest to this pretty girl or to his current petite amie?"

Rachel nodded. "To both. To Catherine, seven and a half thousand euros. To the girl, Elisabeth," she swallowed, "twenty thousand euros."

"Oh, là là!" Despite herself, Rachel smiled; she still couldn't believe the French actually said that. But Kiki was genuinely shocked. "And to Mathilde herself?"

"Ten thousand."

Kiki gasped. *"Mon dieu!"* She put a hand over her mouth. "Are you sure?"

"Yes." Rachel leaned forward. "Why?"

Kiki put her hand down. "Well, obviously to get less than the pretty young girl . . . And if she was not even Edgar's *fruit vert*, so much the worse." She inhaled. "But also, you see, some years ago, before she died, Mathilde's mother visited her in Paris. There was a *petit souper*—Mathilde gave it—in her honor. Madame, it seems, was not very good with champagne, and after a couple of glasses she began crowing that Mathilde was so unique, so memorable, so *ravissante*, that Edgar had recently assured her that in his new will—and this was years after the divorce—he had still left her fifty thousand euro.

"And then . . ." She shook her head, tsking. "Perhaps, a month ago? Genette—you know, my friend who still telephones me—told me she had had a narrow escape. Her moneyman, last year he tried to persuade her to invest in oil. He told her it would go up and she would do very, very well. She didn't do it—she doesn't like risk. And she was wise, because of course oil went down. But, you see, she told me"—she met Rachel's eyes—"her money man is also Mathilde's money man. And Mathilde said yes. So . . ."

Rachel caught her breath, anticipating the end of the sentence.

". . . now there is less than enough."

Rachel remembered Mathilde's flinch at the reading of the will. *Surprise, certainly, almost certainly anger, but maybe,* she thought now, *also disappointment and fear?* Any combination of those ingredients had the potential to be highly combustible.

But for the moment she kept those thoughts to herself. She and Kiki talked for a while longer, Kiki polishing off the chocolates, until at last Rachel stood to go. "You've been so helpful." She put her hands on Kiki's shoulders, feeling bones where she'd never felt them before.

"Anything, of course!" Kiki took Rachel's face between her hands. "It's so good to see you. So well and so"—she gave a tiny wink—"curious. You must come again soon." She smiled. "And bring more goodies."

On the Métro home Rachel mused on what she'd been told. It hadn't done any favors to anyone mentioned. Catherine was so bad at managing money that it was common knowledge; Mathilde was someone who would do almost anything for the sake of money and pride. But that was the question: Would she do anything or only *almost* anything? There was a big difference between being bad at managing money and killing for it, and a long way from losing money to killing to replace it. But what did she know? Both women now had motives that made them excellent suspects, and the desperate didn't think like other people—for that matter, neither did murderers. Maybe if Mathilde and Catherine were enough of the first, they could have graduated to being one of the second.

Chapter Fifteen

The next morning, Rachel was preparing to call Magda to share Kiki's revelations when there was a series of sharp bursts on the buzzer. When she opened the door, Magda brushed past her.

"Good morning. How are you?"

Magda took no notice of the reproof. "Have you read your paper today?"

"What?" Rachel thought she must have misheard.

"Have you read your paper today?"

"Yes, at breakfast. I mean, I haven't read the whole thing, but I—"

Magda thrust a newspaper at her, doubled over into a square. "Look."

"What? Why? Can't you just tell me?"

She jabbed the folded sheets at her again. "Look!"

Rachel took the paper. Magda had folded it so that one article, barely more than a paragraph, was centered.

Tragedy in Central Paris

A woman fell to her death yesterday from a window in the third arrondissement. Catherine Nadeau, 41, owner of boutique Le Cindy in the first arrondissement, fell from the window of her salon into the courtyard below at approximately 17:15. She was discovered by another resident at 17:20.

Madame Nadeau had been in financial difficulties recently; she remarked to a neighbor a few weeks ago that she feared she would be forced to close her store or sell her apartment to keep it open.

Madame Nadeau is not survived by any family. Police are not treating the death as suspicious.

"Oh my God, she killed herself?" Rachel sat down heavily. "But she's been texting me all week."

She looked up. Magda was watching her, head to one side.

"What?"

"Read the second paragraph again."

Rachel did. Then she read it a third time. Then she understood. "But she *wasn't* in financial difficulties!" Her voice came out shrill. "She paid for our drinks. At the *Bon Marché*!"

Magda nodded. "And do you remember, when we went to see her, she said"—she put on the quoting voice—"'I have a good plan for the future.'"

"That's right. She did." Rachel remembered. "And she said something similar when she and I met."

"Don't you see?" Magda held out her hands.

"See what?"

"Someone *killed* her!"

"Oh, now." Rachel frowned. "That's jumping to conclusions."

"No, it isn't. She had the money to relaunch her store and to take you out for a drink at the most expensive department store in the city. She wasn't in dire straits." Her eyes met Rachel's, held them. "It's not hard to imagine. Catherine lets someone into her apartment, fixes them a drink—maybe even a glass of rosé. She probably laughs that stupid laugh at some point. And the other person waits, waits for the right moment. Then—" Rachel jumped. "Catherine on the paving stones of the courtyard, blood spreading underneath her, her body twisted like an abandoned marionette's."

"Jesus." Rachel swallowed. "Maybe you should be the writer, not me." She forced her mind back to logic. "But what would someone kill her for? I mean, for what reason?"

"For the money," Magda said, as if this were obvious.

"For seven thousand euros?"

"Seven thousand *five hundred*," she corrected. "And, as I said, people have killed for less."

"People have gone to someone's house and faked that person's suicide for seven and a half thousand euros that weren't physically there? This is like your unnoticed soup drowner all over again. And anyway," Rachel's thoughts had finally caught up with her, "they wouldn't get any money. It says she didn't have any survivors." She put her finger on that line of print. "If you don't have any heirs, everything just goes to the government."

"Not if the original testator leaves secondary heirs."

"Testator?" Who used a word like "testator"?

"The person who made the original will," Magda said, as if Rachel didn't know. "Edgar. Edgar could have made an arrangement wherein if one of the initial heirs dies, he's set up another heir to inherit their money. Like wedding guests," she explained. "You have an A list and a B list."

Rachel was distracted. First "testator" and now "wherein"? Where were these words coming from?

"Have you been reading up on French law?"

"No." Magda's voice was innocent, but she looked down at her shoes. "Well . . ."

"Well what?" Rachel tried to peer into her face.

"Well, I . . ." Was her friend blushing? "I've just been talking to someone about wills."

Rachel tried to imagine that scenario. "To who?"

"To *whom*," Magda corrected, but Rachel knew she was buying time.

"All right. To *whom* have you been talking about wills?"

"Ah, well . . ." Magda finally looked up. "To Benoît."

Rachel was confused. "Who's Benoît?"

"Remember when we went to Edgar's funeral?"

Rachel nodded. How could she not remember?

"That man I was talking to. He's Benoît."

Rachel cast her mind back. That was right: when she had come over to tell Magda her suspicions, there had been a man. "The one with the pointy nose?"

"Well, yes," Magda looked up, slightly resentful. "It's a little pointy, I suppose."

"No, it's pointy. It's properly pointy." Understanding suddenly dawned. Rachel poked her friend, grinning. "You! Always with the pointy noses. That's your thing!"

Now Magda *was* blushing. Rachel remembered that she

hated to be teased about her love life; being single in your forties was tough enough without having your friends make fun of you. She stopped. "Anyway, I'm veering off track. How does Benoît know about wills?"

"He's one of the attorneys at Edgar's law firm."

Rachel was lost again. "But Maître Bernard is Edgar's lawyer!"

"No, he's a notaire. And in any case he deals with Edgar's estate. Benoît is in a whole different area." She cast a puzzled look at Rachel. "Didn't you wonder why you didn't see Maître Bernard at the funeral?"

"No." This question had never crossed Rachel's mind, and it didn't seem to her that it should. Why would you expect to see someone's lawyer at their funeral?

"Well, he wasn't there because Benoît was there. Benoît's the one the company sent to pay their respects."

"Oh." *You learn something new every day,* Rachel thought. "Anyway, now you're seeing each other?"

"Yes. Well, you know, a bit." Magda looked shy, but proud.

"Hold on a sec." Rachel held out a hand. "Could he let us see Edgar's will?"

Magda frowned. "I'm fairly sure that's illegal."

Rachel bit the inside of her cheek, thinking. "Well, could he look at the will and tell us if Edgar left any of these—whatchamacallit—secondary heirs?"

"I don't know."

Rachel kept her voice calm. "Could you ask?"

Magda thought for a second, then inhaled and exhaled

slowly. "All right. I'll ask. But be prepared for him to say no." She smiled proudly. "He's very ethical."

"Thank you." Rachel was careful to keep her face and voice neutral; she knew how easy it was for the maybe-in-love to mistake joyfulness for superiority. "Well, let's call him as soon as we can. In fact," she stood up, "you could do it now."

Chapter Sixteen

Magda called Benoît from Rachel and Alan's bedroom. Rachel longed to sit beside her on the bed, telling her exactly what to say, but recognizing the impossibility of this, she instead lingered in the hall outside her closed bedroom door, listening to a good deal of giggling and a certain amount of murmured conversation. She didn't know precisely what passed between them, but it resulted in an invitation to the offices of Edgar's law firm, where Benoît would do what he could about the will.

So it was that on the Monday of the following week she found herself seated in the gleaming reception area of Cabinet Martin Frères, on the third floor of a Belle Époque building in the second arrondissement. Magda sat next to her, nervously crossing and uncrossing her legs. She looked like a teenager about to introduce her mother to her friends.

Rachel and Alan had an *avocat* of their own, but, as with Edgar's appartement, Cabinet Martin Frères was in an entirely different bracket. The reception area had the upholstered hush that indicates the presence of significant money and the air of discretion that indicates the presence of significant power. All the furniture was in dark wood polished to a high sheen, and the coffee table held glossy magazines like *Art et Décoration* and *Challenges*. The receptionist sat behind a huge desk, a phone so large it was practically a switchboard placed front and center, and a vase of gloriosa on the far corner. She was a cross between Catherine Deneuve in *Belle du Jour* and Evita Perón: blonde hair pulled into a severe chignon, beige wool dress perfectly plain, haughty mouth painted matte persimmon. Under the desk, Rachel knew, she wore those crippling stiletto heels mysteriously loved by fashionable young French women. After she finished work, she would go out to Le Bar Long or Hôtel Costes and allow some very rich man to buy her drinks. Later she would marry another very rich man, possibly even a client of this firm, and when they divorced, she would receive a settlement that left her comfortable for life. This was the kind of place that had such a receptionist.

Had she missed out, not staying with Edgar? Rachel wondered. All the deference and discreet money of this cabinet could have been hers. That appartement could have been hers. Then she remembered that the question was immaterial, since Edgar, and not she, had ended the relationship. And he had been right. She felt more comfortable with Alan—delightful Alan who had learned to like the ballet, who taught her to appreciate modern jazz, who could make her laugh and shiver simultaneously by bending back his double-jointed thumbs. But still she felt a little bit mournful: thankful for what she had, but sorry not to have had the opportunity to experience what she hadn't.

She had just begun to reflect on this paradox when the man from the funeral reception came through an inner door and walked toward them. Now that she wasn't intent on dragging

Magda away, she could pay attention to what he looked like, and what she saw made her happy. His smooth dark hair, brushed back in two wings from a center part, was silvering at the temples; rimless glasses slightly magnified his lively dark eyes. His navy suit was impeccably cut, and he had paired it with a vivid violet tie. As he caught sight of Magda, his professional smile widened and deepened into something more genuine. He held out both hands to her; she rose and took them. Two kisses on each cheek, Rachel noticed, then an extra kiss on one. So much for seeing him a bit! Things were far advanced indeed. Smiling, she rose to greet him.

"Madame Levis." The man pronounced her name correctly as he took her hand. "Benoît Gèroux. What a pleasure. I've heard a very great deal about you. Magda is always telling me what you have said or done, and always with great pride. Now at last we meet!" He smiled. "I'm honored."

He clasped her hand between his palms, kissing her once on each cheek and leaving behind the deep scent of some delicious aftershave. Rachel could feel herself blushing. She felt an overwhelming urge to giggle like a schoolgirl. If the French have a reputation for exaggerated charm, it's because only they are suave enough to carry off that charm without looking farcical.

"Alors," Benoît said as they settled in his office. "I understand from Magda that you wish to see Monsieur Bowen's will." He lifted a manila folder from a pile and put it on the desk in front of him. "Since we spoke, I have located that will." He fiddled with the folder, putting his index finger between the covers and then removing it. "Unfortunately," he said and paused, smoothed the cover with his thumbs, "this will is not out of probate. If you were asking six months from now, I could easily show it to you. But at this time I cannot." He shook his head sadly, an acknowledgment of the ironies of life. "I can only read it and tell you what it says—paraphrase it."

"But I've already heard it paraphrased." Rachel tried to keep her voice calm. Magda shot her a look.

Benoît shrugged sorrowfully again. "Nonetheless, that's all I can do."

She drew a breath. She shouldn't argue. This was Magda's maybe-boyfriend and a lawyer who had to abide by a code of ethics. She tried to concede gracefully. "Thank you."

"It is a pleasure." He flattened the folder open on the desk and picked up the thick document inside, turning over pages as he read them. At last he put it down, folding his hands on top of it. "Monsieur Bowen appoints no secondary heirs and makes no arrangement for consolidation of bequests."

Magda let out her breath explosively. "Dammit." She dropped back in her chair.

But Rachel was not quite done. As Benoît started to close the folder, she said, "I'm sorry." She smiled. "Can I ask you to look at one more thing?"

"*Comme tu veux.*" He gave a little nod. "I am at your service."

She turned to Magda. "I was thinking last night. When Elisabeth was talking to Mathilde, she said Edgar had left instructions that only she was allowed to see his papers, in order to organize them. She said it was in his will."

Magda nodded.

"But I was there when the will was read. And I don't remember the notaire saying anything about only her having access."

Rachel leaned toward her "What if what matters is not that Mathilde wanted access to the back rooms, but that Elisabeth *didn't want her* to have that access? What if Elisabeth is lying, so she can have time to find something that incriminates her?" She clarified, "Incriminates Elisabeth herself, I mean."

Magda thought for a second, then nodded and turned to Benoit. "Please could you check to see if Edgar says anything about limiting access?"

He dipped his head once more. Again he studied the document, again he slowly turned the pages over, again he put it down. "Monsieur Bowen leaves no such instructions."

It was Rachel's turn to fall back. Elisabeth had lied! She wanted to keep others from finding something in Edgar's appartement, something that was damaging enough to lie for. The ingénue was not so ingenuous after all.

"Thank you so much," she said. She and Magda gathered their things. In the anteroom, under the gaze of the supercilious receptionist, she took Benoît's hand and kissed him on each cheek. He had gone out of his way for them, committing what was at least a semi-illegal act, and for all she knew a completely illegal one. Whatever they had or hadn't discovered, she was grateful.

They stopped outside the building's *porte d'entrée*, hunching themselves against the cold.

"So," Rachel began.

"Dammit about Catherine!" Magda cut her off. "I was sure one of them killed her to get her money."

Rachel had never believed that scenario; now she tried to find a gentle way to put forward her own. "Well, I've been thinking about that." She licked her lips, then wished she hadn't when cold air hit the wet skin. She wiped her mouth with the back of her hand and went on. "Just because she wasn't killed for the money, that doesn't mean she wasn't killed."

"What?"

"No, listen. You made a good point: obviously the money from Edgar put her back in the black. From the way she acted at the store and with me, she didn't have any current money worries." Magda opened her mouth, but Rachel plunged on. "But I do think someone killed her. I think they did it because she was blackmailing them. I think she was blackmailing the murderer."

Magda made a face. "What makes you think *that*?"

"A couple of things." Rachel took a breath. "First, like you said, when we saw her, she said she had a good plan for the future. But Kiki said she could never hold onto money. And people who aren't good with money don't think in those terms about the money they have. They might say, 'This will solve all my problems!', or even, 'I have a plan,' but they'd never think carefully or concretely enough to say, 'I've got a good plan for the future.' Even the phrase is too rational, too long-sighted, for them."

Magda opened her mouth, then closed it. Then she opened it again. "That's really smart. I'd never have thought of that."

But Rachel didn't rest on her laurels. "Then, when we were having our drink, all those strange questions about how the people in the household were taking the death, whether they seemed upset or had said anything to me. I thought she might be trying to find out if someone had suggested her as a suspect, but now I think I misread. I think she was fishing to see if someone was feeling nervous—or if they'd outed her as a blackmailer. And I think *that* someone killed her."

Silence. Then Magda nodded. "Yes. Yes. That makes sense. But now the question is, what can we do with it?"

That always seemed to be the question. Rachel cast her mind back over all the methods of further investigation that she'd seen on television, in the movies, in relevant books. She had already consulted her snitch—they knew nobody on the job—neither of them had a confidential informant. "We'll do a house-to-house search! We'll go talk to her neighbors about what they saw." Then she subsided. "Except we don't have her address."

But Magda grinned, at once both joyous and sly. "We don't, but we can get it." She reached into her bag for her phone. "Thanks to the internet."

Rachel held out a delaying hand. "Okay, but please could it be the internet indoors? We've been out here ten minutes, and I think my toes already have frostbite."

Five minutes later they were in a nearby furniture store, sitting next to each other on an overstuffed tweed sofa.

"What is this called again?" Rachel took off her gloves.

"Infogreffe." Magda stared at the screen. "It lists the names and addresses of all companies and company directors in the country. I used it all the time when I was just starting up, to network and find wholesalers. Right—there it is." She tapped letters into the website that had appeared. "Catherine will have made Le Cindy a company. It's required for tax purposes. And as director of that company, she'd have to list her address."

"And this is accessible online?" Rachel thought of animal rights activists, of domestic terrorists, of good old-fashioned burglars.

"Well, you have to pay a fee." Magda was distracted, focusing on what she was doing. Finally, "There you go." She tapped the monitor.

And indeed, there they went. *Le Cindy, SARL,* the monitor said, *Catherine Nadeau, director.* Below it, plain as day, was a residential address.

Chapter Seventeen

Catherine's apartment was on the Rue Pont aux Choux—Bridge of Cabbages—although the street looked as if it had never hosted a vegetable in all its history. Quite the contrary. It gave of being entirely and eternally industrial, flat cream walls occasionally broken by store fronts or lowered metal security rollers. "*Pas de vente au détail*," read a sign in one of the store windows—"*No retail sales*"—and Rachel guessed the street was so empty because many of its stores were wholesale only. Whatever the reason, they made for a road she wouldn't want to walk down alone at night.

Catherine's building had what seemed to be the only elegant façade on the block, oak double doors surrounded by a carved doorframe, their faceted brass knobs polished until they shone, and a gleaming brass plate announcing the building number. Rachel lifted a hand to the entry keypad. Then she dropped it.

"The code." Her voice was flat. She'd forgotten that an address was not much use in Paris without an entry code to go with it. No point knowing where a building was if you couldn't gain access to it.

"Oh, don't be silly." Magda reached over Rachel's head and put her palm flat on the panel, pressing all the buzzers at once. After a few seconds, the door gave its opening click. "Works when you're fifteen, works now." Magda pushed the porte d'entrée open. "Somebody's always stupid."

"Wait." Rachel put out a hand to catch the door. "We need a plan."

"A plan?"

"Yes, a plan. We need to decide who we'll say we are. We can't just show up at people's doors and say we think she's been murdered, do they have any information."

For a minute Magda looked as if she was going to ask why not, but then she said, "Well, we can say we're police."

Rachel thought, shook her head. "Bad idea. No ID."

"Oh yeah." Magda considered. "Then we can say we're detectives. That's even true."

"No." Rachel shook her head again. "We can't do that. No one ever talks to detectives. Didn't you see *Spiral*?" A rhetorical question; they watched the series together religiously every week.

They stood for a while, defeated by both reality and television. Then inspiration struck. "I know. We can say we're reporters."

"Reporters?" Magda looked dubious.

"Yes. It's perfect. What Parisian doesn't want to tell tales to the newspapers? We can tell them they'll be anonymous sources, and I bet they spill everything."

Parisians were notorious gossips. Squashed together into small spaces, with buildings designed so that the windows of their homes faced each other across courtyards, they couldn't avoid watching each other, and they turned necessity into pleasure by talking about what they saw. A reporter would offer another chance to share tittle-tattle, and giving information would show that they were in the know—something else Parisians loved.

"Okay." Magda added, "We can say we're from *Le Trois.*" At Rachel's questioning look, she explained, "It's a local paper. I found it while I was doing my research on Catherine."

Rachel let the door open fully, and they walked into the courtyard. There was no crime scene tape marking off a space, no soapy water splashed on the paving to erase bloodstains. It looked like any other courtyard in Paris, with a few plants scattered here and there and a set of stairs on either side leading up to the apartments. *How fast a life, and an existence, can be erased,* Rachel thought. Seeing the courtyard now, no one would guess that only a few days ago a dead body, itself alive just a second before, had lain on these paving stones.

Magda's practical voice interrupted Rachel's reverie. "Where do we start?"

Her friend might have known the constants of human nature, but Rachel knew the constants of Parisian résidences. "We start by talking to the plump woman in the apron."

Magda looked around. "What plump woman in the apron?"

"Every apartment building in Paris has a plump woman in an apron."

Sure enough, a few seconds later a rotund woman in an apron appeared, a broom in her hand. She made to sweep a corner of the courtyard, but Rachel knew she'd come out to see who they were.

She smiled. "Bonjour, madame." They walked over to her.

"Bonjour." Her brown eyes, two bright buttons in her

plump face, crinkled at the corners as she returned Rachel's smile.

"We are from *Le Trois.*" The woman continued to smile but gave no sign that she recognized the name. *Excellent,* Rachel thought. Their masquerade would go much more easily if no one actually knew the local paper. It removed the risk of awkward questions. "The local newspaper," she explained.

At the word "newspaper" the woman began to look interested. "Ah, *oui*?" She put down the broom.

"Yes." Magda joined in. "We're writing a memorial to Madame Nadeau." The woman's eyes flicked involuntarily to the space behind them. "We were hoping to get some information about her."

The woman nodded. "I can help you. I live just there." She jerked her head toward the ground floor apartment behind her. "And it was I who found her." She looked both discomfited and a tiny bit proud.

It was Rachel's turn to flick her eyes, toward Magda. *Jackpot,* her look said.

"Well," she began, "can you start by telling us a little about her?"

"She was a lovely woman. And so gracious!" The woman gave a shake of her head. "It's so sad. Just at Christmas she gave me the most beautiful orchid to say thank you for taking in her deliveries."

"Her deliveries?" Magda said.

"Oh yes! She receives a package at least once a week, and when she isn't home I hold them for her. You know," the woman leaned forward confidingly, "she has a little business, a store. I think the deliveries are stock."

Neither Rachel nor Magda pointed out that stock would be sent directly to the little business. Instead, Rachel said, "Ah, yes, the store. It was doing well, then?"

"Weeell . . ." The woman squinted her button eyes. "It *hadn't* been doing well, but Catherine told me a little while ago that her affairs had improved."

Rachel said meditatively, "And yet, the way she died. It suggests *some* sort of personal difficulty. Without any explanation, it seems so unexpected. Did she have any other troubles that you knew of?"

"Well, of course her *amoureux* had just died." Again the sorrowful shake of the head. "I happened to be at my window when she heard—I glanced over and saw her on the telephone. And when I met her here in the courtyard a few moments later, she seemed shocked by the news. Over the next days, as well—devastated, devastated. I'm certain his passing influenced what she did." She cast her eyes to heaven. "The death of love is a tragedy.

"And on the day she . . . left us"—Rachel tried to move the conversation as delicately as possible—"did she have any deliveries or any visitors?"

"No." The woman thought back. "It was quiet all day. In fact, too quiet." Her eyes locked on Rachel's. "I don't think anyone would disagree with me when I say there was a sense of foreboding in the air."

She took a breath in order to continue, but Rachel moved quickly: "When you say 'anyone,' did Madame Nadeau have other close friends here we might talk to?" The woman preened slightly at the suggestion that she had been a close friend of a postmortem celebrity, but shook her head. "Or did she have any frequent visitors?"

"Well, of course, her *ami* stopped by now and then."

"Of course." Magda took over. "But more recently? Maybe on the day she passed? Did anyone visit?"

The woman thought for a second, then said, "No, I didn't see anyone."

"Or maybe even less recently?" Rachel tried to keep her voice light. "None of her women friends visited?"

"I don't spend all day peering out my windows. I'm not a spy!" The woman drew back. Then, having made her spotless character clear, she said, "Anyway, I didn't notice anyone else." She reflected for a second, then offered, "Perhaps you'd like to see the orchid? It's very lovely. You could take a photo of it for the article."

"Oh, I'm sorry," and Magda did sound genuinely upset, "but the paper isn't giving us space for photos, except for one of Madame Nadeau. We would like to talk to some other neighbors, though, although I doubt they'll be as helpful as you. Can you point us in the right direction?"

"Of course." The woman nodded toward the left-hand staircase. "She lived on the second floor. Apartment five." She picked up the broom again and watched them begin to climb.

Where did Magda get her skills, Rachel wondered as she mounted the stairs. It wasn't just her boldness or her readiness with a story that Rachel found enviable; it was the ease with which she came up with plausible lies, and her smoothness in telling them. Rachel suspected that was the motto of the true detective: always be prepared with a good lie. They were the anti–Boy Scouts.

On the second landing they rested for a second, then found

apartment five. The door to apartment six stood at a right angle to it, and Magda knocked. No answer.

"Well," said Rachel, "it is the middle of the day."

As if to prove her right, there was no one home at apartment seven either. But at apartment eight they struck gold: not just a neighbor, but a resentful neighbor.

"The woman couldn't stop making noise," he said. "Thumping up and down the stairs every other day with a new package in her hand. And I could hear her laugh through my walls. Really, people who live in apartments should take their neighbors into account."

The man was of a type Rachel knew well. For him, everything that disturbed his peace was an affront, and he lived for such affronts. He would have collected and remembered Catherine's crimes against his tranquility with bitter love. All he needed to make him their ideal source was to be a shut-in who stayed home all day, every day.

"And I heard plenty of her noise," the man continued, "because I'm home all day these days. Since I left my job. Well," he qualified, "they'd probably tell you they let me go, but the truth is I couldn't stand working there anymore, so I let them fire me. They kept changing my hours on unacceptably short notice, no understanding that I might have a life of—"

Magda clicked her tongue. "Some people! So discourteous!" She shook her head at the sorrow of it all. "Like Madame Nadeau. I suppose her visitors disturbed you? You see," she explained, "we're trying to find friends to interview, and we assume some friends visited her. Maybe you can remember the name of a visitor who was particularly thoughtless? To whom you pointed the noise out?"

"All her visitors were thoughtless." He was a king commenting on peasants. "But none of them gave their names."

"Well, do you remember anyone in particular? Someone you could describe perhaps? We rely so much on members of the public for our information."

Magda must have managed the right combination of fawning and need, because instead of making a comment about the uselessness of depending on the public in the modern age, the neighbor said, "Women visited sometimes—friends, I suppose. All Amazons in high heels, from the sound of them. And a man came by a couple of times."

"A man?" Magda had her notebook open in her hand; now she took a golf pencil from the binding. "What did he look like?"

"I hardly saw him." The neighbor shrugged. "He didn't make much noise. He was wearing a coat, and he had dark hair."

That could be anyone, Rachel thought. Magda flipped the notebook shut. "No one else?" Rachel asked hopefully. She tried to prod him as she had the self-appointed concierge. "Do you remember any of the women visiting *recently*?"

"Are you suggesting I'm unobservant?" The man drew himself up. "I assure you I was aware of every visitor. I have the ears of a lynx!"

Rachel hadn't known that lynxes were famous for their hearing, but she could recognize the moment when she lost someone's good will. This man wouldn't tell them anything more. She stepped lightly on Magda's foot to indicate that they should leave.

"What?" Magda said.

"What?" the man was taken aback.

"No, I'm sorry," Magda responded. "Not you."

The man stared at her, bewildered. "What?"

They could be on that merry-go-round all day. Rachel broke in again. "I'm sorry, but we need to go. We're on a deadline. You've been most helpful."

"Well, if you don't have time to listen to what I have to say . . ." He shrugged, then closed the door. Even the air pushed out from his apartment felt aggrieved.

Magda and Rachel looked at each other, managing not to laugh. They went down the stairs and crossed the courtyard; the unofficial concierge watched them from her window as they left.

"Well, that was pointless." Out on the street again, Rachel felt gloom descend. Another idea proved barren.

Magda was cheerier. "I wouldn't say so."

"What would you say? Stairs climbed, neighbors plumbed, and nothing but that there were a lot of deliveries!"

"Well, that in itself is useful, actually. The fact that she was a personal spendthrift adds weight to the idea that she was blackmailing someone: she needed the money at work *and* at home."

Rachel grunted, simultaneously accepting the point and finding it inadequate. "Yes, but apparently she didn't have any recent visitors, which cancels out the idea that someone pushed her."

"The neighbor said a man visited her."

"And the woman said Edgar visited her. Two plus two equals they were the same person." When Magda looked as if she would protest, Rachel added, "And even if not, he said the man had dark hair and wore a coat—so he could be most of the men in Paris. And more to the point," she said, her voice rising in despair, "he said he hadn't seen any women lately!"

"No, that's not what he said." Magda kept her voice level. "He never said whether or not he'd seen any women: that was the moment where he got on his high horse." She looked at Rachel. "He has the ears of a lynx, you know."

Now they did laugh. "All right." Rachel felt her frustration loosen a bit. "So your feeling is what? That we should ask someone else?"

"No, I'm not sure that would do us any good. If you're being blackmailed by someone and have come to kill them, it's more likely that you'd take care *not* to be seen. So I doubt we'd have much luck finding a witness. I think our best bet is to try to figure out who has the most reason to be blackmailed."

"And that leads us back to Elisabeth and Mathilde, and via them to the mystery item in the appartement."

Magda nodded.

"And your idea is that if we can figure out who has the most reason to kill Edgar, we can then work to connect them to Catherine's murder? Inductive rather than deductive reasoning."

Magda nodded again.

To Rachel this approach seemed an awful lot like guessing, but it did have the benefit of linking to their only piece of certain evidence, Mathilde and Elisabeth's argument. She acquiesced. "All right. We're back to whatever's in Edgar's belongings. Well, since it's small enough for Mathilde to be able to refer to it as a bibelot, it can't be anything very large. And since Elisabeth's reference specifically to Edgar's papers suggests it's some sort of document . . ."

"But what sort of document?" Magda frowned. "And why would Mathilde and Elisabeth want it?"

Rachel had a thought. "What if they didn't both want the same thing? We only assume they're looking for the same thing because one wanted to fetch something and one wanted to hide something. But the two somethings don't need to be connected." She warmed to this possibility. "In fact, there's no real indication that Elisabeth, at least, actually knows what's there." She put up a hand to keep Magda from speaking. "She lied, but that doesn't mean she *knows* anything for certain. In fact, put that together with her stumble in the library and the fact that she's still lingering around the appartement, and it all suggests she doesn't know if there's something there, but she's afraid there is."

"Something incriminating. Yes, that makes sense." Magda crossed her arms and tucked her hands under them. "God, it's cold."

Rachel drew her down into the nearby Métro station. Warm air gusted out from the platform into the ticket area; Magda began to take off her gloves. "What about Mathilde?" she asked. "Do you think what she wants is incriminating?"

Rachel replayed the confrontation in her head. She remembered the outrage in Mathilde's posture and her voice. But how do you guess the source of outrage? Mathilde had been too angry to reveal anything beneath. She shook her head slowly. "I don't know. I've thought about that before. I'm sure what's back there is valuable to her in some way. But beyond that, I don't know."

Another "I don't know." *We've been saying "I don't know" over and over since we started this enterprise,* she thought. It wasn't very detective-like. Did Mr. Monk say, "I don't know"? Did Nero Wolfe? She supposed that she and Magda were like detectives in that they found things out and tried to draw conclusions from them, but so far they were unlike detectives in that they hadn't found out much and they'd been unable to draw any conclusions. But now it was enough: this was the "I don't know" that broke the camel's back. It was time for a bold move.

She steeled herself. "I don't know, but I'm going to find out."

Magda looked disconcerted by this sudden vehemence. "How?"

Rachel's lips thinned. "I'm going to search the bureau. I'm going to go and find whatever's back there, and then we'll know."

"But David is living in the appartement now! And Elisabeth is still spending all day there, actually in the bureau."

Rachel brushed these aside. "I haven't seen David since the first week. From what Fulke says, he often stays out all night. And he sleeps a lot. And as for Elisabeth"—she had no answer for that—"I'll figure something out."

"You sound like me." Magda frowned. "That's not reassuring."

"Don't worry," said Rachel grimly. "It'll all be fine." She fumbled in her pocket for her Navigo pass and waved it at the barrier sensor. Over the sound of the ensuing bleep, she said, "Trust me."

Chapter Eighteen

But for a large portion of the following week, it was all fine only in the sense that she could do nothing. Fulke was a constant in the appartement, and Elisabeth never seemed to miss a day or take a lunch. What's more, David had apparently let his nights become days and vice versa. He sometimes stumbled into the apartment hours after she'd arrived to work, and Rachel didn't relish the idea of his encountering her as she headed toward the back rooms.

At last, after what seemed an eternity but was really only five days, the stars aligned. When Rachel arrived on the Friday morning after the visit to Benoît, the house was even quieter than usual; Mademoiselle des Troyes, Fulke confirmed in answer to her question, was at home with a cold.

"And David?" Rachel asked.

"Monsieur Bowen has not yet returned from his night out."

It wasn't ideal, Rachel thought as she entered the library and closed the door behind her, but if David didn't come home before Fulke left, she'd have to seize the opportunity and explore. She might never get another chance. Slipping off her shoes and putting down her purse, she smoothed her skirt and sat down. She didn't even to pretend to catalogue lest the scratching of her pencil mask the click of the closing door; she just remained motionless. Since her conversation with Magda, she'd decided that if she was going to risk searching, she would do more than just search the bureau, so she used these waiting seconds to make a mental list of what she wanted from her exploration.

Certainly she wanted to find out what Elisabeth might have lied to protect, and what Mathilde might have desired so urgently. But she also wanted to get a sense of the appartement's layout. She could map the basic floor plan of the front rooms—the long formal dining room on the left, the salon on the right with the bureau behind it. But of the other rooms and the details of the place she had no idea. She and Magda were convinced that Edgar had been killed by someone who knew him, but the more logical side of her mind had to acknowledge that there was no concrete evidence for that. Could a stranger—an opportunistic thief or perhaps a drug addict who'd been able to access the building—have entered unnoticed? Despite what she'd said to Magda, she wanted to map the appartement to know if there was there a way in which a stranger could have performed such a tidy murder.

In fact, her logical mind had to acknowledge that they still didn't have much evidence of murder at all. Some wine and some revelations of financial need and greed, some abrupt pauses, and one lie from a pretty girl did not automatically make a crime. Her logical mind wanted to find some sort of hard, incontrovertible proof that her instinct was correct: a bottle of poisoned rosé poorly hidden, a series of letters revealing some nefarious act committed by Mathilde, or some such.

She heard the soft click she had been waiting for: Fulke had left, and she had half an hour in which to search. She decided to start with the dining room: she felt it would help her to see the actual scene of the crime. She crossed the entrance hall, with its thick cream-colored carpet that extended down the corridor into the main part of the appartement, guaranteed to muffle any approach to the dining room. One point in favor of the murderer's being able to sneak in. Then she noticed the front door. It was elegant, but it was still the heavy metal common to Parisian front doors, with the same complex double-rod locking system as her own. It would be nearly impossible for anyone, known or unknown, to open it without being overheard. One point in favor of it not being a murder at all.

She turned the knob of one of the dining room's double doors, opened it softly, and stepped into the room. Here, carpet was replaced by dark wood covered with an oriental rug. On the left-hand, deep red wall, there hung an oil painting of a hazy lakeside. A minor Impressionist, she guessed. It didn't seem valuable enough to be what Mathilde could have wanted—or to murder for—but maybe it was worth more than she thought. She made a mental note and moved on.

The walnut dining table she had glimpsed on her first visit stood in the center of the room, spread with a runner on which stood two multibranched candelabra, polished to gleaming. Surrounding it were ten chairs with solid, oversized backs, each perfectly parallel to the table edge. This was hardly a spot for cozy dinners *à deux.* She remembered her feeling that Edgar had needed to lure Elisabeth into whatever wrongdoing they had committed; the sense of privileged intimacy produced by dinners for two in this grand setting would dazzle anyone.

And she could easily imagine the rage inspired by learning that such intimacy had been a ruse, not a friendship.

Opening a swing door in the right-hand wall, she found herself in a narrow room with a black-and-white tiled floor, walls lined with cupboards and drawers. The butler's pantry. Considering the admirable state of the silver in the dining room, she wasn't surprised to see a cloth and apron hanging neatly on a hook near the cupboards. Considering Fulke's devotion to cleanliness and order, though, she was taken aback when she spotted a pile of paper slips on the windowsill. Her heart beat faster. Bills? Was the household drowning in debt? Or could they be gambling receipts? Or . . . *blackmail letters*? She held out a thumb and forefinger and plucked the pile from where it lay, using her breath to fan out the sheets and twisting her head to read them. Congratulating herself on her skills in evidence handling, she saw that she had found a collection of receipts for the pressing—household linens and suits, and the one on top for a black velvet blazer.

Her cheeks burned. She put the pile back and hurried through the door next to her, another swing one. Behind it lay the kitchen, with white walls and a practical gray linoleum floor. A counter held the usual cooking implements and a bowl of fruit, and there was a small zinc table, just big enough for one person to eat at, with a single chair.

Next to the table stood a massive stainless steel refrigerator. Given the number of people who actually lived in the appartement, Rachel thought, its size must be more a statement than a necessity. It certainly seemed so when she opened it, for it contained only a packet of prosciutto, some fresh pasta, a container of milk, and a half-full bottle of sweet white wine. No rosé.

Checking again, she saw no bottle on the counter either. Nothing to suggest that rosé was still drunk here, nothing to link rosé to anyone currently in residence.

She calculated that she must be standing right across from the bureau, and turned to go into the hallway. To her surprise, though, there was no direct door from the kitchen to the corridor: her only options were to retrace her steps back to the dining room or to keep going deeper into the appartement via a door off the back of the kitchen. Well, it was better to go forward than to go back.

The door led to a small bathroom containing a narrow sink and a toilet. *You'd have to be a member of Cirque de Soleil to hide or retrieve anything in here,* Rachel thought, although she did admire the ingenuity that had allowed for fitting two doors in this bathroom, the one to the kitchen and one that, she found, opened onto a storage room. A folded cot in one corner suggested this had once been a bedroom, but that must have been quite a while ago, because the uncarpeted floor was now crammed with household detritus: a couple of tea chests, some suitcases, an assortment of boxes of various different sizes and origins, and—unexpectedly—a bag of onions and one of potatoes, balanced on what seemed once to have been a desk. Despite the hodgepodge, Rachel knew almost instantly that this space was under Fulke's control: there was no dust, and the various items, although they filled the room, were tidily arranged, a life-size Chinese box puzzle. Then she noticed another door in the far corner. Well, she thought, that cancelled out the difficulties of the front entrance. If this door were left unlocked, someone could easily get in and creep through to the dining room. One point for a possible stranger murder. But if the door was locked, you would need a key to enter the appartement this way, and she had to admit that she couldn't imagine Fulke ever forgetting to lock a door. So once again, murder by an intimate was on the table. She smiled grimly at her own pun.

There was also a door built into the right-hand wall. It led into the hallway, which extended for only a few more feet before opening onto a narrow passage with steps leading both up and down. This must be the door she heard click each day. Like most nineteenth-century Paris résidences, this one kept its servants' quarters on the top floor, with a separate staircase leading from them directly down to the appartements and into the courtyard. Edgar's appartement would have come with a set of those attic rooms to house whatever household staff its owner might have—in Edgar's case, Fulke. She looked at her watch: fifteen minutes.

Somewhere in the house something rustled. She froze, straining her ears, but all was silent once more. One of those receipts, dislodged by a breeze? The cloth in the butler's pantry, brushing against the wall behind it? She waited, holding her breath. When she still heard nothing, she checked her watch. Thirteen minutes. Enough time to work her way down the other side of the appartement if she hurried. She closed the door and gently opened the one opposite.

Edgar's bedroom. The bed was a huge sleigh in dark wood, flanked by leather-topped night tables and with deep-piled dark-brown carpet flowing around and under it. It suddenly came into her head that the whole place was well padded. Only the storage room and Fulke's areas were free of thick carpet, heavy furniture, tufted leather. As David's stories suggested,

Edgar had become a man who enjoyed having money and spreading it thickly.

As if to prove her point, a marble sculpture on a shelf on the far wall caught her eye. Was that a Jacob Epstein dove? She moved closer. My God, it must be worth thousands. She knew Edgar loved Epstein, but when they'd been together he certainly hadn't had the money to buy one. She rested a hand on it. It could easily fit beneath a coat, although not without drawing some attention.

She forced herself to put this thought aside and hurry on, moving to the en suite bathroom. It was full of David's toiletries and the detritus of his pockets: an electric razor and toothbrush, toothpaste, a washcloth and soap, some small change, and a credit card left neatly aligned with the counter's edge. She opened a mirrored cupboard set into the wall. No bottles of pills, no digoxin, not even an antacid: nothing to suggest Edgar had heart trouble, but nothing to suggest he'd been helped on his way either. Of course, the contents would likely have been removed in anticipation of David's arrival. And they would have been thrown out anyway: doctors told you to dispose of any leftover medication when someone died. She closed the mirror and returned to the bedroom.

Again a rustle; again she froze. This time, though, there was *not* silence. This time, after a pause, there was a second rustle. She looked at her watch. Five minutes. Her intuition told her that she was alone, but also that she was running out of time. And she needed to see the bureau; it held Edgar's business papers. She cursed herself retrospectively for deciding to start with the dining room. Had she really needed to see the scene of death? She refocused: she could berate herself later.

Straightening her mental spine, then her physical one, she put a hand on the door to the bureau, turned the knob, and opened it.

Elisabeth was bent over a box, her hands among its papers, flicking swiftly through them. What Rachel had heard was the rustle of documents being leafed through by shaking, hurrying fingers. Hearing the door, Elisabeth lifted her chin and her gray eyes, made even more enormous by the angle of her head, looked up at Rachel. Her face flushed.

"Elisabeth!" Although Rachel was as surprised as the girl who faced her, she had the happy fortune of remembering quickly that the best defense is a good offense. She made her voice sharp. "You're supposed to be sick at home. What are you doing here?"

Elisabeth's eyes darted left and right. "I–I–I was looking for a pen." She inhaled. Having found a metaphorical straw to clutch, she gripped it tightly. "I was working with Edgar's papers, and I needed to make some notes, but I couldn't find a pen. I thought there might be one in a box."

Oh, please! Rachel scoffed inwardly. "Never mind what you're doing at this moment," she said. "Why are you here at all?"

Elisabeth put a hand through her hair, then yanked her sleeves down over her hands. She took another breath. But just as she opened her mouth to speak, there came the sound of a key turning in the back door. Fulke was home.

Chapter Nineteen

"That's enough." Alan crossed his arms. "This has gone far enough."

"Do you want me to stop?" They were sitting on the bed facing each other as Rachel told him about her adventure. She had just reached the point where Fulke opened the door.

"Yes. I want you to stop. If you had told me earlier what you were doing, I would have wanted you to stop then. Now I want you to stop now. Stop the detection nonsense; stop the story. *Stop.*"

"Nonsense?" Rachel remained leaning against the footboard, but her expression grew mutinous. "You're calling my interests nonsense?"

"I'm calling this whole escapade nonsense."

Rachel narrowed her nostrils at "escapade," but he kept going.

"When you first told me that Edgar had requested in his will that you catalogue his books, and that you thought it must be because he'd mentioned at a party that he'd read your work and liked it, I knew you were lying. Who *would* believe a story like that? But I also know you have this notion that I'm an insanely jealous man, so I thought, 'All right, I'll let it go.' But now you tell me that not only did you begin to think that he might not have died naturally—based on what sounds to me like no real evidence—but also that you, along with Magda, have decided on suspects. And when one of your suspects died, you concluded, despite evidence of suicide, that she must have been murdered by one of your other suspects."

Rachel was outraged. "You *are* a jealous man! And we have *evidence* that it wasn't suicide!"

"In which case not only have you spent the last month 'detecting'"—he made quotation marks in the air—"without saying anything, but you've also spent the last week investigating a real murder—a not-undangerous situation—without telling me, too. And then, to cap it all off, you decided that the best way to proceed was by prying around the inner recesses of your original murder victim's apartment, whereupon you surprised your current prime suspect in the middle of doing something suspect! And you kept all this from me, your husband, the man you supposedly love and trust and respect more than anyone else. You're only telling me now because you couldn't think of an alternate story quickly when I asked why you were so jumpy at dinner. So if I don't call this nonsense, I'll have to call it demeaning and hurtful, and in any case, yes, I want you to stop."

He paused to draw breath. Rachel, her cheeks red, kept her eyes on the sheets. She'd never thought about it his way; she'd just thought it avoided all sorts of awkwardness if she didn't tell him what she was doing. She was overwhelmed by sudden shame.

"My love," Alan said, "you are not the police. You are not even a detective"—she opened her mouth to protest—"in any trained way. And you were wandering through what, if you're right, is a crime scene. On your own. And then you're surprised by not one, but two possible murderers!"

Rachel wasn't too ashamed to try to regain superiority. She waved a hand. "Oh, please. I was surprised by a Girl Friday and a butler. That's hardly a murder about to take place."

"If your description of everything leading up to your sneaking around"—she opened her mouth again, but once more he didn't pause—"is accurate, you think a murder occurred there and that this Girl Friday might be the murderer. So your idea of how best to deal with a murder scene is to poke around in it. And when you unexpectedly encounter a possible murderess, your idea of how best to deal with that is to confront her! You can't say the circumstances suggest murder and then say you're perfectly safe!" He repeated "I want you to stop."

Like anyone who has behaved foolishly and been confronted with her foolishness, Rachel's blood was up. Who was Alan to tell her she'd done wrong? Who'd died and made him Inspector Morse? "Well, I'm not going to stop."

Alan sighed. "No, of course you're not." He took her hand and rubbed her fingers with his own, then gave another sigh. "Well, would you be willing to take a break?" He looked at her. "To allow me to recover from the shock?"

"A break?"

"Just a few days. A week."

Rachel frowned.

"Including a weekend. So, five business days. Would you be willing to wait for five business days, just to think about whether you want to keep going and how?"

She considered. Taking a break wasn't a bad idea. She saw now how much her keeping secrets must have hurt him, and agreeing to his request would go some way toward making it up. Plus, although she'd never admit it, she had been frightened by the abrupt end to her exploration, and she could use a few days to catch her breath. Maybe more importantly, she wasn't yet sure what she'd learned, or what its value might be. A few days to gather herself and sort through the information might be good.

"Fine," she said. Then, more for show than anything else, "But only one week."

He exhaled heavily. "Thank you."

Rachel nodded acknowledgment, then took his other hand and held both on the covers between them. "Now," she said, "do you want to hear what happened next?"

"Of course." Alan sat back.

"Well, Elisabeth and I were in the bureau. We didn't have time to get out of the room and close the door, and obviously if we'd gone in and closed it, Fulke would have heard. It would have seemed as if we were hiding. Plus, we panicked. So we were still standing there when the door opened and Fulke saw us. For a second he stopped—but just for a second. And then he looked at me and said, 'Madame Levis.' You would have thought I stood in the doorway to the bureau every day."

* * *

"And what did you say?" Magda leaned forward. Rachel was telling her the story the following afternoon in Coffee Parisien, a dimly lit café near Rachel's apartment. Surrounded by chattering students and clusters of Parisians who had paused for an aperitif, Magda was riveted, her *café americain* untouched before her.

"I said I'd heard a noise and gone to investigate."

"Did he buy it?"

"How could I tell, with Fulke? He didn't turn a hair. All he did was look at Elisabeth and say, 'Mademoiselle.'"

But Fulke's change of focus had given Rachel a second in which to think. "It *is* a surprise to find her here, isn't it?" she said brightly. "She was just telling me that she'd decided to come in because she was feeling better."

Luckily, Elisabeth's fading blush hadn't quite left her cheeks; it was just as plausible that she might be a woman with a mild cold. Even better, when she spoke, the constriction of her throat made her sound as if she had a blocked nose.

"Yes," she said, her voice shaking slightly. "I was just sorting some papers when Madame Levis opened the door unexpectedly."

It was impossible to tell if Fulke believed this either: his face remained smooth save for a touch of mild confusion. "I see, madam," he said to Rachel in English, giving one of his small bows. Then he turned to Elisabeth. "Mademoiselle," he continued in French, "I have a superb tisane for the nose and throat. Allow me to prepare some for you."

He nodded, then proceeded toward the dining room, his canvas bag of fruit and vegetables tucked under his arm.

Casting Elisabeth a look that she hoped said, *I'm not finished with you*, Rachel hurried back down the passageway.

"So you never saw what was in the bureau." Magda's tone was full of sympathetic frustration.

"I know. And those bills!" Rachel shook her head ruefully, "I felt like I was in *Northanger Abbey*."

Magda respected her embarrassment with a short silence. Then she said, "Well, do you think you found *any*thing that could be useful?"

For once, the answer was not going to be "I don't know."

Rachel cleared her throat. "Maybe."

"Maybe?"

"Well then, yes." She paused. "Maybe." Seeing Magda's expression, she explained, "I found something Mathilde might have been after. In the bedroom. A sculpture of a dove by Jacob Epstein."

"*The* Jacob Epstein?" When Rachel nodded, Magda gave a low whistle. "That must be worth a pretty penny."

"And it would fit under a coat. Just. It would've been bulky, but not too heavy."

"D'you think that's what she wanted?"

Rachel shrugged, but Magda's voice sped up. "It's not hard to imagine. She kills him for the money she thinks is coming to her in the will, and then when it turns out it isn't as much money as she thought—as she feels she deserves—she decides to top it up with the sculpture. But Elisabeth catches her on her way in to take it." Satisfied, she switched focus. "Which reminds me: Elisabeth. You found her rifling through some papers when she was supposed to be out sick? Sneaky."

"She must have come through the back door when I was in

the dining room, and I was concentrating too hard to hear her." Chagrined, Rachel changed the subject. "But you know what was really weird?"

"What?" Magda leaned forward.

"None of the rooms between the dining room and the back of the appartement have a door to the hallway. If someone wants to go out, they have to do it either from the dining room or from the storage room."

Magda crumpled her forehead, no doubt as she tried to imagine the setup, then pushed a paper napkin at her. "Draw it."

Rachel sketched a floor plan and slid the napkin back.

"Why would you build your house that way?" she asked.

Magda frowned. "I'll bet it's a leftover," she said finally. "I'll bet that when the place was first built, that back room was a sort of preparation room—you know, what they used to call 'offices.' The servants would come in there and never be seen as they worked their way forward to the public rooms or back to the offices. And if they needed to clean the other side of the place, they could just cross the hall in the back. Very discreet." She squinted at the napkin, a conclusion dawning. "But that means that if you wanted to get into the dining room to kill Edgar, you'd only have two options. You could start in the back room and work your way forward, or you could go through the double doors from the hall. But you said the dining chairs had solid backs—really tall, solid backs. So if Edgar wanted to see who was coming through the double doors, he'd have to stand up. And if he stood up, either there would have been a struggle with the person who'd come to kill him, or he would have been killed from the front." She paused. "But we know there was no struggle, because we know there was no

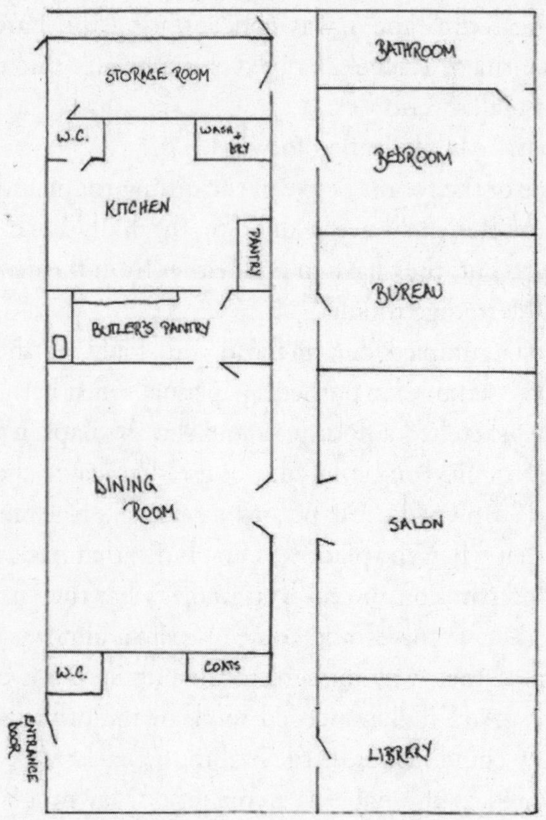

mess to alert the police that anything untoward had happened. And we know he wasn't killed from the front because he was facedown."

"But he wasn't killed from the back either," Rachel pointed out. "I mean, he wasn't struck from the back. There wasn't a mark on him."

"No, but even if the murderer just drowned him, they couldn't have done it after coming in through the double doors, because Edgar would have had time to stand up and defend himself. And if someone's risen and is facing you, you're not going to be able to persuade him to sit back down, and then stand behind him and drown him, without disturbing anything. So the murderer must have come in through the butler's pantry."

"Because then Edgar could see them without standing up."

"Yes." Magda looked at the map again. "There wasn't any rosé in the kitchen or dining room, right?"

Rachel was caught off guard by the change of subject, but she said, "No. A sweet white wine in the fridge, but no rosé." Then, "Why?"

"Well, the fact that there was rosé on the table when he died and now there's none in the house suggests that someone who liked rosé was eating there at the time, but now they don't eat there anymore. And the fact that he didn't stand up suggests he wasn't surprised to see whomever he saw. And those *together* suggest the murderer wasn't a random stranger, but rather a rosé drinker he knew."

"Which means Mathilde or Elisabeth."

Magda nodded, looking pleased with herself—as well she might, Rachel thought. Now, entry via the back door meant having a key, but presumably Elisabeth or Mathilde, or probably both, did have a key. So the vital question was, which one would Edgar have expected to appear at that door? Or at least, she added hastily, not been startled to see at that door?

"It was Elisabeth."

Magda looked surprised. "Why her?"

"First, Mathilde would never enter a dining room via the butler's pantry or a storage room in normal circumstances, so

Edgar would have been surprised to see her. And second, even if she would, she couldn't have entered through the storage room without any noise, because you'd have to move things to make a path. And she couldn't have made the path before because someone who went into the storage room might notice." When Magda didn't respond, Rachel continued, "But Elisabeth must have come into the dining room via the butler's pantry a thousand times. She said she was like family, so her entering through the back would be plausible. And she was there often enough to have made the path some other time without its seeming strange, since she was a sort of an odd-job girl. And I just realized something else I learned." Out of air, she took a gasping breath and went on. "Whatever Elisabeth is after, she wants it badly. Either she pretended to be ill so she could sneak in unnoticed in the hope of finding it, or she came in even though she was ill in the hope of finding it. And she's been in that bureau every day, presumably also looking for whatever it is. Whereas Mathilde has only come by irregularly."

"Maybe Mathilde's wily enough to be playing it cool."

"If you've killed someone and now want to steal from them, you can't risk playing it cool. And that's the scenario we're assuming, right?"

Rachel could see Magda considering possibilities, adding up evidence in her head. Finally she said, "What exactly was Elisabeth doing when you found her?"

It was Rachel's turn to think. "She had her hands in a box of papers. And there were stacks that looked like she'd gone through already."

"Personal papers or documents?"

Rachel cast her mind back. "Documents."

"Did they look official?"

"Yes."

"All right. So we know she was looking for something bureaucratic, something publicly or legally significant. And she got into the house unnoticed, which tells us she has a key, and it would seem a key to the back door, too." Magda paused to add all this up. Then, "I'm not going to say she's our only suspect, but you're right, she's our strongest suspect: someone who has access to the house and whom Edgar wouldn't be surprised to see there; someone who's done something involving him that she wants to cover up. And now"—she licked her lips—"now we have something on her. You caught her doing something she didn't want to be caught doing. You know it and she knows it. So now you have an advantage. You can confront her and demand some answers."

She was right. Rachel felt her heart lift. Then she felt it fall once more. "Not for a week."

"Not for a—?" Then Magda too remembered. "Oh, right."

They sat disconsolate. Rachel gazed grouchily into her half cup of cold chocolate. Shouldn't it make a difference that she'd promised Alan before they had a lead, when it looked as if the whole investigation was going to end up going nowhere? It should, she answered herself, but it didn't. A promise was a promise, especially to a spouse, especially after her recent behavior. Any other way was a step down a dangerous path. She heaved a sigh that out-sighed any sigh she'd ever heaved.

"It's not so bad." Magda said, mistaking the source of her dejection. "A week won't change the fact that you did find her in suspicious circumstances. In fact," she said, her tone growing crafty, "a long wait may wind her up to such a pitch of fear that when you confront her, she blurts everything out. Or she might be lulled into a false sense of security by five days of nothing."

"Six," Rachel corrected. "And she won't be the only one lulled by it." She bit her thumbnail, contemplating the yawning days ahead.

Chapter Twenty

It was a long week. Rachel knew from experience that it was impossible to write good poetry under a time limit, so she didn't even bother to pick up her pen. Instead, she attempted to occupy herself by being a domestic goddess. She cleaned the apartment, then cleaned it again; for the first time in years, she ironed all of Alan's shirts herself. She binge-watched all the episodes from the last season of *Law & Order*. But she still found herself at loose ends by Thursday evening.

"One more day," she pointed out to Alan as they sat down to oxtail soup with warm bread, to be followed by baked Alaska.

"Mmm." He swallowed his spoonful of soup, then looked up at her. "Why don't you invite Magda over for dinner tomorrow?"

"Magda?" Rachel sipped from her own spoon. "Why? I've seen her every day this week. I'm sure I'll see her tomorrow too."

"Still, I think you should invite her to have dinner here. I have some things to show you." Seeing her face, he said, "Good things, good things. Come on. Invite her."

* * *

The dinner was an awkward affair. Rachel, frustrated by her imposed hiatus, emanated boredom and irritation; Magda, having received angry daily updates, didn't want to risk setting her off again and so stayed quiet. Still, as he finished his meal, Alan seemed serenely cheerful.

"That was delicious." They had eaten coq au vin with new potatoes, with *tarte tatin* for dessert. Now he drank the final sip from his wine glass. "So." He poured himself some more, tilted the bottle to Magda, then to Rachel; both shook their heads. "How has everyone's week been?"

"Boring," said Rachel. She sounded fifteen years old. "Buh-oring. And worrying, because I know there's a murderer wandering around, but I haven't been allowed to do anything about it."

Alan smiled.

"Do I amuse you?" she asked.

"Always. But that's not why I'm smiling."

"Then why?"

"I'm smiling because you're angry with me, but I know that in a minute you're going to be very happy, and very happy with me." From under his chair he drew a pile of papers and laid them on the table.

"What's that?" She reached out, but he pulled the stack toward him.

"This," he said, "is the reason for Edgar's 'affection and gratitude.'" He tapped the pile twice on the table, laid it down again, and looked at each woman in turn. "Shall we begin?"

"Alan—" Then Rachel decided to let him have his moment. "Yes."

"Very well." He ruffled the papers he'd just tidied. "When you described your conversation with Elisabeth in the library, and the exchange between Elisabeth and Mathilde in the hall, and then again when you came home from . . . looking around Edgar's house, I did think things sounded strange, even if I didn't say so. And as I thought about it more, I realized that the one common strand in everything you described—Edgar's death and his will, the Nadeau woman's death, the girl sneaking in to rummage around in Edgar's bureau—the one common strand is money." Again he looked at the women, who nodded. "Now," he went on, "I didn't know Edgar Bowen very well, and I don't know this des Troyes girl or Catherine Nadeau at all, but I do know money. So over this past week I had a look at some money. I wanted to see if your thinking could be plausible." He rapped his knuckles against the pages. "And I found something interesting."

"Interesting?" Magda bit her lower lip.

"Well . . ." He raised his eyebrows. "A wise woman once told me that there are four main motives for murder: jealousy, fear, revenge, and—"

Rachel breathed the final word like Howard Carter at Tutankhamen's spy hole: "*Theft*."

Alan nodded. He picked up the first sheet. "Edgar had quite a bit of money. I won't tell you how much because the total is irrelevant, but I will tell you that my job has taught me you don't make that much money without having a very good business head. And without cutting a few corners."

"How do you know he had that much money?" Rachel hated to think of book-loving Edgar, cat-loving Edgar, even newly ostentatious Edgar, as a criminal, never mind how minor.

"I looked at his business expenses: his payroll, his taxes, and the taxes of the people he employed."

"How did you find all that?" Magda was always curious about processes, but Alan, who also loved them and normally was happy to explain them in minute detail, now became vague.

"I'm in banking. There are certain computer frameworks. Certain"—he thought for a second—"means for finding out about people's money."

"Are these legal means?" Rachel wasn't sure which answer she wanted.

"They're means available to anyone who works in banking at my level."

Which wasn't exactly an answer to her question, Rachel noted. But as she was asking herself if she cared, Magda leaned forward and said in a clipped tone, "Did you take, move, or otherwise interfere with any of this money?"

"Is what you found helpful to us?"

"Potentially."

"Are you going to get caught?"

Alan looked at Rachel as he answered. "Very unlikely."

Magda sat back. She put out a hand to Rachel, as if demonstrating something.

Rachel sighed. "Okay. Go on. You checked the taxes."

"Yes, I checked the taxes." Alan's tone became professional again. "The unknown factor here was Elisabeth des Troyes, so I focused on her. I knew her name, obviously, and from Edgar's payroll information, I found her bank account. She *was* Edgar's . . . well, I guess 'aide de bureau' isn't a job title. He listed her as his *secrétaire de direction*, and he paid her by direct deposit. But"—he picked up the second sheet, on which was printed some sort of table—"he paid her quite a bit. Much more than you'd normally pay for that kind of work. Three thousand euros a month."

Jesus, thought Rachel, *give me* that *job.*

Alan put the second sheet to one side, picked up another two or three, then began again. "Many people who make above a certain amount incorporate themselves—you know, they become a company for work purposes." Rachel nodded. "Well, Edgar paid his employees as Edgar Bowen, the company. But he still had bank accounts and money, et cetera, as Edgar Bowen, the person. And that matters," he said, looking down at the papers, "because Edgar Bowen, the company—Edgar Bowen, SARL—paid Elisabeth des Troyes. And *that* matters"—unable to resist, he paused to build suspense—"because Elisabeth des Troyes then paid Edgar Bowen, the person."

"What?" Rachel and Magda spoke together. They leaned forward.

"*She* paid *him*?" Rachel said.

"Yes." Alan took two of the remaining pieces of paper from the stack and turned them to the landscape position, laying them side by side in front of him. "It looks that way. Every month, Edgar Bowen, SARL, would pay her by direct deposit. And late every month, she would remove fifteen hundred euros in cash from her account. And the following month, Edgar Bowen the person would deposit about a thousand euros in cash into his personal account. He must have kept some of the money and used it. Look." He shoved the papers across to Rachel. "You can see."

Rachel looked at the printouts for a second, silently thanking Alan for pretending she could understand them when he knew she was terrible with numbers. She passed them to Magda.

"So," said Magda, accepting them but still looking at Alan, "he was robbing Peter to pay Paul." She frowned. "I don't understand."

"That's because," Alan said, "you need the final piece. And here it is: Edgar Bowen, SARL, less in employer taxes and contributions than Edgar Bowen the person would have paid in income tax. Not much, but over time not much adds up to a lot. And anyway"—again he looked from one to the other—"any good businessman knows that every bit helps."

Rachel couldn't believe it. "Fraud!" she said.

"Well," Alan's tone was forgiving, "pilfering. And by the way," he added, "this explains why he invested in Catherine Nadeau's store. He wanted the tax credit."

Rachel sat still. Edgar had committed fraud. She tried it Alan's way: Edgar had pilfered. It didn't sound any better. The Edgar Bowen she had once known intimately, the Edgar Bowen she had been kissing on the cheeks at cocktail parties all these years, had conspired to cheat the government out of money every month. *And not even big money!* she thought. Compared to his salary, compared to his style of living—piddling sums. Now there was a phrase that really didn't sound good. Would he seem less grimy if he'd gone big? Would great sums have given him a sheen of grandeur? She suddenly remembered an old joke her father loved: "The food was terrible—and such small portions!"

Magda squinted at the sheets. "But cash is notoriously difficult to trace."

Don't say television never taught us anything, Rachel thought. "Given that, how can you be sure what was happening?"

"Good question." Alan nodded. "And that may be why Edgar varied the amount of his deposits. You're right: there's no way to be one hundred percent certain about what was going on. But Elisabeth paid all her major expenses from this account before she took out the fifteen hundred every month, so she wasn't using it to cover rent, or utilities, or another large item. And there's a consistent pattern. She takes out fifteen hundred late each month, and early the next month Edgar always deposits not quite the same amount."

Rachel put her hands up to the sides of her face and felt the skull beneath her skin. "But surely he'd be caught?"

"Eventually, yes, probably. But these were very small amounts, relatively speaking. And for our purposes, all that matters is that he hadn't been caught yet."

"And now he never will be," said Magda solemnly. Then, "So *this* is why he left Elisabeth the money! In affection and *gratitude.* She'd worked this scheme with him, and he was grateful."

"Yes. And she'd done well out of it. Fifteen hundred euros a month is a nice amount for picking up someone's dry cleaning. But he must have promised her, or wanted to give her, something bigger at the end." Alan regathered the papers and knocked them back into shape on the table, his face a picture of satisfaction.

For a few seconds no one spoke. Finally, "Thank you," Magda said. "You worked hard, and you didn't have to do any of this."

"Yes," Rachel echoed, "thank you. Truly." She took his hand. "You're wonderful." But her voice was quiet.

After another moment's silence, Magda turned to Rachel. "This means Elisabeth didn't kill him."

Rachel was taken aback. "What?"

"Well, she wasn't going to kill the goose that was laying the golden egg every month!"

"But maybe she'd had enough. Maybe she wanted to stop."

"Maybe?" Magda said pointedly. "If I said that, you'd say I was speculating. Where's your evidence?"

Both of them had forgotten Alan. They spoke only to and for each other.

"She's looking hard for incriminating documents," Rachel said, "which suggests she wants to be rid of the whole mess. She couldn't turn him in because she'd be turning herself in too. Killing him was her way out."

"It seems an extreme solution."

"Not if she knew it would lead to a much bigger payout in his will."

"That doesn't make sense." Magda made a face. "It's self-contradictory. She killed him because she wanted to stop getting money illegally but also because she knew she was bequeathed more money in his will? Murder is illegal too."

But Rachel was stubborn, and right now she wanted a villain who would out-villain Edgar. "It makes sense of her reaction." Her voice began to quicken as she put pieces together. "That's why she was surprised in that strange way. Remember, I said she seemed as if she were overacting something she genuinely felt. She was expecting a bequest—but then it turned out better than she ever could have hoped."

"Edgar mentioned she was in his will, but not for how much, and for that unknown sum she was willing to cut off a steady income by killing him?" Magda's tone suggested what she thought of that scenario.

"You thought Catherine Nadeau would kill for seventy-five hundred euros! Plus"—Rachel's voice took on a note of triumph—"guilt! The way she behaved when we first talked in the library makes it plain she felt guilty about the whole thing. Guilt and greed!"

"No." Magda shook her head. "I don't buy it. This"—she gestured at the papers—"seems to me a strong reason for her *not* to kill him. As long as he was alive, no one was going to be going through his estate and possibly discovering tax cheats. No," she repeated, shaking her head again, "this information makes Mathilde the prime suspect."

"Mathilde!"

"Yes. She knew the house, and there's no real reason why she couldn't have come in the back. You just think she didn't because it 'doesn't seem like her.'" Rachel ground her teeth at both the tone and the accuracy of the observation. Magda went on, "Elisabeth's rooting around in the bureau shows why she wouldn't have killed him. With him dead she has no way of knowing if there's any remaining evidence of their scheme. She might have twenty thousand euros, but she also has a lot more worry and potential trouble on her hands. Whereas Mathilde . . ." She raised her eyebrows. "We both agree she's cold as ice. Kiki told you she was greedy and proud. *You* told *me* it seemed likely Edgar would have said something to her about the contents of his will. If she knew what was in it, who knows what she might have done out of revenge? And greed. Revenge and greed!"

"*If.* If, if." Secretly, Rachel thought Magda had made some good points, but she wasn't ready to give up her suspect while there was evidence to support her. "And what about the rosé?"

"What about it?"

"We know Elisabeth was the person Edgar ordered it for, and we know it was on the table when Edgar was found. Now that she's not dining at the apartment, there's none there. That seems pretty conclusive proof of her guilt."

"How?" Magda's voice rose on the word. "Absence proves nothing. Catherine drank rosé. And Mathilde drinks it too! *And* David told you she still came around! Plus," she calmed down, "from what you told me, Elisabeth is slim—and timid. Would she be able to throw Catherine out a window, or even force her out of one?" The question hovered in the air as Magda threw down her trump card: "Whereas Mathilde . . ."

Even incomplete, the sentence rang true. Rachel crossed her arms in sulky rage; Magda repeated the gesture in satisfied triumph. They faced each other across the table.

Rachel gave in first. "Fine. You have a point. So what do you think we should do?"

Magda considered. "I don't know," she said at last. "What do you think we should do?"

Alan cleared his throat, reminding them of his existence. "You should go to the police."

They turned to him.

"We can't," Rachel said.

"We still don't have enough concrete evidence," said Magda. "We're building a picture."

"Of *course* you are." He nodded gently. "And I don't

suppose you'd consider the possibility that the lack of definitive concrete evidence means Edgar just had a heart attack and died?"

"No!" they said in unison, their tone firm.

"Even though the sum total of your current evidence is a bottle of wine, the lack of a door, and some minor tax fraud?"

"I know he was murdered," Rachel declared in the same second that Magda said, "He hated rosé."

Alan exhaled through his nose. To distract him, Rachel put her hand on the stack of print-outs. "But what are *you* going to do? About this?"

He shrugged. "Nothing. I can't do anything." Then, after a pause, "Sometimes you know how to do things you're not actually supposed to do. So the knowledge is just ours." He paused again. "Well, yours."

Rachel nodded. They all sat for another moment before Magda stood to leave.

Chapter Twenty-One

Later, Rachel lay in bed in the dark. Beside her Alan breathed evenly, sleeping the sleep of the just and the just made love to. She was wide-awake.

Edgar had been a white-collar criminal. Edgar! In the simplest language, unadorned by comfort, he had been a thief.

She hated crying when she was lying on her back. The tears trickled unnaturally toward her ears, and when she tried to sniffle up the excess mucus, it never worked; the thickness just moved slightly deeper inside her nostrils, blocking them even more. But if she sat up, Alan would wake—he always did when she made any big movement. So she lay, miserable and made more miserable by her miserable state.

Edgar the thief. She revised: Edgar the pilferer. That was worse; "pilfer" was such a silly word. She felt two tears begin their sideways journey from the corners of her eyes. Cat lover, book lover, gracious older lover, and that was the truth of him: he was a . . . pilferer. She snuffled softly. Had that been him all along, and she'd just missed it? Was her judgment that bad?

She reminded herself of her feelings as she walked around Edgar's appartement, seeing the luxurious public and personal rooms and the sterile other spaces, the barren refrigerator. Maybe she was surprised by tonight's revelations only because she had been too much of a coward to admit earlier what she already knew: that her first great love had become a shallow plutocrat. She sniffled.

But wait. She wiped her temples with the heels of her hands. That he had been a thief was the truth of *this* action, certainly, but was it the truth of him? He *had* been a cat lover; he *had* been a book lover; he *had* been a gracious older lover—and he had been a gracious man, period. He had loved her—she was sure of that—and when he left her, he did it tenderly, without any pleasure or glorying in the heart he'd broken. Maybe as his income had grown, so had his greed, but that didn't mean he'd become only that greed. When Elisabeth had nearly cried in the library, it hadn't been over the loss of Edgar's monthly payments or over her sudden windfall: she had wanted to cry for the loss of the man who'd talked to her like a friend, who'd taken an interest in her life and her self. And while he might have left her money as a kind of postmortem payoff (*might*, Rachel stressed to herself), he'd left Mathilde money as a way of thanking her, acknowledging her value too. Even Catherine, with her terminal profligacy, had been cared for in his will, and what he had asked Rachel to do, she knew, sprung out of a real desire to give pleasure to another book lover. And his crime wasn't really very large; it *did* seem outweighed by the love and thought behind these actions. She suddenly remembered the feel of his hand on her lower back, guiding her through a crowded room. That hand had shown care and caring, a warmth that wasn't just physical. Yes, she knew criminals could be warm and caring—she remembered the cliché about every thief loving his mother—but that was surely proof that no criminal was purely criminal, that each one was also a person, multiple and human.

Oh, people! She thought. *Why must they be so complicated?* Why must it be that every relationship, every thorough knowing of another person, required readjustment? One had to learn that the unpleasant had their own troubles and possessed unexpected decencies, and one had to discover imperfections in the pleasant. There was never a place of rest, never complete knowledge. Why did personhood involve so many layers? And, given that it always did, why did that always come as a surprise?

But she was tired and had wrestled with enough weighty thoughts for one night. Tomorrow she would talk to Elisabeth and see what she could find out there. She turned on her side, gave a deep, nostril-freeing snuffle, and pressed herself against Alan's warm back. She slipped her arm around him and drifted off to sleep.

Chapter Twenty-Two

The next day brought sun, a little more warmth in the air, and a general sense that February might not last forever. What it did not bring was Elisabeth.

All morning Rachel kept an ear open for her arrival, via front door or (would fate be so kind?) back. But there was nothing. Finally, as Fulke held her coat when she was leaving, she said, "Fulke, I'm wondering if Mademoiselle des Troyes has recovered from her cold." Weak, she thought, but it took her where she needed to go. "Do you think I could speak to her before I leave?"

"Mademoiselle Elisabeth has not been here today." He spoke from behind her head.

"Oh?" She kept her voice light. "Is she still stick?"

"I don't know, madame." He settled the coat on her shoulders and took a step back. "She hasn't been in contact."

Something in the way he said it gave her pause. "Since when?"

"Since the day she was ill last week." His voice held not a trace of irony. "I assumed she was too unwell to call."

Rachel turned to face him. "She hasn't been here for five days?"

"Six," Fulke corrected gently. "Seven, if one includes today."

Out in the street, she called Magda. "Elisabeth hasn't been to Edgar's for a week."

"A week!"

"Fulke told me." Rachel felt the wind pull a strand of hair forward. She tucked it behind her ear and leaned more firmly into the phone.

"You don't think . . ."

In that pause Rachel heard all her own thoughts: *You don't think I was wrong and now she's an escaped murderer? Or that I was right and now something's happened to her? You don't think the real murderer has* done something to her*?*

"No, no," Rachel replied to all these unspoken worries. "No, surely not." Promise of warmth or not, Christ, the wind was cold.

"But what should we do?"

What should we do? Rachel thought. What should you do when one of your chief suspects hasn't been seen for six days? When one of your chief suspects might be in the process of turning into your third victim? "We should go to her house."

"We don't have her address," Magda pointed out.

Rachel felt the wind whip her legs and rued her decision to wear a skirt. "We don't," she said, putting from her mind frostbite and whatever chilblains were, "but we can get it."

* * *

"This is not. How I envisioned. Spending lunch. Today."

They were on their fourth flight of stairs in a six-story

building in the eleventh arrondissement, and Alan's words came in small bursts. When they reached the landing, he stopped, bracing himself against the banister.

"Detective," he said, "was not on my job wish list when I was a child."

Rachel shrugged. "Well, if you hadn't insisted on coming along instead of just handing over the address, you could have avoided this."

At last they reached the sixth floor, a long hall off which opened a warren of tiny rooms. A hundred years ago they had been *chambres des bonnes*, squashing maids into what were not much more than cells. Now, Rachel knew, half of them had been converted into kitchens, and the other half served as rooms cheap enough for students, blue-collar workers, and the occasional single professional trying to save money. Because this was Paris and people would live anywhere if it was affordable, she also knew that half the landlords of these rooms hadn't provided any heating or cooling. In winter they would be freezing; in summer they would be stifling. And the arrangements the tenants made to combat this would increase the fire hazard level to one she didn't want to think about. Once again she was grateful for her access to money.

Their footsteps echoed on the wooden boards as they walked down the hall, looking for number 27, Elisabeth's room. It was at the very end. Rachel saw that it was actually two rooms knocked into one, and thus twice as large as the others. Its white metal door seemed simultaneously pure and vulnerable, although she recognized this as projection. She pressed the buzzer next to the door.

There was no answer. She pressed again, and when nothing

happened, she banged on the door with the side of her fist. Nothing.

"What should we do?" Magda whispered.

"I don't know." Rachel was determined to speak at a normal level. "I don't know what we *can* do."

"What if she's in there?"

"She's not answering, which suggests she's not in there," Alan pointed out.

But something about the long hall and its echoing air had spooked Magda. She clutched Rachel's arm and hissed, "What if she's in there and she's *dead*?"

"No one's in there dead!" Rachel shook off her hand. Then she softened; the cold and silence did make the place eerie. She patted Magda's arm reassuringly. "Anyway, if there were a murderer in there waiting, I promise I'd save you."

Suddenly a dark-haired girl in jeans and a peacoat appeared at the top of the stairs. Without looking up from her portable, she walked down the hall toward them, her left hand groping in her pocket for a key. She seemed to know the distance to her own door by muscle memory, for she never looked up from her device as she stopped at a room maybe three yards away from where they stood. In fact, she probably wouldn't have noticed them at all had her key not scratched the door plate instead of finding the lock. Thus thwarted, she glanced upward and, in doing so, saw their shapes out of the corner of her eye. She jumped, let the hand with the key fall, and turned to face them. "Can I help you?"

Rachel and Magda froze, but Alan kept his cool. He took a step toward her. "Bonjour, Mademoiselle. I am Monsieur Field, with CorBank USA, and these are my . . . associates, Madame

Levis and Madame Stevens. We are looking for Mademoiselle des Troyes." He held out one of his business cards. The girl took it, glanced from it to them and back again. Maybe it was the card or maybe it was the fact that criminals do not usually come in groups of one man and two women, but she relaxed and nodded acknowledgment.

"She's not there."

"Not there?" Rachel said. "Has she been there at all today?"

"Today?" The girl gave a humorless laugh "She hasn't been there since last week."

"Did you see her leave?" Magda stepped slightly forward, making it easier to see and be seen.

"No. But I know she isn't home because I keep hearing her portable ring, and no one picks up."

Rachel yelped, "She left her portable?"

The girl looked dubious. "Why are you here, exactly?"

"We have a check for Mademoiselle des Troyes," Alan said smoothly. "As you may know, she inherited a large sum recently, and she asked for it urgently. We have been trying to contact her so she might collect it." He gestured lightly at the shut door, suggesting that their many messages lay in the abandoned portable within. "And now, because it's Friday and we believed she needed it urgently, we've come to give it to her."

Rachel was taken aback to discover that her husband also possessed the true detective's way with a lie.

Surprisingly, this story mollified the girl. "All I can tell you is that she isn't there. Have you tried slipping the check under her door?"

Alan looked outraged. He had obviously taken to his role. "Mademoiselle, we are a bank, not her mother dropping by! We cannot slip checks under doors!" He shook his head sorrowfully. "Ah, well, we'll just have to keep trying. Thank you very much."

"Thank you," said Rachel and Magda, echoing him. As they trailed back up the hall to the staircase, they heard the girl unlocking her door.

Once the porte d'entrée clicked firmly shut behind them, Magda stopped abruptly. "She's not in there," she said, as if they hadn't been right next to her all the time. "She hasn't been there for a week."

"And her phone's still there," Rachel added.

"Kids don't go anywhere without their phones," Magda said. "You saw that girl just now; she couldn't move without hers."

"Maybe Elisabeth forgot hers?" Rachel was hopeful, but even to her that idea sounded implausible.

"Or it fell out of one of her bags when she picked them up to leave?" Magda's attempt was equally feeble. They looked at each other.

"I don't . . ." said Magda.

"I'm not . . ." said Rachel.

They both stopped and then Rachel spoke. "What should we do?"

Alan said, "You should go to the police."

This time, they had to agree.

* * *

They sat in the *Commissariat de Police* on Rue Vaugirard. It had taken some to persuade him, but Alan had returned to work. Then Rachel and Magda had come to this, the commissariat closest to Elisabeth's building. They had explained their concern to a young *gardien de la paix* whose Adam's apple stuck out in his throat like the metal tab in an umbrella shaft. He in his turn called a slightly less young *brigadier*, who sat across from them and listened intently to their story. Now the brigadier had vanished into the recesses of the building, and they sat alone under the fluorescent striplights of the reception area.

This was decidedly not a domain of walnut furniture and chic receptionists, Rachel reflected. They sat in the curious metal and plastic chairs so beloved of municipal entities, fashioned so that the sitter inevitably ended up with a backache. Where the ceiling above them was once-white plaster now made gray by decades of ingrained dust, the floor below them was once-gray linoleum now made white from years of footsteps and chair legs dragged across it. There was a table with magazines, but it was scuffed oak-look chipboard, and the magazines were *Voici* and *Oops!*

"Do you think there's a hot drinks machine?" she murmured to Magda. The place was too depressing for full volume.

"You could ask." Magda tilted her head toward the gardien, who was staring at the logbook in front of him with the intensity of a man who yearns to be on the internet. Rachel was just preparing to rise from her seat when the door to the inner recesses swung open and a middle-aged man with salt-and-pepper hair, his sport coat open over jeans and his rumpled shirt tucked in, appeared. The brigadier trailed slightly behind him.

"Bonjour, *mesdames*." The older man put out his hand. They rose and shook it, first one and then the other. "I am

Capitaine Boussicault. My colleague tells me you are here about a girl who has been missing for a week?" They nodded. "Come with me."

He led them through the door and down one or two identically drab corridors until they reached a large room filled with desks; off the side of it was a smaller room with only one desk and three chairs. He nodded at them to precede him, and they all filed into the smaller room. He gestured for the two women to take the chairs in front of the desk, then shut the door and sat behind the desk. The young brigadier, his hands in his pockets, leaned against the far wall, near his superior, but not next to him.

"Alors," said the capitaine. "A girl is missing. She has been missing some time?"

Rachel cleared her throat. "Yes. Elisabeth des Troyes."

"Bon." He pulled a pad toward him, wrote on it with a pencil he found on the desktop. "How old is she?"

Rachel gave her best estimate. "Twenty-one?"

"And one of you is . . . her mother?" He looked questioningly from one to the other.

"Oh no!" Rachel was too worried to be offended. "We're no relation to her."

"You're friends?"

"Nooo . . ." Rachel didn't feel she qualified as Elisabeth's friend.

The capitaine looked puzzled. "All right." He put the pencil down. "How do you know this girl?"

What could she say? Rachel wondered. She's the employee of my former lover? She and an old boyfriend of mine were working together to defraud the government? How could she define her connection to Elisabeth in a way that was accurate but also sounded sane? She thought for a long moment before she spoke, choosing her words carefully: "We were beneficiaries of the same estate."

"Ah." He seemed to accept this, because he picked up the pencil and prepared to write. "Whose estate was that?"

"A man named Edgar Bowen."

"Edgar Bowen!" He put the pencil down again and looked at the brigadier, who had straightened up.

"You've heard of Edgar Bowen?"

"Madame," the capitaine said, his voice urbane, "everyone here has heard of Edgar Bowen. He's The Soup Man." For a moment, his tone became confidential. "Policemen love a striking death."

"It's funny you should say that," Rachel began, but Magda interrupted by clearing her throat with a loud hacking.

"So sorry." Magda waved a hand. "Dry indoor air." She beamed. "All better now."

Knocked off his stride, the policeman latched back onto the original conversation. "*Bon*, so you were both beneficiaries of Edgar Bowen. And you became close?"

Why not? Rachel thought. It sounded plausible. "Yes."

"And you noticed her missing because . . . ?"

"Well, we're both working in Edgar Bowen's appartement at the moment, but she hasn't been there for a week." She added, "And before that she came every day."

"What does she look like?"

Rachel gave as complete a description as she could of

Elisabeth, also describing the various changes of clothes she had seen her in. The capitaine wrote it all down.

"And I understand you went to check on her, but she didn't answer the door?" Even though his superior wasn't looking, the brigadier nodded, confirming it.

"Yes."

Finished writing, the capitaine looked up. "Perhaps she is ill."

"She isn't ill," Rachel said. "We rang the bell and pounded on the door, but no one answered."

"Perhaps she had just gone out. Perhaps—forgive me," he put up a hand, "she is avoiding you."

Magda took over answering. "Well, her neighbor says she hasn't seen her for a week."

"But people—even young ladies—do go away for a week. That's not unusual."

"But her neighbor says she can hear Elisabeth's portable ringing and ringing, which means it must be in her room. And what twenty-one-year-old do you know who would go away and leave behind her portable? That *is* unusual." Magda sat back in triumph.

The capitaine looked down at his pad, drew a deep breath, and made his hands a steeple in front of his chin. For a second he gazed into the middle distance; then he let out his breath. When he spoke, his voice was measured. "My dear mesdames. What you are telling me is that a young woman of legal age, and of whose life you know little, has not been seen by her neighbor for a week and seems to have left her portable in her home for that same amount of time. Now, I don't know this young woman even as well as you do, but there doesn't seem much here to cause alarm. The young lady may have gone on vacation and forgotten her portable, or it may have slipped out of her pocket or baggage as she left."

"We thought those things!" Rachel interjected. "But then we also thought—" But remembering Magda's signal earlier, she stopped short.

"You also thought what?" The capitaine's face was open, his curiosity unfeigned.

The room became very quiet. Rachel could hear the humming of the computer fan and make out the sound of the brigadier rubbing the cloth of his pocket between his fingers. She thought how she'd wanted to go to the police at the start. Now here they were. And Elisabeth could be in real trouble: girls did not just vanish for a week with no cell phone and no word to anyone. They did not. She looked at Magda, whose eyes were pleading with her.

"It's because of Edgar," she said.

Magda let her breath out in a gust.

The capitaine took his hands out of the steeple and clasped them on the desk. "Explain, please." He watched her intently.

"Elisabeth was very attached to Edgar. They worked together closely. And we—we think . . ." She stumbled over the last phrase.

Magda sighed, but finished for her. "We think Edgar Bowen was murdered."

The capitaine's expression changed from serious to astonished, from astonished to amused. He let out a short bark of laughter, then exchanged a glance with his junior before turning back to Magda. "Murdered! And what leads you to this conclusion, that an open-and-shut case of accidental death that occurred when the victim was home alone is, in fact, a murder? Where is your evidence?" He laughed again.

Rachel was stung. "It's the wine." Then, hearing how thin that sounded, she explained further. "There was rosé. Edgar didn't like rosé. He wouldn't have had it on the table."

"So you think Monsieur Bowen was murdered because the wine is wrong?" He shared another amused glance with the brigadier. "Truly, madame, you have lived here long enough to become French."

Rachel flushed. "It isn't only that. In fact, it isn't only Edgar." This time she didn't stop. "We're also worried about Elisabeth because another woman close to Edgar died."

"Ah?" Although the capitaine's tone was neutral, his lips twitched. Rachel's face burned at the knowledge that he was humoring her, but she kept going.

"Catherine Nadeau, Edgar's companion. She's dead, and the newspaper report of her death said it was suicide over money worries. But we saw her only a week before she died, and she was perfectly cheerful and told us she was solvent. In fact," she drew a victorious breath, "she had just reopened her store!"

"Yes." The capitaine nodded, his face and tone no longer patronizing. "I read reports on that event too. The police were called to the scene." He clicked his tongue. "Always a painful business, such deaths." He leaned forward and held Rachel's eyes with his own. "You know, of course, madame, that many suicides seem more cheerful in the days before their deaths. You know that often the decision to end everything, the sudden certainty after a long period of confusion, cheers them. And you know that in many cases suicides occur after people exit depression, for before that the person is too depressed to act on her wishes." He leaned back in his chair and stared at the ceiling, once again steepling his fingers. "And doubtless you have considered that many people who say that they are solvent do so to save face and, in fact, are nothing of the sort." He thumped down the front legs of his chair and gazed at her, his expression bland.

Rachel sat mute. She pinched the bridge of her nose, squeezing the tender bulbs at the inner corners of her eyes, and looked at the wall behind the capitaine. She knew that to the two men it would seem as if she were weary or embarrassed, or both, but really it was to stop herself from crying. She was worried about Elisabeth; she was a bad detective; and now this man was taking pleasure in humiliating her. She blinked hard to force back the tears.

"And in the case of Monsieur Bowen," the capitaine continued, his voice now serious, "no, mesdames, I am sorry to disappoint you, but the police investigated. It was the butler's night off, and before he left, he fixed vichyssoise for Monsieur Bowen to eat. When he came home late, he went straight up to his rooms, and the next morning, when he came to clear away the dishes before arranging the room for breakfast, he found Monsieur Bowen. Found him dead." He opened his arms and displayed his palms in an expansive gesture. "There was an autopsy, which proved that he drowned in his soup! It was in his lungs. That is all there was to it, wine or no wine."

"We disagree," Magda said coolly.

"You may disagree all you like." He made the exaggerated moue and propulsive exhale that constituted the typical French expression of dismissal. "But the story is very straightforward."

He shrugged an equally dismissive French shrug. "Now"—as he spoke he rose from the desk—"I thank you for coming in. I *will* look for this young lady, for, like you, I find the situation unusual. And if you leave your contact information at the front desk, I will let you know what I discover."

This was, Rachel knew, his way of being kind. But she couldn't forgive him because of it.

As if to prove her right, he added, "But we will say no more about this nonsense of Monsieur Bowen. *C'est finis.*" He reached out and shook each of their hands. "My colleague will show you out."

When they finally stood outside the commissariat, Magda took Rachel's hand and squeezed it. She looked serious, and when she spoke her voice was solemn. "You know," she said gravely, "I think that young guy kept his hands in his pockets because we gave him a hard-on."

Rachel was still laughing as they went down into the Vaugirard Métro station.

Chapter Twenty-Three

For Rachel, the rest of that day and the morning of the next seemed to inch by, all of the hours filled with questions about Elisabeth. *Could* she be on vacation? She dismissed that as too much of a coincidence: the timing of her disappearance connected it clearly to recent events. But how? This was the question that drummed in her head. Was Elisabeth, conniving fraudster and murderess, on the run? Or was Elisabeth, unwilling partner in crime and unexpected heiress, the victim of a ruthless killer? Was this Godard's *Breathless* or one of those documentaries where the victim lay buried under the floorboards?

And as the hours went by, she began to face up to other, more complex, questions. If Elisabeth was a victim, whose victim was she? Parisians noticed their neighbors, watched them. Look at the two they'd spoken to at Catherine's. Mathilde could never have passed up Elisabeth's stairs without comment; her clothes alone would have made her the subject of gossip. She supposed it was just possible that she'd arrived when all the neighbors were looking the other way, but admitting that this was only a possibility meant acknowledging that there must be other possibilities too. Who else would want

Elisabeth out of the way? And Catherine? Who else would want Elisabeth *and* Catherine out of the way? Her head began to spin.

Then, very softly, a thought began to make itself known. There *was* someone else who might have committed all these murders. She and Magda had been working on the assumption that Mathilde's financial woes and wounded pride lay at the bottom of everything, but someone else might have needed money too—in fact, someone had lost his home because he didn't have enough money. What if the person they should be considering wasn't Mathilde, but David?

As Magda had said, he'd gained the most from Edgar's death. Catherine had told her he'd been evicted for nonpayment of rent; Edgar's death solved that problem. And the only visitor Catherine's neighbor had remembered was a dark-haired man. They had assumed that was Edgar, but now she realized that they hadn't asked whether he'd been seen before or after Edgar's death. Catherine could have been blackmailing David over some slip, and her visitor could easily have been him, arriving to pay his blood money or to—she swallowed. And David was young enough not to attract much attention among Elisabeth's neighbors. He could have been taken for someone's boyfriend or a new tenant. In fact, she suddenly realized, Elisabeth might have been blackmailing him too—who knew what she'd unearthed in Edgar's papers or what David had accidentally given away? After all, they saw each other daily in the appartement.

What if, a niggling voice whispered, Magda were right?

But there are certain things a mind, even the mind of a natural detective, shrinks from. The toddler Rachel had known, his hands held up to his father when he was too tired to walk anymore, his face rapt while that same father read him a bedtime story—that toddler could not have killed that father. And hadn't Catherine displayed only boredom at her mention of David? Surely if she'd been blackmailing him, she'd have shown some greater reaction to his name. *Good points, Levis,* she applauded herself. She scoffed at the voice that was cynically suspicious, that knew David less well than she did.

She was assisted in this dismissal by her portable, which rang out the "Imperial March" from *Star Wars*: Magda. She swiped the screen. "Hello?"

"Do you want to look at dresses before we eat or afterward? Only, before might be better if we want to have flat stomachs."

Rachel had no idea what she was talking about. Eat what? What dresses?

"Oh, don't tell me you've forgotten. You *can't* have forgotten!"

It came back to her in a rush: they were going to buy dresses for the *Bal Rouge*. Magda had been asked as Benoît's guest, and they'd decided to add lunch to the shopping. "I haven't forgotten," she said. "We're going dress shopping for the bal." She flared her nostrils. It had completely slipped her mind that the charity gala was this weekend. Looking at her book-chipped nails, she wondered if she had time to fit in a manicure before the big event, as well.

"Let's start at Galeries Lafayette." Magda's excitement was barely contained.

After her first experience of it, the bal had never loomed large on Rachel's horizon. She was no fan of listening to performances by Opéra apprentices and speeches from titans of international finance, all the time wishing it were polite to ask for a second dessert or a larger glass of champagne. But like most things, the bal shone more from a distance, and for years Magda had listened yearningly to her morning-after descriptions. Now at last she was attending, and her joy at the prospect of experiencing it for herself was dizzying.

"Galeries Lafayette would be excellent." Rachel reflected that, if nothing else, the process of preparing for the bal would free her mind from thoughts of Elisabeth and attendant troubling questions. "I'll meet you there in a couple of hours."

Chapter Twenty-Four

"Oh, you never told me everyone looked so *good*!"

Unlike Rachel, Magda was finding *Le Bal Rouge* hugely enjoyable, even from up close. Rachel quashed her vague sense of testiness; Magda's positivity had long been one of her more irritating qualities. No doubt she'd love the performances and find one dessert sufficient, and Rachel would have to sit through it all with a false smile of shared enjoyment on her face.

On the other hand, she had to admit that everybody did look good. The only thing better on a man than a sharp suit was a tuxedo, and here the room was crowded with a hundred James Bonds. The women were equally elegant, the brilliant colors of their gowns catching the light and throwing it back. A murmur like the buzzing of contented bees rose from the room.

She considered her own quartet. Alan was always handsome, but set off by a white shirtfront and studs, his blue eyes shone, while Benoît's smooth elegance was burnished by formality. Magda gleamed in maroon taffeta that complemented her warm skin. Even Rachel had managed to find a perfectly acceptable navy velvet dress, although its boned bodice left very little room for dinner.

"Not bad for a group of people who eat reheated croissants for breakfast," Alan remarked. Benoît looked taken aback at this revelation, but he beamed nonetheless. Benoît, Rachel thought, was one of life's suns; his pleasure warmed everyone around him with its rays. Beneath his smile, she once more felt the desire to giggle. She turned her face so Alan wouldn't see. No matter what he said, she knew he was jealous.

The dinner, alas, was just as she remembered: perfectly good but nothing special. The dessert was poached pear tart with a cardamom coulis, more unusual than delicious (although she still ate it, and Alan's). The entertainment was grueling. As an apprentice with the Paris Opéra began Brünhilde's third-act aria from *Götterdämmerung*, she distracted herself by thinking about Elisabeth. Could she be perfectly safe somewhere, as the capitaine had suggested? If that was so, why did Rachel have such a bad feeling? Had the eeriness of Elisabeth's hallway infected her instincts, making her unnecessarily suspicious? But even if that were true, Elisabeth still hadn't been seen for more than a week, and twenty-one-year-olds were nearly attached to their phones. Rachel bit her thumbnail, wishing the singer would just be quiet and let her think. To distract herself from both the noise and her own aimless worries, she watched Magda, whose delight shone on her face.

But even with Magda's evident enjoyment, she couldn't sit through the next offering, a well-known mime's routine of building a house that turned out not to have a door. Claiming a need to use the bathroom, she excused herself. She would wait in the mezzanine until she heard the applause that signaled that the mime had finished.

This year the bal was held in one of those immense former residences that the French do so well, a *hôtel particulier* converted to a party venue, all marble and gilding and thick carpet in the public spaces. The mezzanine had a circle of small balconies, each one embraced by two rose marble columns rising out of an equally rosy balustrade, and each offering a view up to a ceiling mural of cherubs in filmy draperies and down to a floor mosaic of elaborately intertwining vines. She stood on one of these balconies, thoughts about Elisabeth beginning to bubble up into her mind once again. She gently eased the boning of her bodice away from where it dug into her waist. Maybe one dessert was enough after all. Realizing that as soon as the mime finished, the ladies' room would have a line out the door, she decided to make good on her excuse and go now.

Turning around, she nearly slammed into Mathilde.

"Rachel! I thought that was you." The older woman stood still, her posture ramrod straight as always. She wore a long black gown that Rachel recognized as Chanel, utterly without accessories except for a leather belt, her smooth silver hair parted in the center and pulled back into a low bun. She smiled frostily.

"*Bonsoir*, Mathilde." Rachel tried to appear as cool as the woman in front of her. "I didn't expect to find you here."

"Of course not." Mathilde shrugged, making it plain that the very idea of her attending such an event was ridiculous. "But an old friend asked me to accompany him, and I didn't like to say no. And it isn't the worst evening I've spent. Although," she jerked her head toward the doors behind them, "that woman! I never understand the attraction of this make-believe nonsense."

Rachel relaxed a little. "I know what you mean. Building nothing from nothing . . . Now, if she *actually* built a house onstage, that would be something to stay for."

Mathilde snorted appreciatively. "Yes. Perhaps bringing all the bricks and mortar hidden in her unitard."

"Of course." Rachel raised an eyebrow and dipped her chin. "In France the real trick would be to find workmen who would build it without going on strike."

This time Mathilde gave a real laugh. She looked Rachel up and down speculatively, something new in her gaze, then came to stand next to her, close enough to speak low and still be heard. Rachel could feel her breath on her cheek. "Tell me," she said softly, "you know that girl, Elisabeth, Edgar's little *aide*?"

Rachel was taken aback at this abrupt switch into confidence. Apparently shared contempt was the way to Mathilde's heart. She swallowed hard, nodded. "Yes. Yes, I remember her."

Mathilde's voice remained low. "It seems she has disappeared." She paused to gauge her effect; Rachel tried to look both shocked and unlikely to say anything. This was no easy task, but her expression must have satisfied Mathilde, for she pursed her lips and continued. "My son told me a policeman called the house to ask Fulke about it." She shook her head. "First that Catherine"—was there the ghost of a pause?—"killing herself, and now this one goes. It's like one of those old films, *hein*? *The Lady Vanishes.*" She gave a wintry smile of amusement. "Or in this case, the *young* lady vanishes."

Rachel swallowed again. What was the correct response to this unsolicited disclosure, to its motiveless and only thinly veiled malice? What would Nora Charles do? Rachel tried for an excited but humble tone, an acolyte inquiring of the keeper of knowledge. "Do they know where she is?"

It seemed to work. "The policeman only asked, my son said, didn't answer." Mathilde shrugged. "This girl does not seem to me like someone who would be missed at all, never mind by the police." Suddenly changing tack, she said, "She was at the same *université* as my son, you know." Rachel, who had not known that David attended the Sorbonne, was fascinated by the way Mathilde lingered over the words "my son," obviously sweet as honey in her mouth. "Only in a much easier course." She unfurled a long-fingered hand dismissively. "That CELSA, where they study *le culture pop*. And—of course! You were there when she kept me from collecting some *objets* Edgar would have wanted me to have."

Rachel said nothing. What could she say? That even she knew CELSA was France's best school of media studies? That she knew Edgar hadn't left Mathilde any objets in his will, and that therefore the hypothetical "what he would have wanted" was irrelevant? That over a box of candy Kiki Villeneuve had revealed Mathilde's vanity and sense of entitlement, and now Rachel viewed her with a weather eye? Since she could think of nothing else to offer, she concentrated on maintaining a neutral expression.

Mathilde's eyes rested on the elaborate design of vines and flowers below. She said idly, "I never liked the idea of my husband's money going away from his family. So *désagréable*. And to waste it on an improvident woman and an employee." She shook her head. "I don't speak of receiving it myself, you understand, but better left to his son, *n'est-ce pas*? And now . . ." She tapped her nails on the marble balustrade. "First the death of that woman, and now the girl has vanished." For the first time in Rachel's acquaintance with her, she gave a genuinely delighted smile. "It almost seems as if the money my husband gave away is cursed! Of course we won't get it back, but it's pleasant to know no one else will be using it either."

Suddenly she blinked and held up a hand. "Ah! There we are."

Rachel could hear the sound of applause from inside the ballroom.

Mathilde gave another of her taut smiles. "I must hurry if I want to use *les cabinets.*" The skirt of her dress wrapped around her as she turned, but it made no difference to her progress. She would easily beat all other contenders in the race to relief.

* * *

"Holy shit," Magda said. She was seated on a toilet lid in one of the cubicles of the now-empty ladies' room, Rachel standing over her. "Holy shit."

"I know." Rachel crossed her arms under her breasts, squeezing her shoulders forward.

"That's what she actually said?"

"Yes, that's exactly what she said. She stood there dressed like some Anna-Wintour-*The-Devil-Wears-Prada* devil doll and told me she found her husband's leaving money to Elisabeth untidy."

"You said 'devil' twice."

"Once as a noun, once as an adjective. Anyway, she's worth it! Trust me, she was terrifying enough for two devils."

"But," Magda said, smoothing her taffeta skirt, "come on!

You don't think she was *telling* you anything? I mean, you don't really think she was telling you she'd done something to Elisabeth?"

Rachel took a deep breath, calming herself. "I don't know." She shook her head. "At first I couldn't understand why she was even talking to me. And then what she said was so allusive." She swallowed. "But the tone! She sounded, well, 'gloating' is the only word that springs to mind. Allusive, but gloating."

"Could we get out of this stall?" Magda tried to rise, but she couldn't with Rachel standing where she was. "I can't think when we're squashed in here."

"I don't want to go outside. I don't want anyone to surprise us."

"We'll be the ones doing the surprising if they find us in here together. Come on." Magda struggled again. "If we go out we'll be able to hear anyone coming in. And see them, for that matter."

Rachel reluctantly slid the bolt back and, with some shifting, managed to step out into the sink area. She and Magda crept to the anteroom, sitting down on one of those curious round couches that live nowhere except in the anterooms of plush women's restrooms. The shape meant that one of them needed to sit sideways if they wanted to see each other, but Rachel had to concede that it was better than being squeezed into a stall.

"Now then," Magda said. She took a deep breath. "How did she seem?"

Rachel thought. "Pleased."

Magda rolled her eyes, "Could you be more specific, Monsieur Poirot?"

"Pleased with herself."

Magda didn't laugh.

"Well . . ." How *had* Mathilde seemed? "Almost eager. It was strange. She scarcely knows me, but it was as if she was just longing to unburden herself."

"About what, exactly?"

Good question. "Well, she mentioned both Catherine and Elisabeth. She said she didn't like the idea of money leaving the family—"

"Yes, yes!" Magda waggled her hand impatiently. "We know that. Skip to what she said specifically about Elisabeth and Catherine."

"All right. She said she couldn't see why Edgar would leave so much to anyone outside the family. Especially not to . . . she called Catherine 'an improvident woman' and Elisabeth 'an employee.' And she said it was true that she and David couldn't have the money back, but it was *pleasant* to know that"—she made her voice precise and ominous—"'no one else will be using it either.'"

"Did she sound like Inspector Clouseau when she said that?"

"No." Rachel was confused. *Should* Mathilde have sounded like Inspector Clouseau? Would that mean something?

"I only ask because you made her sound like Inspector Clouseau. 'No one *ailss* will be using it *ayzair* . . .'"

"I did not sound—" Rachel stopped herself. "Do you really think this is the time for that?"

"Well, you just made a joke. I thought it might lighten the mood."

Rachel fixed Magda with a deadening gaze and said slowly, "Edgar. Possibly Catherine. And now Elisabeth."

Magda stopped smiling.

Rachel continued, "Edgar for the money she needed. Catherine over blackmail about Edgar. Then Elisabeth because she found something in the bureau that linked Mathilde to Edgar's death. It all fits together. And if you think about it, it explains everything."

Magda thought about it. She put a hand to her mouth. "Wow. I know she's cold, but *that* cold?"

"Trust me: she's that cold. I think if she knew Edgar had made a will reducing her bequest, and in favor of Elisabeth . . ." Rachel shook her head. "Or even if she still thought she had fifty thousand coming, and she needed it to cover her investment losses. I said it at the start: I wouldn't put murder past her. And now she's gloating about the disappearance of the girl who got her money, and whom her husband valued, *and* who tried to keep her from something incriminating in the back of the appartement? And we can guess how she feels about employees!" In case Magda couldn't guess, she added, "They're expendable!"

Magda went very quiet. At last she said, "Should we telephone the capitaine?"

Rachel considered. "No. You're right; we still don't have any evidence that the police would be willing to act on." She frowned. "Besides, he was mean."

Magda nodded: he *was* mean. They sat disconsolately on the tufted pink velvet until at last Magda sighed, slapped her hands softly on her thighs, and rose.

"Well," she said, "we can't change anything tonight.

We have to get through this evening and tomorrow before we can do anything, so we might as well go back in. Kristin Scott Thomas is going to perform a monologue from *Phèdre* before the head of BNP Paribas speaks."

Normally, Magda's ability to compartmentalize would have grated, but even Rachel loved Kristin Scott Thomas. She hurried out behind her friend.

Chapter Twenty-Five

When Rachel arrived at the appartement the Monday after the bal, Fulke's greeting was scarcely more than a murmur. "Monsieur Bowen only recently returned from his night out," he explained quietly, "and has just now gone to bed."

The result of this was exactly what the results of such announcements always are: Rachel crept around the library as if it shared a dividing wall with the bedroom and her lightest movement might jerk David from his slumber. She removed and replaced books stealthily even as she inwardly cursed the fact that David, at last present and a potential source of evidence, was unavailable to her. Over the course of the hours since the bal, she had managed to calm herself down about her encounter with Mathilde, but even when she considered it with a more level head, it marked Mathilde out as a very plausible suspect indeed. Meanwhile, her anxiety about Elisabeth had not subsided one bit. Taken together, these made her very anxious to talk to the man who knew Mathilde best.

After an hour or so, she had to accept that she probably wasn't going to see David that morning. After another hour, she had come up with a new plan. When Fulke began to leave after delivering the mid-morning tea, she put out a hand to halt him. "Fulke, may I ask you a question?"

He stopped. "Of course, madame."

Rachel breathed in, then plunged ahead. "Were you here the night Monsieur Bowen died?"

If Fulke was surprised by this seemingly random question, he didn't show it. "I was here until five p.m., Madame Levis. Then I went out for my evening off."

Oh, right: Rachel remembered that both the woman at the funeral and the capitaine had said it was his night off: he wouldn't have seen anything. Unless—"Do you know if Monsieur Bowen was expecting any guests?"

"He was not, madame. I kept a record of all the late Monsieur Bowen's social engagements, and he had none that evening."

Wait a second. "You have a list of all his engagements?"

"Yes. The police retained it for their inquiries. They have yet to return it."

Damn! Night off, no visitors, an engagement calendar dangled in front of her but then snatched away—what to do now?

"Did you go far? For your evening off?" If he'd stayed in the area, he might have seen someone entering or leaving the building, or even just recognized Mathilde on the street. Or maybe he himself had . . .

She heard Magda's voice in the depths of her mind saying, "The bottom of the list."

"No, madame. I crossed the river and went to Le Champo cinema. I wanted to attend their showing of *The Servant*. I admire Joseph Losey's work very much."

Rachel reflected that this was the closest thing to an

intimate revelation that Fulke had ever made to her. Yet even as he said it, his impassivity somehow removed it from the category of personal admission.

"And did you come back right away?"

"I had dinner after the film, at a café near the cinema. I try to eat one meal a week that I don't prepare myself."

Was this meant as a reminder of his position? Again, his face and body gave nothing away, but Rachel's ears burned with shame at the knowledge that she was prying into the private life of a man Edgar had valued and trusted implicitly. The thought of that had been distasteful when she stood at the door that led to his quarters upstairs, and it was distasteful now.

"Of course, of course," she said hurriedly.

But even as she fell silent, she couldn't help continuing to think. All right, Fulke hadn't been in the appartement or anywhere near it that night. She could easily check the showtimes of *The Servant*, so he'd be a fool to lie about going. And why would he be lying anyway? Looking at his smooth face, she was reminded once more that he'd only had things to lose from Edgar's death. But still, maybe he'd seen something, some suspicious behavior before or after Edgar's death.

"Madame Bowen has been here since the reading of the will?" She didn't know why this came out as a question.

Fulke nodded. "Yes."

"And did she seem different to you? From her usual self, I mean."

Fulke wrinkled his brow, but he didn't speak. Rachel understood: he would be loyal to the tact his position expected. She thought for a second, then tried a different approach.

"I saw Madame Bowen on Saturday night, at the *Bal Rouge*.

She seemed anxious, and I was worried." She frowned as proof of this. "I know Monsieur Bowen's death must have been a terrible shock for her, and I wondered if you had noticed any changes in her behavior. Whether she seemed tense to you too." Shared concern: it was weak, but it might work.

But Fulke said only, "Madame Bowen has always been . . . taut."

"No more so recently? Over the past few weeks?" Rachel knew she was pushing her luck, and indeed Fulke gave one of his small closing bows.

"Madame Levis. A butler neither hears nor sees."

"Oh, dear." She looked up at him from the ottoman. "I apologize for my presumption. I don't want to know family secrets." *Yes, I do.* "But I am worried." She still didn't say about whom.

He looked at her carefully. He was assessing her, but what aspect of her? Whatever aspect, she must have passed, for he said, "I have not noticed any increase in strain in Madame Bowen." Then he unbent a fraction more. "It seems to me that she was more tense in the days before Monsieur Bowen's passing."

"Oh?" Rachel kept her voice steady.

"I heard her raise her voice to him in the bureau on one or two occasions. And when she left afterward, she put her coat on more roughly than usual."

You could write a dissertation on the way our observations are determined by our jobs, Rachel reflected. Would a cleaner have said Mathilde seemed more untidy than usual; a dancer more graceless? But this wasn't the time for such thoughts. "You heard her raise her voice to Monsieur Bowen?"

"I do not like to say so." His pained tone backed up the statement, and he hesitated before he continued, "But I gathered the discussions were about financial issues."

"Always a tense topic," Rachel said sympathetically. "But at least she confined her tension to the bureau." Again her tone remained flat.

Fulke looked sad. "I'm afraid that was not always the case. She made Mademoiselle des Troyes—" He broke off, discretion reasserting itself. "She was ungracious to Mademoiselle des Troyes."

"I see. And all of this even before the shock of Monsieur Bowen's death." She felt this sentence was a particularly crafty enticement to reveal more, but Fulke said nothing. Rachel took a chance and didn't speak. She would outwait him.

Seconds passed as agonizing hours.

"Madame Bowen remained tightly wound after Monsieur Bowen's death," Fulke said at last. Rachel felt her back muscles unclench. "She expressed strong opinions about Madame Nadeau in the week or two afterward, and she remained unkind toward Mademoiselle des Troyes." He then uttered the only full disloyal sentence Rachel ever heard him say, "Madame Bowen is not a woman who forgives."

"Forgives the living, or the dead?"

Fulke repeated, "A butler neither hears nor sees."

Forgives neither of them, then, Rachel thought. She saw that Fulke was beginning to regret his revelations, so she chanced only one more question, and on a different topic. "And you're sure Elisabeth said nothing to you about taking a vacation before she left or about taking a few days' rest because she was feeling ill?"

He shook his head. "She said nothing. Although . . ."

"Although what?"

Again he said nothing for long seconds; again his face gave nothing away. Finally he said reluctantly, "Although I know that when Madame Bowen came to see Monsieur David last week she seemed more relaxed."

Then, obviously feeling he'd said too much, he bowed and left the room. When he helped Rachel on with her coat at morning's end a few hours later, he acted as if their conversation had never occurred, and Rachel, sensitive to his embarrassment, said only, "Thank you," as the appartement door closed behind her.

She put out her hand to press the call button for the building's elevator, and as she did so, as if by magic the doors opened in front of her. Out stepped two men. One was very thin and wore a black suit made of some shiny fabric, cut close to his body; a white shirt beneath with its first three buttons undone; and the pointiest shoes Rachel had ever seen. His companion, smaller and fatter, wearing a puffy vest over a t-shirt and low-slung sweatpants, seemed to be from another subculture entirely, but the way he looked at the thin man made it plain that he was with him.

The thin man stopped and pressed his hand to one of the elevator doors, forcing them to stay open. He smiled at Rachel, but his face was so bony that the expression seemed more the grimace of a skull than a welcome.

"Thank you." Rachel stepped into the elevator.

He kept his hand on the door, nodding acknowledgment. "You are a friend of David Bowen?" He nodded again, this time toward the door of the appartement. His hair was cut very close to his ivory scalp, and when he spoke, she could see that his teeth were sharp and discolored. He eyed her up and down speculatively.

"Not of David." She put out her hand to press a button, trying to seem calm. "I knew his father."

"Ah, his father! The rich man whose fortune David takes over."

"Well, I wouldn't put it that way." She managed a smile.

"You wouldn't?" He cocked his head. "How would you put it?"

"I would say he was a good father who loved David enough to leave him well off."

But the man's interest had wandered. He must have caught something in her accent, because he leaned closer and said, "You speak English?"

Rachel tried not to take a step backward. "Yes. Yes, I do."

"Ah! *Scarface*, hein?" With his free hand he gestured at his outfit. She had no idea what he was talking about, but she smiled politely. Then he grinned again. "Did you inherit some of the good father's money too?"

God, would he never let the door close? Rachel could feel her stomach jumping, and she was desperate to pee. "No, I'm just . . . I was asked to organize his library."

"A library!" Finally he let go, making a dismissive click between his teeth. He turned and retreated, the smaller man falling in behind him in a lazy strut. As the elevator doors shut, Rachel saw that the suit trousers fit with scarcely a wrinkle; they made his legs look like pipe cleaners. She would have liked to laugh—it deserved a laugh, this stylishness gone terribly wrong—but he had shaken her. In fact, between his death's-head attempt at charm and what Fulke had revealed, she felt completely off-balance. What she needed was a nice cup of tea.

* * *

Half an hour later, she wiggled into a more comfortable position in a Starbucks chair as she waited for Magda to return with their drinks. Normally, she refused to go to Starbucks on principle—Paris was full of small family-run cafés—but if you wanted a decent cup of tea in the city, it was the only place to find one. If you ordered tea at a real Parisian café, you received a tiny stainless steel pot of hot water with a teabag beside it, possibly with a grudging slice of lemon expiring on a separate saucer. Corporate logo mugs filled with preposterously named brews were galling, but they were positively Merry Olde England compared to a cup of tepid Lipton-flavored water and an outraged glare when you asked for milk. And, she reflected as she tilted her head back, if you were going to go to Starbucks, you couldn't do better than this one near the gilded Palais Garnier. She considered the ceiling's gilt swags and faux-baroque murals, meant to invoke and poke gentle fun at the Palais's decadent Beaux-Arts origins, and for a minute it wasn't so hard to be a woman living in Paris who hated coffee.

"I was stuck behind some students." Magda looked put out when she finally appeared, clutching their drinks. "They kept changing their minds." She slipped into the chair opposite Rachel and took a settling breath. "Now, what was that about two men in the elevator?"

"Oh." Rachel sighed, but lightly. Somehow her communion with the ceiling had made that encounter seem less important. “When I was leaving Edgar’s I was waylaid by these two really unpleasant men.”

“Waylaid how?” Magda looked concerned. Like any big city, Paris was filled with men who harassed women on the streets, but here they were especially persistent, sometimes following for blocks, making remarks and threats. Any such encounter was cause for commiseration.

“Oh, not that kind of waylaid. I was getting in the elevator as they were getting off, and one of them just . . . lingered.” But she shivered. “He gave me the creeps. But I don’t want to relive it. Just let me just tell you what Fulke said.”

Magda listened carefully as she recounted the conversation. When Rachel finished, she said, “That really doesn’t look good for Mathilde.”

“But it’s still not concrete evidence.”

Magda sighed. “You’re right—it isn’t.” She went quiet. Rachel waited for the usual reinvigoration, but none came. Instead, Magda stared into her mug. Eventually she looked up. “I’m out of ideas.”

It had never occurred to Rachel that Magda, so full of determination and purpose, might someday exhaust her resources. Of the two of them, Magda had always been an optimist, able to meet any setback with new hypotheses and cunning plans; if she couldn’t see any way to move forward, the situation must be bleak indeed.

Perhaps they should give up, she thought. No one would ever know they’d backed down except a capitaine they’d decided not to call and Alan, who might tease her once but then would never mention it again. But she looked at her best friend’s troubled face. Magda downcast was a rare sight, whereas Magda supporting her was a common one. Maybe the best response was for her to switch roles too.

"So," she spoke crisply, "we need clear evidence of Mathilde's wrongdoing. No more hints or interpretations."

"Yes." Magda nodded.

"That means we need something like . . ." She considered. "A journal of Elisabeth's?"

"Well," Magda crumpled her face, "that's a little *Gone Girl*, but . . . yeah. Or, I don't know, some evidence of what Elisabeth stopped herself from telling you. Or that she was scared of Mathilde, or of Mathilde's doing something to her. Or even evidence of what she found in the back rooms." She lifted a weary hand. "Just evidence of *some*thing."

"Well." Her list had given Rachel time to think. "It seems to me that those are all the sorts of things that might be found"—she delayed for a delicious second—"in someone's apartment." She wiggled her eyebrows at Magda and took a sip of tea.

* * *

Listening to excerpts from this conversation in bed that night, Alan said, "It's a good thing the two of you found each other, because it's clear you were meant to be."

"What's that supposed to mean?" Rachel turned to look at him.

"You're equally crazy. You've worked yourselves up into a conviction based on what is essentially speculation, and you completely believe your own creation."

"This is not speculation!" Rachel was stung. "Elisabeth is missing! Catherine is dead! Mathilde's behavior has been suspect!"

Alan snorted, but only said, "All right."

"You don't believe me."

"I said, 'All right,' didn't I?" He was quiet for a second, then risked again. "Wasn't this all supposed to be about Edgar?"

"What are you talking about?"

"Well, when you began, you thought someone had killed Edgar, and two weeks ago Elisabeth was your main suspect. Now you're envisioning some grand web of crime involving multiple deaths and a disappearance; Elisabeth's turned into a victim, and Edgar seems to have become a detail."

Rachel's tone was dignified. "Our net is widening, yes."

Alan snorted again. "What does that mean?"

"It means there's every possibility—it's more than likely—that Edgar's death, Catherine's murder, and Elisabeth's disappearance are related."

"'Catherine's murder, Catherine's murder.'" He was exasperated. "As far as you have proof, she committed suicide or fell out her window! The only reason you think her death is related to Edgar's is because she was openly happy that he'd left her money. That's hardly a solid lead!"

Rachel tried to control her sense that he had a point. "Two people who knew each other are dead, all right? And another person who knew *them* has just disappeared. You feel comfortable calling that coincidence? Okay, what if Elisabeth isn't dead, but only not dead *yet*? What if she's being kept somewhere and there's still time to find her? Do you want me to focus on someone who's already dead and sacrifice a young girl's life? Is that what you'd prefer?"

"All right, all right." Alan surrendered. "Yes. I see the logic of it. You should focus on Elisabeth's suspect disappearance, which may turn out to be related to Edgar's suspect death."

They sat in longer silence. At last Rachel said, "Which will probably turn out to be related."

Alan did not tear his hair or clench his jaw, or even sigh. He simply turned on his side away from her and switched off his bedside lamp.

Left with no opponent, Rachel snapped off her own light. Lying in the dark, she reflected that she'd been right to hold back some information from him. Given his objections, suggestions, and caveats, she had a good idea that he would not approve of what she and Magda had finally decided to do.

Chapter Twenty-Six

"Here we go." Standing in the freezing hall outside the door to Elisabeth's room the next morning, Rachel took a card of bobby pins out of her bag. She held it up for Magda to see. "*Les pinces à cheveux*. I never knew they were called that in French."

"Why can't we just use a credit card?" asked Magda.

"Because credit cards only work with cheap slide locks. I spent the whole morning reading up on this. I'm an expert on lock picking."

"Well, in theory." Magda's voice was a raised eyebrow.

Rachel ignored her. She unfolded a bobby pin and bit the rubber bulb off one tip. "Make a slight bend in the end," she whispered to herself, quoting the instructions from the internet. She curved the naked metal about forty-five degrees and held it between her teeth. "Bend another pin at a right angle to make a lever," she muttered. "Now insert lever into keyhole and put rotational tension on it." Sliding the bent bobby pin into the bottom of the lock, she twisted it slightly to one side. "Okay. Insert the pick into the lock and feel for seized pins." She gently poked the unbent bobby pin in on top of the first until it came to a halt. "Yes, yes!" she whispered excitedly. "Now I just have to open the pins. There should be an audible click."

She wiggled the unfolded bobby pin up and down. There was no click. But it had worked in the video!

"Why didn't it work?" Magda hissed.

"Just wait a sec. Go in my purse and get my notes."

Magda rummaged, withdrew a sheet of paper.

"What does it say about opening the pins?"

"Uh . . ." Magda moved her eyes over the sheet, then read out loud, "'Open pins by wiggling pick gently. There should be an audible click.'"

"'Gently.' Okay, gently." She relaxed the arm that held the second pin and breathed in deeply through her nose. "Be the bobby pin. You are the bobby pin." She delicately wiggled the unfolded pin up and down. There was an audible click. "Holy crap!"

"It worked!" Magda whisper-screamed.

"Wait." Rachel kept wiggling the unfolded pin until there were two more clicks. "Turn the handle! Turn the handle!"

Magda turned the handle, Rachel let go of the bobby pins, and the door swung open.

"Oh. My. God." Magda's voice was filled with wonder. "You're awesome! You're like Pierce Brosnan in *Remington Steele*."

Rachel smiled sheepishly. "I owe it all to the internet." She shut the door behind them. A quick glance showed that the room was empty, and a breath of its stale air made it clear that it had been for some time. "She hasn't been back yet. Let's get to work."

"All right." Magda started to turn around. Then she swung

back to face Rachel. "Can I just say, first we picked a lock, and now we're casing a joint! I feel as if I should be wearing a trench coat."

Rachel, who felt much the same, nonetheless also felt it was up to her, the housebreaker, to keep them focused. "Later, later. C'mon."

In any sane housing area, the room would have been a prison cell or a large storage closet. In Paris, it had been made into a studio apartment. A window glinted on the far wall, a single bed under it. Against the wall at a right angle to the bed was a small desk, three book-filled shelves above it, and facing the foot was a narrow closet. Next to the closet a counter acted as a room divider. In the space beyond it was a sink with a draining board, two electric burners set into the counter next to that; beneath the counter a small fridge; and above it a row of cupboards. Disbelievingly, Rachel saw that the far corner held a shower cubicle. It was as if someone had won a contest to fit a complete apartment into the smallest possible area. The counters were white Formica; the bed had white sheets; and someone had painted the walls white. On the dark floorboards was a blue-and-white rag rug, and facedown on the rug was a cell phone.

"The portable," Magda breathed, stepping forward.

"Don't touch it!" Rachel whispered.

Magda stopped.

"We should leave things as they are."

"Right. Okay." Magda moved to the kitchen area and opened a cupboard. Rachel went to the desk.

It held only a blank writing pad. Opening the center drawer, she found pens and pencils, a ruler, and other miscellany of student life. In the top left drawer lay a series of notebooks filled with neat notes that she didn't bother to read—work from college courses, clearly. The second drawer down held a jumble of loose sheets of paper and file folders; under them was a small hardbound notebook. Rachel flipped it open and riffled the pages. The writing in this one started on the back page, a list of numbers and notations that told her Alan had been correct in his conclusion. Elisabeth was not so simple, after all, she thought, if she had the sense to keep accounts, and to write them in a notebook in such a way that anyone opening it wouldn't immediately notice them.

"There's nothing here." Magda was opening the cupboard over the sink in the kitchen area. "But she does have nice dishes. In fact," she turned around, "the whole place is quite nice. Sort of a Swedish feel. To give it more room, I suppose."

"Yeah." Rachel was digging through the bottom drawer. "I thought that too."

Magda came and stood next to her. "What did you find?"

"Nothing in here." She shut the drawer. "In the drawer above, just a notebook where she wrote down how much she received from Edgar and how much she gave back." She sighed.

"Well, since there's nothing else, can we . . . ?" Magda nodded toward the cell phone.

"Yes, fine." She reached into her coat pocket and pulled out her gloves, realizing too late that she should have worn them all along. "Do you mind if I do it?" she asked.

"Hell, no. You're detective of the day!"

Rachel picked up the phone by its edges. It was off. She pressed the power button, felt it vibrate to life, and swiped her finger across the screen. Nothing happened. She took off a glove, swiped again. Nothing. She tapped twice; suddenly the screen bloomed into color. *10 messages,* it announced. Then the tiny battery icon blazed red and the phone died. *Of course,* Rachel thought. Even French phones aimed for maximum drama.

Her voice was irritated. "It's run out of power. From two weeks on the floor, I suppose."

"Never mind." Magda's voice was flat.

"What never mind? It's the only concrete clue we have! Should we try to find a charger?" She looked up and saw Magda staring fixedly at the rug. She followed her line of vision. In the place where the phone had rested, revealed by its removal, was a round rusty circle of dried blood.

Their eyes met.

"It's nothing," Rachel said. "How long has that rug been there? It could be an old stain." But she peered at the fabric more closely.

"Look." Magda bent almost double, pointing to the floorboards. There, nearly blending in with the color of the wood, was a line of similar stains leading from the rug toward the door.

Rachel became aware of how cold the room was: she could see her breath. But it wasn't just the air, she knew. She had gone cold inside. She suddenly understood that up until that second everything about the case—Elisabeth's absence, Catherine's death, even Edgar's murder—had all been in the realm of the abstract, words and theories with no reality attached. That, she now saw, was another meaning of "no concrete evidence." But these blood drops were concrete evidence, and they were concrete evidence of violence.

"We need to go," she said. Magda didn't argue. Rachel

wiped the phone's screen and put it back over the first bloodstain. Their footsteps magnified by the floorboards, they hustled out of the room, closing the door behind them. They didn't care that the lock, having been picked so successfully, could not be relocked. They had other things on their minds.

* * *

They went to another café. This time the situation seemed to call for stronger stuff: Rachel ordered a pastis, Magda a cognac, and they didn't speak until the drinks came.

"Blood." Magda took a mouthful of cognac.

"Yes." Rachel took a long drink of her pastis.

They stared at the street outside the plateglass window.

"I know we were serious before," Magda finally said, "but that blood made me realize that I hadn't really seen all this as *real*. I was treating it like a book or a suspense film."

"Me too." Rachel took another swallow. "I thought the same thing."

Another silence. Then, "Is she dead?" Magda's voice was a whisper.

Rachel shook her head. "We can't know. Maybe . . . maybe she cut herself when she was packing in a hurry. Maybe she got a nosebleed." She knew she was clutching at straws. Shaking her head again, she inadvertently quoted Magda's words back to her. "It doesn't look good." Then she tried to sound hopeful. "But that doesn't mean it's necessarily bad."

Magda finished her cognac, and when the glass was empty, she put it down very carefully, looking at it for a second. Then she said, "We should go back to the police."

"Yes." Rachel started gathering her coat. "We should."

The ping of an arriving text rang out. She fished the phone from her bag, squinted at it. "Speak of the devil. It's from the capitaine." She moved her chair so they could share the screen.

The text was barely two lines long:

Re. Mlle. des Troyes—carte bancaire was used at a distributeur in Bayonne two days ago.

"He's not very forthcoming, is he?" Magda said.

"She used her card!" Warm relief flooded Rachel. They'd worried for nothing! Elisabeth was fine! But wait. Elisabeth's card had been used, but it wasn't clear by whom. She went cold again. "Or at least, her card had been used." But the user would need to know Elisabeth's PIN, and who would know that besides Elisabeth. But there were all sorts of stories about people being threatened—or worse—into revealing PINs. Elisabeth could be not fine at all; she could be the very opposite of fine.

She turned to look at Magda. "Is this good news or bad news?"

Magda frowned. "I mean, it seems good. After all, presumably she's the only person who could use her card."

Presumably. "But Bayonne? What would she be doing there?"

"She could be on vacation," Magda said. "It's near the beach."

That didn't sound plausible to Rachel. Who went on vacation to the beach in February? And only now, after two weeks, Elisabeth was using the card? But she wanted to believe. "Okay."

"Well," Magda's voice was determinedly reassuring, "look

at it this way: at least this puts Mathilde out of the equation. We know she's not in Bayonne."

That was some relief. "True. The only connection she has to the South is Perpignan. She was born there."

"Perpignan?" Magda grabbed her wrist. "Mathilde is from Perpignan?"

"Yes." Rachel shook free. "So what?"

"Perpignan is near Bayonne!"

"It's on the other side of the country!"

"But they're both in the Pyrenees." Magda spoke as if this sealed some important deal.

"Yes, except one is east and one is west. And separated by two hundred miles." Magda looked unconvinced. "You think Mathilde was paying a visit to her hometown and decided to run over to the other side of France to pick up some shopping, using a carte bancaire she'd stolen from her murder victim?"

Rachel thought this picture made it plain how ridiculous the idea was. Apparently Magda disagreed, because after a moment's pause she said, "Except . . ."

"Except what?"

"Except Mathilde wouldn't have had to kill Elisabeth herself. She could have sent someone to do it. In fact," she paused, "she'd be more likely to do that. It's smarter." Her voice sped up. "It's not hard to imagine. Mathilde's father's free-spending ways put him in the company of some shady people. Mathilde goes home to Perpignan and contacts one. A crony. She says, 'I need you to take care of someone for me.' He's always admired her steel, so for a fee he says yes. She drives back to Paris and has the perfect alibi. And the hit man laid low until he thought enough time had passed and it was safe to use the card. Biding his time. Oh God!" She clutched Rachel's wrist again. "That could have been the man at Catherine's! He could have done them both!"

Once upon a time, Rachel would have tried to bring Magda back to reality by pointing out all the flaws in this scenario. But after their experience at Elisabeth's, it was harder to dismiss.

"Whatever the actual story," she said now, "we found blood. So we can't automatically assume Elisabeth is safe. And we can't automatically assume she's the one using the card. We should talk to the capitaine."

* * *

They scarcely spoke again until they reached the commissariat. "Capitaine Boussicault," Rachel said to a different gardien at reception. *"S'il vous plait."*

He lifted the handset of the desk phone, pressed a few buttons, and engaged in a brief conversation before putting it back. "The capitaine is at lunch. If you would like to wait?"

Lunch? How was that possible? Looking at her watch, Rachel discovered it was one thirty. "Yes, we'll wait." She and Magda returned to their familiar seats, the same disconsolate magazines staring up at them.

After a few long minutes, Magda suddenly mumbled, "We broke in."

"What?"

Not raising her voice, she repeated, "We broke in."

"So what?" Rachel whispered back.

"You picked the lock. And we're not police. So that's breaking and entering."

"But in a good cause!"

"I don't think the cause matters. I'm pretty sure we're criminals, and I'm also pretty sure that what we found can't be used."

Rachel stared at Kim Kardashian's falsely eyelashed eyes on one of the magazine covers. The phrase "illegal search and seizure" swam up from her memory. "Great. So what do we do now?"

Magda thought. In fact, she thought for such a long time that Rachel was about to prod her. Then at last she spoke, but so quietly that her lips nearly didn't move. "We can phone in a tip."

"You *must* be kidding me." For a second Rachel's voice was loud. The gardien looked at them, then went back to his work.

"No. One of us will phone anonymously and say we think the police should go look at Elisabeth's room. We'll do it from a pay phone. You can do it on your way home tonight."

"Me?" Rachel was horrified.

Magda shrugged. "I've got a date." She grabbed her bag and stood up. "We're sorry," she said to the gardien, "but we have to go. We'll contact the capitaine again tomorrow."

* * *

As soon as Rachel closed Edgar's library door behind her that afternoon, she sat down heavily on the ottoman. She knew it was useless to try to do anything without regrouping first.

It seemed to her that the fact that Elisabeth's card had been used was a hopeful sign. But then the blood seemed just the opposite. *Was* Elisabeth dead? She tried compromising with herself. The drops weren't very big; maybe she had just been injured. But it had been almost three weeks since the stains had been made. She wouldn't be just injured anymore. She trembled, feeling her throat close up. She tried to breathe in and out regularly. In an effort to distract herself, she focused on the titles of the books in front of her: *Le Giaour, En Attendant Godot, Considérations Philosophique de la Gradation Naturelles des Formes de l'Être*, the Guten—

But the Gutenberg facsimile wasn't there. Instead, its niche was filled by nineteenth-century editions of *Vanity Fair* and *Pendennis*. Rachel stood up and peered more closely. She hadn't made a mistake; the bible wasn't where it should be. She moved to the start of the shelves, refocusing her eyes in that way that makes everything else fade into the background but allows the item one wants to leap out. Nothing. She focused and searched again, this time methodically. Still nothing. Nor—she checked carefully, twice—was the bible in any of the piles that currently lay on the floor.

She opened the library door and Fulke appeared. "Is David here?" she asked. Then, remembering his recent habits: "Is he awake?"

Fulke nodded, presumably in answer to both questions, and led her down the hall. He opened the door to the bureau for her. David sat at the desk, his eyes closed.

"David?" He jerked his head up, obviously woken from a secret doze.

"Rachel! How are you?" He smiled.

"I'm fine, thank you. Have you seen the facsimile bible I showed you the other day?"

He blinked, trying to shake off the fog of sleep. "Facsimile bible?"

"Yes, the Gutenberg facsimile. The Paris Edition? I showed it to you when we were looking at the books in the library?"

She could see him slowly waking up. "Yes, of course. No, I haven't seen it."

"Well, it's missing from the library."

Light dawned in his eyes. "Oh, wait. The bible in the slipcase?" She nodded. "Yes, I was looking at it. I think I put it back, but now I can't remember." His face creased slightly. "I'm sorry. But I'm sure it's around." He reached in his pocket, drew out a tissue, blew his nose.

Rachel frowned. "It has to be somewhere. Thanks. I'll keep looking." Fulke followed her out, closing the door behind them.

One of the useful discoveries of a life lived in mess is that vanished objects have a way of turning up as soon as you stop looking for them. Rachel didn't stop looking for a long time—she checked the shelves and stacks once more, groped under the chairs and ottoman—but eventually she admitted defeat and placed her hope in this hard-learned knowledge.

Still, troubled by her earlier discoveries, now confused by the vanishing bible, and rattled by the fruitless search, she had to admit that she was in no state to do any useful work. She didn't alert Fulke or David that she was leaving, just found her coat and slipped out the door. She treated herself to lunch at Bistrot Vivienne and a distracting walk around the Marais. It wasn't until she was telling Alan about the missing bible over dinner that she realized she'd forgotten to stop on her way home and phone in the tip to Capitaine Boussicault.

Chapter Twenty-Seven

"How could you forget?" Magda voice was shrill with disbelief. She and Rachel were debriefing on the couch the following morning.

"Magda, you wouldn't *believe* the day I had. It wasn't just going to Elisabeth's. When I got to Edgar's, one of the books had disappeared."

Magda looked confused. Not really surprising, Rachel realized belatedly: unless you knew the circumstances, it was just a missing book.

"Sorry, I should explain." She slowed down. "About forty years ago, a library here in Paris printed up a limited edition of facsimiles of their Gutenberg Bible. Edgar had one in his library, and now it's gone. It's just vanished." Magda's face was still puzzled, so she added, "It's worth about eight thousand euros."

"Oh my God!" Magda's jaw dropped. "When did you last see it?"

"About a month ago." Rachel was embarrassed that she couldn't remember the exact date.

"You're sure it isn't just mislaid? You did say that library was a mess."

"Not any more. And I looked everywhere. I mean everywhere. Under chairs! I even went and asked David if he'd seen it."

"And?" Magda cocked her head.

"And he said he'd taken it out to look at, but he couldn't remember if he'd put it back or not."

"Well, there you go."

"I know. It's just that even the slipcase isn't there. If you took something out, you'd leave the slipcase, wouldn't you? And put the book back in it when you put it back? So it seems to me someone must have taken it after him, slipcase and all."

"Fulke?"

Rachel shook her head. "I don't see Fulke leafing through a facsimile of the Gutenberg Bible—if only because he probably knows the whole bible by heart. Plus, let's be realistic, he would never, ever borrow something of Edgar's. Edgar is the employer: a butler doesn't borrow his employer's things." She heard Fulke saying, "A butler neither sees nor hears," his smooth head bowing. "And now that there's no Edgar . . ." She shrugged. "No."

"So a very expensive book's vanished into thin air." Magda raised her eyebrows. "Okay, I don't blame you for forgetting the capitaine. But," she fumbled for her phone, "we do need to call him; we should have done it already. We better do it right now."

"Wait." Rachel took a deep breath. She'd decided to tell Magda her suspicions about David, but she needed a second to brace herself. She exhaled. "Right. So I've been thinking—"

The doorbell rang. Rachel looked at her watch: five minutes to seven. "Alan's forgotten his key again." She unwrapped the blanket from around her feet. "Stay here; I'll be right back."

"Uh-uh, I'm coming with you," said Magda. "What if you mysteriously go missing?"

Rachel laughed. As she unlocked the door, she whispered to Magda, "Don't mention the bible thing; I'll tell him later." Magda nodded, and she opened the door.

Elisabeth stood on the threshold.

"Elisabeth!" Rachel felt her heart leap. It was as if a vanished love—a soldier lost on a battlefield, a sailor swallowed by the sea—had appeared on her doorstep. She stood mute, staring at the risen phantom.

"Bonsoir, Madame Levis," Elisabeth said. Her voice was not sepulchral; it was not faint. It was the voice of a real, somewhat travel-weary young woman. She carried a slightly dusty black backpack and had a messenger bag slung across her chest. She looked worried and her hair could have been cleaner, but aside from that she seemed fine.

"My God!" Rachel put out her hand. "Come in, come in!"

Elisabeth crossed the threshold, but then she stopped. She looked at Magda, then Rachel, then just looked awkward. It took Rachel a minute to remember that whereas Magda had listened to descriptions of Elisabeth, considered her behavior, and, well, broken into her home, to Elisabeth Magda was just a woman who happened to be visiting Rachel.

"This is my best friend, Magda Stevens," she explained. "I've told her all about you."

Whether it was the use of the term "best friend" by a woman well into adulthood, the fact that at least Magda knew *her*, or just that she had caught her breath and gathered her wits, Elisabeth visibly relaxed.

"Bonsoir, Madame Stevens." She bobbed her head. *"Enchanté."*

"Enchanté," replied Magda. They were like two guests meeting at a cocktail party. Rachel was struck by the surreal nature of the situation: a girl who up until three minutes before might have been murdered was exchanging polite greetings with a woman who one day earlier had been following a trail of that girl's blood across the floor.

She spoke to break the sense that she was in a dream. "Please," she said, holding out her hands to Elisabeth, "let me take your things from you. I'm so glad to see you! Can I bring you something to drink?"

Magda poked her head over Rachel's shoulder. "A coffee or a cup of tea? A glass of water? An apéritif?" Rachel could feel her sizing the girl up.

Elisabeth smiled. "I'd like some water very much, please. I've been on trains all day."

Once they had relieved her of her bags and sat her down on the couch with a glass of water ("And a *macaron*," whispered Rachel; then, "Not the rose petal one!"), they took up positions on the chairs across from her. Elisabeth looked around the séjour, taking in the books and the décor—even turning her head to look out the windows at the view—all the time sipping her water and nibbling her macaron. Neither Rachel nor Magda spoke—what if this were some kind of delicate reimmersion process?

Finally Magda could take it no more. "Where have you *been*?"

Elisabeth looked down. "Bayonne."

It was Rachel's turn. "You *were* in Bayonne?"

"Yes." She didn't look up. "I wanted to be near the ocean, to think."

The two women stared at her. "Did you use your carte bancaire?" Rachel asked.

"Yes, at a distributeur. My cash had run out." She raised her eyes and looked at each of them in turn. "I'm sorry, but I don't understand. How did you know I was in Bayonne?"

"We didn't know," Magda said, "but the police told us your carte had been used there—"

"The police! You have the police looking for me already? Without even allowing me to explain?" She started to rise, but Rachel put out a staying hand.

"Just a second." She kept her voice calm. "I think there's some confusion."

Reluctantly, Elisabeth sat down again.

Rachel said, "Elisabeth, do you know that we've been looking for you for the past two weeks?"

"Looking for me?" The girl looked baffled. "No, I didn't know. I haven't been watching the news or using the internet. I didn't even have my portable."

"We know," Magda said. She paused, cleared her throat. "Your neighbor told us."

"My neighbor?" Elisabeth's volume went up on the last syllable. If possible, she looked even more confused—and scared. "Why have you been talking to my neighbors?"

Rachel again held up a calming hand. "Just one neighbor. We've been very worried about you. We'll explain in a minute. But first, can you tell us what happened to you? You just vanished."

The girl shifted on the couch, thinking. "Yes," she said finally, then held up her glass. "But please can I have some more water first?"

Settled with a full glass, Elisabeth crossed her legs, yanked the sleeves of her sweater down, and began. "After you found me in Edgar's bureau, I went home. I was very worried. You see, Edgar and I . . . well, Edgar . . . Edgar had asked me to do something for him, as a friend, and I had done it. Something illegal."

She looked at Rachel, who said calmly, "Yes, we know about that too."

"You know? How do you know? You are a librarian *and* a detective?"

It was the first time anyone had been impressed by Rachel's detecting abilities, and she sat up a little straighter—but she stayed focused. "We know. Go on."

"I knew you would be suspicious about what I'd been doing. I told Edgar right from the start that someone would catch us." She gazed at them as if hoping this fact might mitigate in her favor. "I told him it was wrong, and we would be discovered. Edgar said we wouldn't be, but I always knew it was only a matter of time. And then, you see? You caught me." She wrapped her arms around herself. "When you found me in the bureau, I knew the time had come."

Rachel interrupted. "What were you looking for in there?"

Elisabeth blushed hotly, a rich pink flood that Rachel thought no longer existed in the shameless modern world. "Anything to do with taxes." She swallowed hard, then continued. "After you found me, I spent the weekend thinking about what to do. But I couldn't concentrate. I was afraid the police would come for me at any moment."

Rachel smiled inwardly at this vision of police officers swarming into Elisabeth's tiny room, but she kept her face straight.

"So I decided to go away. I took some things and just left. I didn' even stop to clean up when I cut myself on my nail scissors while I was packing."

Ah, so that *was* what had happened!

"I went to Bayonne because I knew it from when my family went there on vacation once. I wanted to be by the water, and it was the farthest I could go from Paris. I didn't realize my phone had slipped out of my bag until I was at the station. But it didn't make any difference. I was happier without it, to be honest." She took a drink of water. "I kept cash in my desk—" she hung her head again"—you know, money from Edgar. I took it with me, and I decided that when it ran out, I'd have to choose what to do. And it ran out two days ago." She looked up. "But by then I'd decided to come back anyway. I wanted to come and see you, then turn myself in and go to jail."

For the first time, Rachel thought she might understand how it felt to have a child. The girl sitting on her couch was so scared yet so determined, so set on being noble, and so young, that Rachel longed to put her arms around her.

But Magda was more puzzled by practicalities. "But why come here first? Surely it would make more sense to go directly to the police, not to come see Rachel?"

The girl looked abashed. "I wanted—well, you see . . . I thought if I came here and explained to Rachel, she might help me with the police." She looked at Rachel. "In the library you said you understood what Edgar could be like, the force of his personality. I hoped maybe you would explain that to them, so they would see it wasn't just me. And I thought . . . I thought . . ." She gathered herself. "I thought it would be easier to give myself up if I had the support of a friend."

This time Rachel did go over and give her a hug. "You won't have to go to jail. In fact, it might not even be worth going to the police." She nearly laughed at the mixture of hope and disappointment on Elisabeth's face. "But we'll talk about that later. For now, we're just glad to see you. We've been so worried."

Between the two of them, she and Magda managed to offer a fairly thorough explanation of their activities over the past days, from Alan's discoveries to their message from Capitaine Boussicault. They included their visit to her room with Alan but by tacit agreement left out their visit alone.

When they finished, Elisabeth said, "But I still don't understand. Why were you so worried?"

Rachel looked at Magda. How were they to explain their concerns about Mathilde, the evidence they had uncovered, and what it had seemed to suggest? She took a deep breath, trying to think of where to begin.

"We thought Mathilde had killed you," Magda said. "Or had you killed."

For a second Elisabeth's mouth hung open. Then, unexpectedly, she began to laugh. "Madame Bowen? Why would Madame Bowen kill me?"

Rachel frowned at Magda. "Well, you see, first there was Catherine Nadeau—"

"But Madame Nadeau killed herself!"

Was it worth it? Rachel looked at the girl's anxious face. Was it worth it to take the necessary time, invoke the necessary patience, in order to tell her a story that would make the situation clear but would also distress and worry her? She sighed heavily. "Yes, yes, she did. And after she did, someone mentioned to us that Madame Bowen was very jealous of Edgar. We were worried then that if she thought the two of you were . . . intimate . . ." She swallowed. "Well, we were worried about what she might do. Might have done."

Elisabeth looked incredulous. "But Madame Bowen knows I'm gay!"

Now it was Rachel who was open-mouthed. She had never considered that the lissome Elisabeth could be anything other than heterosexual. She felt her liberal credentials slipping away. "You're a lesb—" She stopped herself. "Mathilde knows you're a lesbian?"

"Yes, she knows. Almost the first thing she did when we met was ask me if I had a boyfriend. Now I see why." She nodded, as if confirming something to herself. "I explained that I liked women, and I had a girlfriend. So she knew from the start." Then, clearly losing interest in the subject, she said, "I would still like to pay back the money Edgar gave me."

Rachel said gently, "We won't worry about that for the moment." She did sound like someone's mother. It was a new experience, and she didn't know how she felt about it. "Just let me ask you one more thing. Did you ever feel that Madame Bowen was angry at Edgar or that she thought he was treating her poorly?"

"Nooo." Elisabeth frowned. "She was a tense woman, but she never seemed tense with Edgar in particular."

"She never seemed angry at him? You never heard her ask him for money?"

The girl shook her head. "I did hear her telling him she was worried once or twice. But she has plenty of money of her own. At least, Edgar always said so."

"And after he died? How was she then?"

Elisabeth considered. "Well," she said, "she did seem more anxious. You saw how she was that day in the foyer." She lowered her eyes and blushed again. Remembering her own transgressions in that encounter, Rachel assumed.

"Yes," Magda said, "Rachel told me about that day. Do you have any idea what she was after?"

Elisabeth shook her head. "She said it was something with sentimental value, so maybe something to remember Edgar by? I know she loved an Epstein sculpture he had. She was always mentioning it."

The dove! Hadn't Rachel also considered the dove, during her search? The dove would easily be worth the forty thousand absent euros.

"So she wanted a memento of Edgar," she prodded.

"Yes, that wouldn't surprise me because I know she was very fond of him, and I know Madame Nadeau, who hadn't known him anywhere near as long, wanted one too."

"I'm sorry what?" Magda's voice was sharp.

"Oh yes," Elisabeth said dismissively. "The day after the funeral, when I was working in the bureau, I took a break, and I ran into her in the hall. She had her overnight things in a little bag, and she said she had come to pick them up and perhaps find some small memento to remember Edgar by."

"Hmm," Magda said.

In the next half hour, they fed Elisabeth some more macarons and forced an herbal tea on her—it promoted calm and fortitude, according to Magda. Rachel promised to arrange a meeting between Alan and Elisabeth so they could discuss whether she would confess herself to the police; although she didn't say so, she thought he'd do a much better job of talking her out of it. She also promised to telephone the commissariat and tell them Elisabeth was no longer missing. Both women invited Elisabeth to spend the night at their respective apartments, but she politely declined. She had been away a long time, she said, and even if it had been by choice, now she just wanted to be in her own home.

They saw her to the door.

"Call your mother," said Rachel, who felt new empathy for mothers.

Only as she was undoing the locks to let the girl out did she suddenly think to ask, "Elisabeth, how did you know my address?"

The girl shrugged. "Edgar had a card with your information on it. I wrote it down after our talk in the library."

After all that time, he kept track of her address. Rachel smiled as she opened the door.

"Thank you," Elisabeth said. She double-kissed them both. "I will telephone you tomorrow."

"Thank *you*," said Rachel. "You've taken a huge weight from my shoulders."

"Yes," Magda added. "It's so good to see you alive and healthy." She smiled. "And to meet you, of course."

The two of them watched Elisabeth walk down the hall, her bag on one shoulder and her rucksack on the other, springy hair bouncing against her shoulder blades. As she reached the elevator, Magda called softly, "Your door might be open." But when Elisabeth turned around, Magda just smiled and gave a little wave. She closed the door.

"Oh my God!" Magda practically jumped up and down. "This is great!"

But Rachel didn't see what there was to be excited about. Elisabeth's return meant the departure of their best evidence for murder. Without the assumption that she had been done away with for money or because of something she'd known, or that she'd fled to escape punishment, once again they had no real evidence of anything nefarious. "I guess," she said.

Magda was taken aback. "You guess? Elisabeth's not dead! And she gave us the link between Mathilde and Catherine's death! There was something in the appartement that incriminated Mathilde—maybe still is something—and Catherine found it when she came to collect her things!"

"No," Rachel's voice was calm, "what Elisabeth gave us was a reasonable explanation for why Mathilde wanted to get into the back of the appartement. She wanted a memento, or she could have been after the dove. And she gave us a reasonable explanation for what Catherine was doing there when Elisabeth came across her: picking up her things and also looking for a memento." She sighed. "So we're back to just our original bottle of rosé as evidence of anything. And our little meeting with the police made it clear how they'll see that."

Magda lapsed into thoughtful silence, then said hopefully, "Or Elisabeth could still be our killer? Her return could be a bluff, to put us off the scent."

This was the second time she'd mentioned bluffs in connection with Elisabeth. Rachel looked at her scornfully. "Magda, think about that girl. She blushed when she confessed to searching for documents! Not even doing anything with them, just hoping to find them! Does *that* girl have the cunning and mettle to be a bluffing killer?"

Magda took one breath, then a second. Finally she spoke. "Well, there is another possibility."

Rachel waited.

"We thought Edgar's death, Catherine's death, and Elisabeth's disappearance were linked, but there's no reason they need to be—we just thought so because of the timing and Catherine's weird questions. But if we leave Catherine and Elisabeth out of it, all the evidence we have, from Kiki, from Fulke, even from David, still makes Mathilde a solid suspect for *Edgar*'s murder. Although," she admitted, "it is strange that Elisabeth never heard the arguments Fulke mentioned."

"Not necessarily." The explanation for that seemed simple to Rachel. "Fulke is a lifelong trusted retainer. Mathilde wouldn't think of him as another person, certainly not another person she needed to be careful in front of. Whereas Elisabeth was a recent interloper. She would've been more circumspect when she was around."

"Mm." Magda nodded. "And in any case, Mathilde did need fifty thousand euros, whomever she did or didn't discuss it in front of. Which makes murder in expectation or in anger at disappointment more than plausible." She considered for a moment. "She could even have used the ten thousand she did get, given that bad oil investment. So she *is* still a very good suspect. In fact, in light of recent developments," she said, gesturing toward the couch cushion just vacated by Elisabeth, "we should move her back to being our prime suspect."

Rachel nodded, but more by rote than for any real reason.

Magda's reasoning made sense, and of course it was wonderful to see Elisabeth alive. So why wasn't she excited? Why did she just want to be alone?

But Magda didn't appear to notice her reluctance. "Didn't you have something you wanted to tell me earlier?"

Rachel shook her head. "No, it doesn't matter. I'll tell you another time." Along with everything else, Elisabeth's return made her suspicions about David seem less plausible and less worth mentioning.

"You sure?"

"Yes. I'll call you later."

Magda might not have noticed reluctance, but she could take a hint. She stood up. "Okay, I'll see myself out. Talk later." She kissed Rachel and made her way to the door.

Chapter Twenty-Eight

When Rachel told Alan that Elisabeth had reappeared, he said, "Do you want to talk about it?" And when she shook her head, he made her a cup of tea, then went into his study. Rachel was grateful for both the tea and the silence, but they brought her no calm. Somehow the apartment continued to hold all the tension and excitement of the last few hours; she itched to get out of it and find peace. Finally, she shrugged into her coat. The Monoprix supermarket, a ten-minute walk away, was a monument to order, and at nine at night it was likely to be mostly empty. She would go there.

To reach the grocery section of the Monoprix, shoppers had to take an escalator down, then walk past a dim space flanked by shelves full of wine and liquor. This descent, coupled with the harnessing of so much potential chaos—so many different types of alcohol that might have been confused but were not, so many different-colored liquids that might have been mis-shelved but never were—always brought Rachel a sense of calm, and the feeling expanded as she encountered the uniform arrangements of fruits and vegetables in the produce section, peppers and apples and avocadoes all organized in cool serried piles. In a good supermarket, civilization reigned: it was always tidy, and no one knew who you were or what you had done.

She was humiliated; she admitted it to herself. She and Magda had made up a story, she now saw, and then called it the truth. Mathilde seemed like a villain—she *cried out* to be a villain—and they'd decided that that made her one. They'd taken an abandoned telephone, a few drops of blood, and some unpleasant remarks on a balcony, and whipped them into a wish-fulfillment scenario they had fully committed to without a backward glance.

Rachel knew that she didn't have small emotions. Her happiness was always bliss, her sorrow always misery. It wasn't really surprising, then, that her embarrassment should feel like complete debasement. Trying to comfort herself she rested a hand on a row of cantaloupes. Nobody looked. Nobody cared, she thought. Nobody here knew that she had got it wrong; that Alan had been right; that the police had been right; that her first foray into investigation had led to a murder victim who was, in fact, alive and well and on holiday in the South of France. In February.

With that thought, her rationality began to reassert itself, and after its brief retreat her good sense kicked in once more. It was true Elisabeth's return made a significant emotional difference to how she thought about Edgar's murder, but did it really make any difference to the actual possibility of that murder? She and Magda had built a case in which Elisabeth's murder bolstered the existence of Edgar's, and vice versa, but did it need to be that way? Now that Elisabeth had returned from the not-really-dead, did they have to admit that Edgar had, in fact, just keeled over at dinner, worn out by greed and . . . pilfering . . . with the favorite wine of whichever woman had been with him left on the table? For the first time since the day Magda had confronted her at Bistrot Vivienne, she questioned herself sternly. Did she still believe Edgar had been murdered?

She looked at the tomatoes. The intense red of their skins demanded similar concentration from her. She focused inward, groping for her animal instincts. Yes, she decided, she did still believe it. Elisabeth or no Elisabeth, the other scenario still felt wrong. Edgar had died at someone else's hand.

She pushed herself harder. All right that was what she felt, but did she have any actual evidence? Not feelings or instincts, but actual, police-procedure-worthy *proof*?

She bit her thumbnail. Well, to start with, there was the fact that, although rosé had been found on the table, neither woman had said she was dining with Edgar. If someone died shortly after you'd had a meal with them, it was the sort of thing you'd mention—even to someone you didn't know very well, even if only in passing. But both Mathilde and Elisabeth had said nothing on the subject. That meant that either neither of them had eaten with Edgar that night—which made the presence of rosé a mystery all over again—or one of them had been there but wasn't admitting to it—which suggested that one of them had something to hide. In either case, something was off.

Ah, here she was back at "a thing is off." But now there was more than one thing as evidence. There was also the soup. She remembered her mother once telling her that you could drown in two inches of water. The average soup bowl probably held about three inches when it was full. That meant that in order to drown in it, Edgar would have needed to be near the beginning of the meal. Suppose she accepted that Edgar had passed out into his bowl, very near the start of his evening meal. Again, the rosé was proof that he hadn't been alone at that meal. And if someone slumped facedown into his bowl while you were beginning to eat with him, either you called an ambulance, or you tried to save him yourself, or you were his killer.

But this was evidence offered in light of the fact that she had suspects available. *Occam's razor,* she reminded herself, *Occam's razor.* Without the complication of specific suspects, was there evidence of murder?

She made herself think very slowly. Elisabeth and David, on separate occasions, had spontaneously mentioned that Edgar hated rosé. The bottle on the table could not, then, be explained away by a gustatory whim or a sudden urge. Someone else needed to be there if its presence was to be explained. This meant not only that someone had been with Edgar at dinner, but also that this person hadn't come forward to admit to that—suspect behavior added to suspect circumstances. Then there was the fact that the Edgar who had been revealed to her by her recent experiences didn't look so decent. He had been a tax cheat, had made and taken back fiscal promises, had coerced another person into committing fraud. Even a love of cats couldn't save such a character. According to Fulke, he'd made his wife furious over money, and by Elisabeth's own admission, he'd made her, his reluctant partner in fraud, terrified and miserable. Who knew how many people of lesser conscience he might have irritated?

Between the wine, the soup, and the facts, she could

rationally say that yes, there was enough evidence to support a suspicion of murder, even by a person or persons unknown.

But really, she acknowledged, she didn't believe it was by person or persons unknown. What about that heavy front door? What about the impossibility that Fulke would ever leave the back door unlocked? And even if you left all that aside, what about the fact that Edgar lived at one of the most exclusive addresses on one of the quietest streets in Paris? Could anyone seriously believe that a stranger could sneak unnoticed into *that* building, on *that* street? No, when she said "person or persons unknown," what she really meant was a person Edgar knew, and when she said a person Edgar knew, what she really meant was Mathilde, with her pride and her need and her greed.

And speaking of greed . . .

She caught sight of her face in one of the mirrors used to help staff spot shoplifters, and she turned away. She didn't have the courage to confront the next thought. She just couldn't push herself to it. Then she turned back. *There comes a time in every detective's life,* she reflected, *when she must acknowledge fully the hitherto unacceptable, consider fully the previously inconceivable, taste fully the heretofore unpalatable—Stop!* she said to herself. *Just face it.*

She began with the two men she'd met at the elevator outside Edgar's apartment. If you can tell a man by the company he keeps, what did this company tell her about David? Not much, her worse angel whispered; nothing good, her better one responded. No one who dressed the way those men did was in any legal business: she was streetwise enough to know that. And then there was David sleeping on a friend's couch rather than at his father's place. Why had Edgar refused to house his son? It wasn't as if there were no space, and there was a fold-up bed in the storage room. Had David been mixed up in something he hadn't wanted to tell his father? But what kind of trouble could a nice boy from the first arrondissement get mixed up in? Or could it be that the two elevator men had known David even when Edgar was alive, had known Edgar was "the rich man whose fortune David takes over," and had done away with him for their own reasons, unknown to David? If Catherine really had been a suicide, that hypothesis was plausible. But *had* she been a suicide? Was David a likely suspect? Or were his two dubious friends likelier ones? She confessed she liked that last possibility best, while also confessing that it was the least likely.

But then she needed to ask herself the most brutal question of all. Did she really want to search for the truth anymore? The fact that there was a mystery didn't mean she had to solve it. Why—to make further discoveries that unpleasant people thought in unpleasant ways, and that pleasant people could turn out to be dishearteningly flawed? To try once more to find a guilty needle in an impenetrable haystack? To have to face off against a policeman who would never believe her, and to be the recipient of more eye rolls from an impatient husband?

The answer that came surprised her. Yes, she did want to keep going. Whatever unsavory acts he had committed, Edgar had also acknowledged those who had played important roles in his life and those to whom he had been grateful. In his will, he had at least tried to pay them back. If she stopped now, she would fail to show him the same respect. She had started her investigation to acknowledge his role in her making; that role still existed, so the investigation shouldn't stop.

She would go back to the library. She didn't have to try to concoct any hypotheses there: she could just go back and see what developed. She could observe, then make sure that any ideas that did occur to her were based on ratiocination—now there was a good old-fashioned detective's word! She would *ratiocinate*. And after all, she pointed out to herself, she hadn't finished the cataloguing. The cataloguing that Edgar had specifically asked her to do. She would return to the library with no expectations, and she would finish the job. Or rather—she corrected herself, giving an orange a satisfied squeeze—finish both jobs.

Chapter Twenty-Nine

The next morning Rachel shouldered her bag with optimism. The sun was shining in the frosty sky and she was filled with a sense of new possibilities. When she arrived at Edgar's residence, her positivity seemed rewarded, for the elevator was resting at ground-floor level, something that had never happened before.

Alas, when the doors opened on Edgar's floor, her luck came to an end. Waiting on the landing were the man in the suit and his attendant. Rachel felt herself flinch (she hoped unobtrusively), but the man in the suit—it was electric-blue this time—seemed delighted to see her.

"Ah, the father's friend!" Again he gave his grim grin, then said in heavily accented English, "We 'ave to stop meeting like *thees.*" He laughed, showing scraggly teeth.

"I agree," said Rachel.

Luckily, he didn't understand the joke. He patted the pockets of his suit. "We are going out for a big day, to spend some money. You'll come?" He winked.

"No, thank you." She took a step toward the door of the appartement. "I have a lot of work to do."

He shrugged. "*D'acc.* Another time." He winked again,

more salaciously. Then, as if suddenly inspired, he pointed to the short man and said, again in English, "Say 'allo to my *leetle* friend!" They both burst out laughing, and as the elevator doors closed, her final glimpse was of the tall man punching at the small one's stomach, stopping just short as he doubled over.

Inside, she said to Fulke as she slipped her coat off, "I met some men outside."

"Ah, yes. Monsieur David came home this morning with those gentlemen. They had coffee before leaving."

Trust Fulke to turn a night on the town into a morning at a gentleman's club. But she noticed for the first time that his usually implacable face was a little pale. She wanted to say something sympathetic, but it was difficult to think of Fulke as needing sympathy. She didn't know where to begin.

"Monsieur David is a young man, with a young man's habits," she said at last.

For a second his features relaxed into fondness, even if his only reply was, "Indeed."

Was he too thinking of David as a small boy? After all, Fulke had been there. But again it seemed somehow improper to say such things, to breach the wall that hid his private self. Instead she gave him a wide smile into which she tried to put all her empathy and sincerity, and went into the library.

* * *

When she stood up at the end of the morning, she was surprised to see that she was very nearly finished. She had put all the shelves in order and moved the books from most of the stacks into their proper places, organized first by category and then by author. There were three or four piles remaining, but in about a week the only task left would be to type up the catalogue, and that she could do at home.

Then she caught sight of the gap still waiting for the lost Gutenberg, and in a second the sense of calm she'd cultivated in the past few days seemed like so much willed foolishness. Not only had she not solved Edgar's murder, but she hadn't even done her duty by his books. Had the volumes of the bible somehow slipped behind the shelves, maybe? She ignored the unlikelihood of this and flattened herself against the wall so she could peer into the narrow gap. But no matter how she craned her neck or what awkward positions she took to look fully behind, above, between, and below the shelves, there was no Gutenberg facsimile.

Her optimism, fragile as any recent vow, cracked. Her eyes filled with tears. What had she achieved, then, on today's grand reentry into the fields of detection and librarianship? Nothing. Murders were not solved, and she couldn't even find a three-volume book! Which meant that, so far, all she'd done for Edgar was lose him an eight-thousand-euro investment. She was not a good friend.

Magda would have lightened her flagellation with a sardonic remark or the observation that excessive guilt was its own form of narcissism, but Magda wasn't there. Maybe that was just as well, because it forced Rachel to scold herself. What had she expected to discover in the last twelve hours? She shouldn't be sulking over the little time she had left; she should be figuring out how to increase it. Should she refuse to type up the catalogue until she'd checked and rechecked every entry? Should she insist on remaining until the Gutenberg facsimile had been found? She sighed. She should call Magda, of course.

"You don't need more time!" Magda's voice sounded crisply down the line. "All the case needs is fresh eyes, and now that we've had a chance to regroup after Elisabeth, our eyes are fresh. Meet me at Bistrot Vivienne in an hour."

As always, Fulke was waiting for her in the entrance hall. For a single, weary second Rachel thought of asking him what he thought on the subject: Who might have killed Edgar, and why? Butlers neither heard nor saw, but they knew everything, and she was willing to bet that Fulke had information that would put her puny investigations to shame. She would never ask, of course. They may have known, or known of, each other for years, but she would never feel comfortable enough with Fulke to be so bold and so frank. That knowledge made her glum all over again: it seemed to her that the fate of a good butler was to remain forever a perfect stranger.

As Fulke helped her into her coat, she was surprised to see David appear. He *looked* as if he hadn't yet slept after a night out, his wide eyes bloodshot, his hair disarranged. He wiped his nose with the back of his hand, sneezed, then had to wipe it again.

"Hello," he said at last.

"Hello." She smiled at him. "Oh, dear. How are you?"

He shrugged. "Well enough." He watched her button her coat, then spoke. "Rachel?" For the first time she heard the boy he used to be in his voice. She nodded encouragingly. "When will you finish the library?"

"Oh, how funny! I was just trying to figure that out." She puffed out her cheeks and thought. "Maybe in two weeks?"

"Oh." How pale he looked! Winter was not kind to people with sallow skin.

"And after that you ought to have the books valued."

"Valued?" His voice was high with confusion. "I thought you knew how much they're worth."

"I'm just cataloguing them. I could guess at some things, but I can't tell you what the whole collection is worth."

"And how long will valuing take?"

Rachel thought. "A month? Depending on how soon they can come and how quickly they research."

She saw the edges of his nostrils pale. He shook his head and his voice rose to a yelp. "No! That's not good enough! It has to be sooner!" Then he halted abruptly. He took a deep breath, made an almost physical effort to relax. The blood came back into his face. "Well, now I know. Thank you." He turned and walked back down the hall.

Rachel stood frozen by confusion. What had just happened? Would David come back? She waited a few seconds, but, no, he didn't, and when she looked at Fulke, he gave no hint about how she might interpret the outburst. Instead, he smoothly opened the door for her.

"Tomorrow as usual, madame?"

With a noncommittal murmur, Rachel walked out onto the landing. She saw her finger shaking as she pressed the button for the elevator; she felt shaken as it descended. She wasn't scared, merely mystified and off-balance. Had she said or done something to anger David? But running over the exchange in her mind, she found nothing.

As she stepped out into the street, she noticed that the air was fractionally warmer than it had been that morning. Spring was coming, however slowly. She would walk home in honor of its approach, and to clear her mind of what had just occurred.

She crossed the Seine via the Pont Neuf, thinking about time and change. This was the oldest bridge in Paris. It had been built in 1604 and officially opened by Henri IV, her favorite French king. But the Pont had now been repaired and restored so many times that it was difficult to know how much of the original remained. So was it the oldest bridge in Paris, or had it become new? Or was it new, but no different? Had it outlasted time or fallen victim to time's passing?

Maybe because of the word "victim," her mind wandered back to her encounter at the elevator and the two grotesque men. *There* was evidence of time's passing. Edgar had probably never even brushed up against such people, and here was his son entertaining them in his home. But she thought of the lines from *Hamlet*: "Your father lost a father; that father lost, lost his." Who knew what David's children would bring home to horrify him when it was their turn? As she passed Café Buci, where breakfast was expensive but the croissants had been perfect for as long as she could remember, she engaged in an enjoyably poignant rumination on the changing of young cubs into old lions. As Kiki had said, time passed. It was inexorable. Time moved on; seasons rolled round; the young Turks became the old guard.

She would have laughed at this foray into metaphysics, but as she passed the hundreds of modern stores squashed into ancient buildings—a spa! a chocolatier! a Marionnaud perfume boutique!—they made abstract speculation all too real. The French were good at preservation, good at lasting. They had a different notion of time and different ideas about survival. She thought of Kiki in her appartement, accepting the inevitability of loss with an equability that would never occur to an American. No matter how long she lived among them, she thought, she would never be French.

She wandered aimlessly down the Boulevard Saint Germain and into the Rue des Carmes, meditating on these topics as she glanced in the passing store windows. Then suddenly she did a double take and stopped short. For there, in the window of P. Brunet, *Livres Anciens et d'Occasion*, was a Gutenberg facsimile.

* * *

"What do you think it means?" asked Magda. She was standing outside the store window with Rachel ten minutes later.

"I don't know," said Rachel, though she had a pretty good idea what it meant.

"Well, are you sure it's Edgar's facsimile? Did you recognize it when they showed it to you?"

"They didn't show it to me. I haven't been in."

"You haven't been in!" Magda gaped at her.

"I just—I just . . ." Rachel couldn't explain that it would be equally awful to know that the facsimile was Edgar's edition or that it wasn't: either way, they would either be back at zero yet again, or she would once more have to face uncomfortable possibilities. "I waited for you."

"Well, here I am." Magda pushed open the shop door.

A woman looked up from a glass counter she was wiping. "Bonjour."

"Bonjour. We would like to see the Gutenberg facsimile from your window." Magda's tone suggested she was an expert in biblical facsimiles, perhaps out shopping for another to add to her collection.

"Of course." Coming back with the books in the slipcase, the woman laid it on the counter in front of them. "A very fine example. In near-perfect condition except for some fading on the case." She turned it on its side to show them.

"May I?" Rachel removed the first volume from the case, carefully opening it and turning the pages. Halfway through the Song of Solomon, she stopped; she reached out an index finger and pointed at a black hair that lay on the page. She looked at Magda; Magda looked back.

"Ah, it must be the seller's!" The woman reached out and gently brushed the hair from the page. "One sees this all the time if one works with antiquarian books. Readers' hairs are sometimes preserved for centuries."

Magda turned back to the bookseller and smiled her interest. "So it could be an ancient hair! But what makes you think it must be the seller's?"

The woman shrugged. "Oh, he had black hair. But as I say, it could be hundreds of years old."

"Did the seller also have a cold?" Rachel's voice shook a little.

"Why do you ask?" The sale assistant peered anxiously at the open pages. "I gave him a tissue and made sure only I handled the volumes. Is there—"

"Excuse us a moment." Magda took the book from Rachel and laid it on the counter. The two women moved to stand beside a glass case filled with religious figurines, including a particularly gruesome crucifixion in which blood coursed from the wound in Jesus's side into a puddle beneath. *Why were early representations of Christ so obsessed with suffering?* Rachel wondered. She remained focused on this statuette until Magda made a noise.

"I'm sorry," Magda pitched her voice low. "I know she hasn't exactly offered us ironclad proof, but . . ." She winced. "I think we really need to talk about David."

Rachel sighed. "I know."

"You *know*?"

"Yes." After the hair, there was no point in keeping her misgivings secret. "You were right. We were suspicious of Mathilde because of her spitefulness and greed, but David is the one who really has the best motive to kill Edgar. All right, you'd hope it would be Mathilde, but whether we like it or not, markets go up and down, and her fortunes could improve on their own. David, on the other hand, actually *became* rich because Edgar died. And he fits the neighbor's description of the man who visited Catherine—I mean all right, eighty percent of the men in Paris fit that description, but he fits it too. And I didn't tell you—I couldn't bear to tell you—that before Edgar died, David was evicted for some reason, and Edgar wouldn't help him. He was sleeping on a friend's couch." She forgot herself for a moment and wailed, "But he was such a lovely little boy!"

The saleswoman looked up, but quickly back down. She turned a page of the bible with ostentatious concentration.

"I just meant we should talk about him and the bible," Magda said. "But yes. Absolutely. He obviously did benefit most from Edgar's death. And he was sleeping on someone's couch? I'd like to hear more about that."

Her interruption, however, had given Rachel time to doubt. "Wait."

Magda lips thinned. "Yes?"

"He did have a motive, it's true. But motive is irrelevant

unless there's a reason to suspect the murderer acted on it. Our problem with Mathilde is that we have no solid proof that anything actively pushed her to murder, right?"

Reluctantly, Magda nodded.

"Well, it's the same with David. Just because he benefited from Edgar's death, that doesn't mean he was responsible for it. He has something that could be a *motive*, but we don't know if he has any actual *motivation*." She shook her head. "The David I've been talking to over the past few days had less than no reason to kill his father. He and Edgar adored each other."

But Magda's patience had apparently reached its limit. "Stop," she said. She repeated it as if it were a calming mantra. "Stop, stop, stop." Then she collected herself and smiled at the woman. "Thank you so much. We just need to confer further before we come to a decision." She reached for the door.

Out on the sidewalk, Rachel could see the assistant's hands in the window, putting the bible back on display.

"Someone killed this man," Magda said, her words angry clouds in the cold air. "We've never doubted that. It's pretty clear Elisabeth is no longer a viable suspect. Mathilde is, but we have questions. But here is a person who, as you just pointed out, benefitted from the death, made use of those benefits quickly, and has some strange habits and even stranger friends. He walks like a duck; he talks like a duck; he *hangs out with ducks*! You need to at least consider that he is"—she paused awkwardly—"our duck."

Rachel stood there. It was true; it was all true—it was even her own ideas repeated back to her. She had to stop allowing the David she'd known as a child to make excuses for the adult David's behavior—and like it or not, the adult David did look like (she clung to euphemism) a duck. Why had he slept on a friend's couch rather than ask for Edgar's help? Why was he such close friends with those two menacing figures? Why had he—it still pained her to think it aloud—taken and sold the facsimile? Could there be *any* other explanation?

"All right," she said. "You're right. But here's the thing: we were sure it was Elisabeth, and we were wrong; we thought it could be Catherine Nadeau, and we were wrong. My point about the difference between motive and motivation is valid. Before we end up wrong again, please could we do some more digging and *then* draw our conclusion?"

"Brilliant!" Then Magda sobered. "Yes, absolutely we should find out more about him. We could . . ." She thought for a second; her brightness dimmed a little. "We could . . ." Finally she said, "Do you want to go see Kiki again?"

Kiki did seem to know everything about everyone, Rachel reflected. But really she only knew everything about a certain portion of everyone: elderly and middle-aged people from long-established families who moved in the same circles she did. David fit only one of those criteria.

"No." She shook her head. "We need someone closer to David, in age and in culture. Someone who knows him or, if they don't know him, might know people who know him. Someone who can give us the kind of information only young people know about young people."

They considered. It was the informant problem again, Rachel thought, except this time she needed a young one. God, did she even know anyone young anymore? She tried to make a list of friends who fit that description and quickly realized that it contained only one name. "Elisabeth."

"Elisabeth?"

"She might not be close friends with Davi near each other in age, and they must have talk when they were both in the appartement. Or sh seen those men at some point. Or known abou could hear her suggestions sounding more and m so she fell back on the truth. "She's all we have."

Magda smiled. "Well, she is your *friend*."

"Oh, don't." Rachel winced. "I felt so bad wh that. It was like when Rosie McAllister told me I'd b to her than anyone in her life. Remember?"

"Because you listened to her cry for one after Charles Lautremont ended it with her!"

Rachel clenched her teeth at the memory, and for the two women reflected on the awkwardness of uneve Then Magda said, "Rosie McAllister is head of cre LaMarchant advertising now."

"So I was right. Charles Lautremont didn't know was missing out on."

"My point was that sometimes asymmetrical frie are worth cultivating."

"I knew what your point was." They were near some she could feel it. That she also felt uncomfortable about e ing someone else's attachment to her must be ignored. V Sam Spade quibble over that? Would Shaft? She pulled o cell and dialed quickly, giving herself no time to get in t with her finer feelings.

After she disconnected, she looked up. "We're going to her Sunday night."

"Not 'we.'" Magda shook her head. "I can't go. I have a da

"Another date!" Rachel raised her eyebrows. "Benoît?"

"*Mais bien sûr!*" She looked abashed, but also happy.

"Oh, Magda." Rachel smiled. "I'm so pleased."

"I am too." She grinned. "Or I kind of am. Now I wish I [were] coming with you."

"Don't worry." Rachel waved a hand. "I'll tell you [ev]erything."

Chapter Thirty

Elisabeth had pulled heaters from somewhere, and her room was cozily warm. Rachel tried not to notice the fire hazard of extension cords that made the heat possible. Elisabeth had obviously settled back in: a towel was flung over the door to the shower cubicle, and a rack of clothes drying in the kitchen filled the air with the scent of laundry detergent. Warm and homey, the room scarcely seemed to be the same place where she and Magda had stood a few days before. Rachel couldn't help thinking of the attic of Sara Crewe, child heroine of *A Little Princess*, and its transformation from garret to cocoon of luxury.

"Thank you," she said, taking the cup of herbal tea Elisabeth held out. The girl put a *Folies Bergères* coaster on the desk, then sat on the bed. Her cheeks were pink, her eyes bright.

"What can I do to help you?" she asked.

Looking at Elisabeth's earnest face, at the sleeves that were, of course, pulled down over her hands, Rachel wondered for a second if she should just drink her tea and go home. The little girl who had wanted to turn herself in to the police and give back her inheritance was unlikely to know anything about

David's seedy friends. Then Rachel hardened her heart and made an effort to see Elisabeth in a different light. Never mind bright eyes and pink cheeks: this little girl had been willing to participate in an illegal enterprise for her own benefit. Besides, she really was all they had.

Rachel took a deep breath. "Tell me about David."

Elisabeth looked away, stayed quiet. Rachel understood: the girl was a fellow member of The Young, trying to protect David from The Old. Rachel would have to move more delicately.

As if to prove her right, Elisabeth said warily, "What do you want to know?"

"Just what he's like." Rachel was reminded of her conversation with Fulke: similar loyalty, albeit to a different tribe. Maybe a similar approach would work. "I'm worried about him. He seems tightly wound. I just want to get a sense of what normal is for him. You're around the same age; you must have talked sometimes. I thought maybe you could help."

Elisabeth frowned. "We did talk sometimes when we were both at Edgar's." She looked into the distance, considering. "He seems nice. He's graduated." She made it sound as if this removed him to a country far away, one she could only imagine. "He would ask about my course, sometimes compare it to his. He's very clever. He studied architecture, I think. But he isn't an architect."

Get to the bad stuff, Rachel wanted to shout. But by this time, she knew that slow developments could sometimes yield unexpectedly good results. "Yes, he mentioned that he was looking for a job. Do you know what he wants to do?"

"Well," Elisabeth looked confused, "I'm not sure. I think maybe nothing at the moment. I heard Edgar say that to him once."

"I'm sorry?" This *was* unexpected. "When did he say that?"

"Maybe September? When David's landlord evicted him. I was arriving one afternoon when I—" She stopped and looked worriedly at Rachel before continuing. "I wasn't eavesdropping, but if you hear two people in the middle of a conversation, you wait until there's a pause to interrupt."

Rachel nodded. "I agree."

Thus supported, Elisabeth went on. "I heard Edgar say, 'You have an excellent degree. I can't understand why you can't find a job. I think you don't *want* to do anything.'"

This was not the sort of thing that David's version of Edgar would say. Maybe there was more to it. "Did . . . did he mention anything about bad influences or friends who seemed to be encouraging David in bad habits?"

"What? No." Elisabeth clearly had no idea what Rachel could be talking about. "The two of them were quiet, and then David said, 'Thank you.'"

Rachel knew that silence. It was the sound of an exasperated parent giving money to a troublingly needy child, and she had been on the receiving end of it several times. Suppressing those memories, she tried again. "And did Edgar say anything else? Anything about things that should change, or . . ." She stopped. She didn't want to lead Elisabeth.

Elisabeth shook her head. "All he said was, 'You *should* say thank you. You spend it fast enough.'"

Rachel looked at her carefully, assessing. What reason did she have to lie? And how much skill at lying did she really have? She thought of Magda's suggestion that Elisabeth was bluffing. But here, now, Elisabeth's doll face showed no hint of guile, and Rachel recalled her rich blush when she admitted her own wrongdoing a few days before. Yes, she knew that people could be consummate liars, but *this* consummate? Was Magda right, and Elisabeth was telling stories in order to cast suspicion on David? Could it be that Rachel now needed to double back on her previous doubling back, that she should reconsider Elisabeth as a murderer, one who was fabricating stories to remove suspicion from herself?

The girl blinked, apparently puzzled and eager to help, and Rachel couldn't accept the possibility that she was a cold-blooded psychopath. Better to let the evidence do the work: as Elisabeth continued, she might trip herself up—or future research might show whether she was telling the truth.

She cleared her throat. "And do you know if David ever did stop asking his father for money?"

"I don't know. I don't think so, because I know he knew David had been evicted in November and moved in with friends. If he'd been giving him money, he would have given some for his rent, yes?"

Rachel nodded again.

Elisabeth said firmly, "But I know he had faith in him—continued to have faith in him. He said David had pulled himself back together so well that—"

"Excuse me." Rachel was lost again. "'Pulled himself back together'? Back together after what?"

Elisabeth colored at her slip, but she couldn't unsay it. Now she had to explain. "Well . . . the *désintox*."

"Rehab?" Rachel nearly shouted, dropping back into English in her astonishment. Why hadn't Kiki mentioned *that*?

"Mais oui." Elisabeth nodded gravely. "About eighteen months ago. Edgar tried to keep it very quiet. It was only for a month, and when David came out, he was fine."

Rachel bunched her hands into fists where they lay on her thighs. This changed everything. Everything. She felt embarrassed for her prior clueless self. She thought of David's red eyes, his nights out that became days out, the nagging winter cold that made his nose run all the time. She cringed, remembering the way she thought he'd been struck by the beauty of the Gutenberg facsimile—he'd just been struck by its potential resale value! And that credit card in the bathroom hadn't just been random pocket contents: he used it to cut cocaine in there! He had a habit, and he needed money to fund it. *That* was the kind of trouble a nice boy from the first arrondissement could get mixed up in.

Then she felt embarrassed for her present enlightened self. Magda *had* been right all along. She thought of the man in the suit and his companion, of David's sudden outburst the day before. He'd needed money to pay those men, and maybe other men before them. And when he couldn't persuade Edgar to give him money anymore, he had to find another way, and in the end he'd killed his father to achieve it. Catherine had probably found out—about the murder, about the drugs; about something big enough to make the police pay attention anyway—and David had taken care of her when she'd tried to get money out of him. Murder *would* seem an extreme solution, but when you're a desperate coke addict, probably nothing seems extreme.

"Excuse me." She put her cup down and stood up.

* * *

For this visit, Rachel didn't ring the bell of Edgar's appartement. She banged on the door with the side of her fist, feeling the metal shake as the sound bounced off the walls of the landing. If David had murdered his father, the crime didn't merit quiet social niceties. It demanded disturbance and outrage, and she would provide them.

Fulke opened the door. "Madame Levis." He was only slightly ruffled.

"Fulke." She dropped her fist, "I want to see David."

The butler indicated his surprise by raising his eyebrows. "I did not expect visitors at this hour. I had just finished closing the front rooms."

Rachel crossed the threshold into the entrance hall, panting slightly. "I need to talk to David, and I need to talk to him right now. It's vital."

"Monsieur David is in the bureau. I'm sure he'll be delighted to see you." Fulke turned to lead her.

But Rachel had no interest in a decorous walk. She darted down the hall. Fulke would want to open the door and announce her, but she wanted to catch David off guard, with no time to prepare a face or an alibi. She felt that if she surprised him with the question, if she appeared unheralded and asked, "Did you kill your father?," she would know if he were telling the truth. Somehow she would be able to read his features.

But it wasn't David's features that greeted her when she thrust the door open. Instead, she was stunned by the sight of him lying facedown across the desk. Where the back of his head should have been, there was a mess of blood-soaked hair and bone. More blood radiated out from that central well in splashes and long streaks, spreading across the surface of the desk and around David's down-turned face. Blood spotted the papers on the desk in front of him; a spray of it decorated the bulb of the desk lamp. Beside the desk, bent and dented on the carpet, lay one of the dining room candelabra.

Chapter Thirty-One

Someone brought Rachel a cup of hot sweet tea. Someone brought a blanket and put it around her shoulders. Someone asked her if she wanted anyone contacted, then went to telephone Alan. Behind all these things there was a constant bustle, a to-ing and fro-ing and arriving and talking and photographing that continued while she sat in the entrance hall in a chair someone had supplied for her, and tried to keep memory from her mind.

She stared into her tea, noticing that the cup had come without a saucer. Fulke would never have allowed such a thing. He must not have made the tea. He must be somewhere else. Maybe with his own blanket and his own tea, although Rachel couldn't imagine Fulke with a blanket around his shoulders, and she definitely couldn't imagine he would take his tea with blood in it. Blood? She turned her mind away. No, no, *sugar*—Fulke didn't seem like a sugar man.

"Madame Levis?" The name was hers, but the voice was unfamiliar. She looked up, confused, and slowly recognized Capitaine Boussicault.

He put a hand to his chest. "Boussicault. We have been in touch by text."

"Yes." She nodded. "Yes, yes, I remember. Bonsoir."

"Bonsoir." His voice was surprised, but gentle. "Why are you here?"

"I—" She cleared her throat. "I came to see David." Realizing he might not know the name, she clarified. "The man who lives here. Edgar Bowen's son." She tried to smile, aiming for something of her usual self. "What are *you* doing here? Isn't this outside your normal area?"

Smiling back, he shrugged. "Policemen love a striking death." He squatted down beside her, his trench coat brushing the floor. "No, no. This came up as a bulletin, and of course I remembered the name. And I remembered your story too. So I thought I'd come down and have a look." He peered carefully into her face. "Will you excuse me? I'm an outsider here as well, so I think I'll find a chair and join you."

She didn't know how long he was gone, but when he came back, he brought not only a chair but a fresh cup of tea. He handed it to her. "You've had a shock," he said. "And this tea is stronger than the other was."

She took the cup as he put the chair down next to her and sat, gathering his coat around himself and staring straight ahead. After a few seconds, he spoke. "In fact," he said conversationally, "hot drinks are not a good idea for people in shock. They find drinking difficult, or often they drink too quickly and burn their mouths. But," he continued, his tone mild, "it doesn't seem to me that you are *in* shock. You have only *had* a shock. Such differences are important. A cup of tea will comfort you, and a bit of sugar will help you." He smiled at her. "Try to drink it all."

She took a sip. It was certainly sugary.

"When I was waiting for the *bouilloire*, I had a chat with the *lieutenante* in charge. She tells me you found the body."

"Yes." Rachel shivered, gathering the blanket more securely around her shoulders.

"You had come here why? Remind me."

"I wanted to talk to David. I—" She caught herself before going on. Better not to reveal her suspicion and give him more reasons to believe she was foolish. "I'm cataloguing his father's library, and he told me earlier today that he wanted to sell it. I wanted to show him which were the especially valuable books."

The capitaine nodded, although whether or not he believed that Rachel had come around at ten at night to offer a book valuation she couldn't tell. At least he didn't ask for more details.

"And Monsieur Bowen was as you found him?"

"Yes. I didn't touch anything."

"Yes." He nodded, casting her a conspiratorial smile. "I remember that you are something of an aspiring detective—you and your friend."

"Magda," she clarified.

He stared straight in front of him once more, then shook his head. "This is a bad business, Madame Levis. It's unfortunate that you should be mixed up in it."

"How is it a bad business?" He said nothing. "What"—she swallowed—"what do you think happened?"

"Well, Monsieur Bowen's maître d'hôtel has told the police

that Monsieur Bowen had some particularly unpleasant friends, and one or two neighbors support this."

The men. "Yes, I've seen them."

"Ah!" The capitaine raised his eyebrows. "Well, apparently they came to see Monsieur Bowen tonight. The maître d'hotel let them in, and Monsieur Bowen said he would see them out when they had finished. The maître d'hôtel went to his quarters and"—he gestured back into the appartement—"as you see." He clicked his tongue. "Young people, drugs—we see it all the time. It's too bad." He shook his head sorrowfully.

Rachel drained the sludge at the bottom of the cup. She turned to face him. "Why are you being so nice?"

He looked taken aback. "You say that as if I were an ogre!"

"Not an ogre, but last time you laughed at me and had your junior officer hustle us out. Now you're . . . like an uncle."

He smiled. "That is also a new description for me." He met her eyes. "Madame Levis, in my job I meet many fantasists. Often they are ladies, and sometimes they even come to speak to me with their friends. But never—*never*—has one come to see me about imagined crimes only to be involved with a real crime shortly afterward. This is unusual enough to warrant a personal visit and some serious reconsideration." He patted her hand where it lay on her left knee. "So here I am, being nice."

She smiled back.

"Rachel?" She heard Alan's voice before she saw him. Then she was pressed against his cashmere front, hearing his heart beat fast through his clothes. "My God! Someone telephoned and told me you'd found a body. Are you all right?" He brushed her hair out of her eyes and searched her face, kissed her, kissed her again.

"I'm fine," Rachel said.

"Monsieur Levis." The capitaine rose.

"Field." Alan turned to him. "Alan Field."

"Monsieur Field." The capitaine held out his hand and Alan shook it. "I am Capitaine Boussicault. Your wife did indeed find a body, but she has told my colleagues all about it." *Did I?* Now Rachel vaguely remembered a woman sitting with her, asking questions about David and the state of the bureau, writing her answers down in her notebook. "She's free to go." The capitaine's face was solemn as his eyes met Rachel's. "We may want to see her again, but for now *ça suffit*. You may take her home."

Rachel was suddenly completely exhausted. She felt like a dishrag that had been used and wrung out. "Thank you," she said as Alan helped her up. She leaned against him, wishing he would open his coat and hide her inside.

Alan must have noticed her exhaustion because he said nothing in the cab home, just kept his arm around her as she slumped against him. When they arrived at their apartment, he put her to bed. A few minutes later, he brought her a cup of warm milk. She hadn't finished half of it before she fell asleep.

Chapter Thirty-Two

Alan took the morning off work, and he and Rachel stayed in bed. She didn't want to talk, or sleep, or even have sex. Instead, she lay with her head on his chest and her arms tight around him, her hands clasped together on his other side. She squeezed him closer and closer, feeling his soft skin and the rough poke of his chest hair, smelling his familiar scent of citrus, faint sweat, and deep darkness. At some point the squeezing must have become uncomfortable, even painful, but Alan kept his arms around her, his face in her hair, not moving.

"Tell me how we met," she said to him at last.

"How we met?" Alan was surprised. But he understood why she wanted the story, so he began. "Well, it was July of two thousand and three, and I'd just been sent here. I didn't know anyone, and my French wasn't that great, so of course I decided to go to a talk by Bernard-Henri Lévy."

Rachel laughed against his chest.

"I knew his name, and I'd read something of his in translation, and I wanted to feel . . . French."

She felt his ribs rise as he breathed.

"So I went to the Pompidou Center, and I listened, and I

understood maybe one sentence out of every five, but I watched him toss his hair and wear his shirt with too many buttons undone and generally make it plain that his real goal was to show us that he was even greater than sliced bread." He paused. "And afterward there was a wine reception, where you could have a plastic glass of Chardonnay and buy the great man's books. And I was looking at some impossibly French treatise he had written when this beautiful woman came over and stood next to me."

Rachel poked him.

"Hey! I'm just telling it like it was. You came over, and you stood next to me, and you said, 'Bernard-Henri Lévy is an ass.'" He paused, just as she had then, and when he spoke again she joined him. "'But he has great hair.'" He took a breath. "And that was the start of us."

Rachel squeezed him tighter.

* * *

By mid-afternoon Rachel was feeling much better. It wasn't so bad, she decided, seeing a dead body. Doubtless it was the sort of thing detectives did all the time; they learned to look on death with a steely eye. She felt she could do that. She tried making a steely-eyed face.

A knock at the door announced Magda. She stood on the mat, brandishing a roll of Oreos. "I thought you might want a taste of home." She grinned. "Fresh from the stash in my kitchen cupboard!" She kissed Rachel on the cheek, followed her into the kitchen to put the packet down, then kissed her again, this time enveloping her in a hug. "Golly," she said. "What a life you lead."

"I know!" Rachel pursed her lips and rolled her eyes, playing along. She could feel Magda's watchful eyes on her as she filled the *bouilloire*.

They sat on the couch, each holding a mug and neither speaking. At last, abandoning joviality, Magda asked, "How are you?"

"I'm fine," she said lightly. Magda's face demanded honesty. "No, really. I'm pretty much recovered, I think."

Magda leaned forward and opened the Oreos. Rachel stared at her tea. She saw the liquid jiggle back and forth, its surface quivering, then rippling, then cleaving into miniature waves. She made an effort to still her hands.

"Have a cookie," Magda said.

As the first bite of Oreo crumbled in her mouth, Rachel made a noise somewhere between a sob and a laugh—a kind of ragged hiccup. The cookie tasted of a thousand rainy afternoons with nothing more important to do than watch *Brady Bunch* reruns and dream about Duran Duran. She took a second bite, closing her eyes for a moment. When she opened them she said, "I've never seen a dead person before." Her voice shook.

Magda didn't speak.

Rachel remembered the emphatic un-aliveness of David's corpse. It hadn't looked dead the way her first pet, Wilfred the hamster, had looked the day she came home from school and found him cold in his cage. Wilfred had looked like Wilfred, only unmoving, but David's body seemed to have no connection to the living David. In some atavistic, instinctive way, it had been definitively *not alive*. For the first time she had understood the difference between sleep and death, between unconsciousness and death—between passivity and emptiness. And her confusion at being faced with this utterly new experience meant that for two or three long seconds she hadn't processed what she was seeing; she'd observed it but hadn't grasped it. When those seconds passed, the horror came, with enormous force, but even now she could remember the scene with objective clarity. And that memory, of slaughter as tableau, somehow made it worse. Maybe looking on death with a steely eye wasn't such a good idea after all.

"It was awful," she said, because there were no better words.

"I'm so sorry." Magda sighed. She waited a long time before she spoke again. "How—well—I mean—how did you come to be there?"

Rachel shook her head. "I went to Elisabeth's, and she told me—" She caught herself; she wasn't sure she could handle Magda's glee right now. "—some things that I put together with other things. Suddenly I thought he'd murdered Edgar. So I went to confront him."

"What things?" Magda tried to keep her voice even, but Rachel could hear the hint of excitement. *Well,* she thought, *I'll have to tell her everything at some point; might as well get it over with.*

"Um, you know." She shifted uncomfortably. "She mentioned some facts, some issues he'd been having . . ." She gave up. "He was a coke addict."

"I *knew* it!" Magda drew in her breath sharply, smacked a couch cushion in satisfaction. "I knew it all along!" She snapped her head down in a satisfied nod. "Didn't I say it was drugs all along? I said it was drugs all along."

"You *did* say it was drugs all along," Rachel said. Then she added, "However, you said drugs made David kill Edgar, not that drugs would make someone kill David."

"Whatever." Magda waved a hand. "The two possibilities aren't mutually exclusive."

Thankfully, the doorbell rang. Rachel held up a finger, slipped her feet from the blanket, and went to answer it. The visitor was the capitaine.

"Madame Levis? I'm sorry to surprise you. I wanted to stop by to see how you were." The corners of Boussicault's eyes crinkled as he smiled, but he watched her closely. "I persuaded someone to let me in at the main door."

"I'm feeling better, thank you." She tried to sound as if seeing a corpse were all in a day's work. Eat your heart out, V. I. Warshawski!

He smiled again. "And also I wanted to tell you how our inquiries are progressing."

Where Magda's enthusiasm hadn't touched her, this announcement did. She was getting a police update. She was on the case! V. I. Warshawski indeed. She stood back to let him in.

"Ah!" He said when he reached the séjour. "And here is your partner in crimes. Madame." He nodded and Magda nodded back, moving her legs off the couch to a normal sitting position.

"Would you like coffee, or tea?" Rachel turned toward the kitchen.

"No, no, thank you." He dipped his head. "But a seat, perhaps?"

"Of course!" She gestured at a chair, then sat down on the couch again herself.

The capitaine waited until she had settled before he spoke. "First, I have a little follow-up information. A mixture of good and bad. The good is that my colleagues were able to learn the names and addresses of Monsieur Bowen's two little friends."

What little friends? Edgar didn't have any little friends, Rachel thought. Then she realized that his Monsieur Bowen was David, and that the little friends were the two men she'd met at the elevator.

"That *is* good," she said. "Are you allowed to tell me?"

He smiled. "Their names, certainly. One is Matthieu Mediouri. He models himself on Al Pacino in *Scarface*, apparently."

Well, Rachel thought, *that explains the references.*

The capitaine continued, "The other is called Laurent Brabinet. Although it seems he prefers to be known as"—here he said in a very nasal American accent—"L-Brah." He returned to his normal voice. "They're known to the police. Mid-level drug dealers. I'm sorry to have to tell you that Monsieur Bowen made frequent use of their services."

"That's all right," Magda cut in. "We already knew."

The capitaine looked nonplussed. "Ah bon? Yet again you surprise me." He clicked his tongue. "Well, it seems that Monsieur Bowen had somewhat overextended himself, and they felt he had imposed on their good natures for too long. They sought to remind him of their relative positions."

My God, thought Rachel, *Stendhal has come back as a policeman.*

"We spoke to Monsieur Bowen's mother. An indomitable woman. She absolutely rejected the idea that her son was involved with drugs or that he would even have known Mediouri and Brabinet. She assured me that both things were impossible." He shook his head. "But I have dealt with many mothers, and all their sons have been beyond reproach. So at your suggestion, Madame Levis, we spoke to someone at Pierre Brunet Livres." He consulted his notebook. "Camille Murat, a book valuer and buyer. We showed her a photo of Monsieur Bowen, and she confirmed that he was the man who came to the store a few days ago and offered her a very good copy of the Paris Edition of the Gutenberg Bible. She bought it for three thousand euro."

"Three thousand!" Rachel was irate. "That's less than half what it's worth!"

"And of what she's selling it for. Nonetheless, Monsieur Bowen accepted without haggling, she tells us. And Pierre Brunet's bank tells us that a man matching Monsieur Bowen's description cashed the check on the account the same day." Here he paused to draw breath, then continued, "This three thousand euro is nowhere in the appartement. We have searched thoroughly. And Monsieur Bowen's maître d'hôtel told us that Monsieur Bowen had received a visit from Mediouri and Brabinet last night. As I told you, Monsieur Bowen said he would see them out. So, unfortunately, the man doesn't know when they left. Or," he added delicately, "what Monsieur Bowen's condition was when they did."

Rachel was impressed by the police. It wasn't even twenty-four hours since they had arrived on the scene, and already they'd managed to gather more evidence than she and Magda had in three weeks. Well, she supposed it *was* their area of expertise. Then she remembered that they had closed Edgar's case without so much as a cursory investigation, and she felt newly unforgiving.

"What's the bad news?"

"Yes, well, the bad news . . . There are two pieces of bad news. For your purposes, the first piece is that I was unable to find any connection or encounter between these men and Madame Nadeau. In fact, I was unable to find any indication that Madame Nadeau was anything but a suicide." He looked at Rachel. "And I made thorough inquiries." She knew this was his way of apologizing, and she nodded her thanks as he went on. "The further bad news is that we haven't yet been able to track these men down." He looked disappointed. "We've talked to our *mouchards*, but so far nothing."

"Well," Magda said, "from what Rachel said they're pretty easy to spot, so it probably won't be long."

"Yes, maybe." But Boussicault didn't look as if he meant that. After all, "easy to spot" was relative. "Still," he brightened, "we do have something else to check out, just to be sure. We found no fingerprints on the candelabrum, which means the case against Mediouri and Brabinet is so far circumstantial. In such cases we like to follow other leads, even if only to rule them out. And there is one that is very interesting. The maître d'hôtel tells us that shortly before he was murdered, Monsieur David Bowen made a will. The man had put it in the post to Monsieur's Bowen's avocat that very evening. We may find more worthwhile information in it."

"Ah." Rachel kept her voice level and steady. "Another will."

"Yes." Boussicault shrugged. "I suspect his lawyer suggested it right after the reading of Monsieur Bowen's will. Where large sums are concerned, they like to have all eventualities covered as soon as possible. So tomorrow we visit"—he checked his notebook again—"Cabinet Martin Frères, the Bowen family's lawyers. After which," he said, beginning to rise, "I will report to you ladies again. And in the meantime, if you think of anything you feel might be helpful, Madame Levis, please telephone me. Any time." He fished a card out of his pocket and presented it to her.

His rising prompted Magda to glance at her watch. "I need to go too. I promised I'd call my mother at eleven her time, and it's nearly that now." She looked carefully at Rachel as she stood up. "But I can stay, if you want me to. She'll understand."

"No, no." Rachel shook her head and smiled at both of them. The capitaine's report had reenergized her. Her mind was full of unarticulated possibilities and near-conclusions, and she wanted some time to grasp them. "I feel just fine. We'll talk later—I'll check in, I promise. Go on."

At the door, the capitaine helped Magda with her coat, then smiled at Rachel again. "I'll call the *ascenseur*. Madame Levis, as I said . . ."

Rachel nodded. "Thank you."

As the capitaine loped down the hall, Magda put her arms around her and searched her face once more. "You're sure?"

"I'm sure."

"Well . . ." She looked uncertain. "Call me later, all right?"

"I promise." They kissed. Rachel closed the door behind her, checking that both locks were tight. Tonight she would ask Alan to buy a chain.

Chapter Thirty-Three

That night Rachel barely slept. Her mind spun. She couldn't stop asking questions, trying to arrange evidence into a solution. One of their original suspects was now irrelevant: Elisabeth wouldn't have killed Edgar, couldn't have killed David because she'd been with Rachel at the time, and probably didn't have the strength to kill Catherine (Rachel refused to accept that Catherine's death was a suicide, no matter if all the police in Paris said so). One of their suspects was impossible for one murder, but (she had learned her lesson from the business over Elisabeth and Mathilde) that didn't rule him out for the others—David hadn't killed himself, but he still could have killed Edgar and Catherine. Mathilde was a possibility for Edgar's death and Catherine's, but Rachel couldn't believe she would kill her beloved son. In other words, this most recent death once more threw all possibilities into confusion.

But now they had a new element to consider: the two men. What were their names? Mediouri and Brabinet. They could have killed David, or both Edgar and David, and they seemed like exactly the sort of people who would throw someone out a window. In one way it seemed more likely that they had killed Edgar than that David had. You wouldn't kill your father, but you might well kill the rich father of your neediest customer. But that depended on whether Mediouri and Brabinet had expected to benefit from Edgar's death—and, she reminded herself, on whether they had even been in the picture when it occurred. They also seemed likely suspects for killing David. They were more than capable of it, she was sure, but what reason could they have? If he'd handed over what he'd made from the Gutenberg, they had just received a tidy sum, and given what he would have when the will came out of probate, there was the promise of plenty more. David was young; he might have been a source of income for years to come. It would be bad business sense to kill him.

But then this will . . . She thought back to what Boussicault had said: David had signed it only very recently. Conceivably, if she discounted filial instinct, David could have killed Edgar for his money, then made Mediouri and Brabinet beneficiaries in order to keep the supply coming, which in turn prompted them to kill him. She bit her thumbnail. It wasn't beyond the realm of possibility. Making them beneficiaries wasn't smart or well thought out, but drug addicts weren't known for their orderly thinking, and David would have had no reason to think he was going to die soon, but every reason to want a regular supply of what Mediouri and Brabinet had to offer. Then, with the promise of a large lump sum coming to them after his death, the two men had little reason to keep supplying him and an excellent motive for murder.

The question was, had David done that? Was his making a

will related to his murder, or was it merely coincidence? It seemed to Rachel that young men, even young men who had just come in to a great deal of money, did not rush to make wills. There had to be another reason.

Finally she gave up trying to clear her mind. She got out of bed slowly; Alan grunted and opened his eyes but didn't fully wake. In the séjour, the window was black. The sun wouldn't rise for another two hours. She sat at her desk in her robe and wrote a list of all her unanswered questions, then tried to answer them, then balled up the list and threw it in the trash. She knew what she wanted to do. She went back to the bedroom, dressed as quietly as she could, left a note for Alan on the table, and went out. She would've liked to walk through the Luxembourg Gardens, but the park didn't open until the sun came up, so instead she turned left out of her building and shivered her way to the Port Royal Métro station. In fifteen minutes she was at Cadet, the stop closest to Magda's apartment.

She paused outside the station: even in her anxiety, morning in Paris arrested her. The early sunlight casting its haze down the Rue La Fayette granted a moment of grace; the unvarying flat facades and even roofline of the long boulevard were at once aloof and soothing, their white serenity announcing an indifference to temporary upheavals. She gazed down the street's long length, breathing in the blank morning air before starting up the hill toward Magda's apartment.

At the top of the long hill of the Rue de Rochechouart, the white dome of Sacre Coeur turned pink, then yellow, under the brightening sky. The air smelt of warm butter and yeast, and the curbs glistened where the cleaning vans had sprayed their water along the gutters. An occasional workman strolled by, thumb and first two fingers clamping a cigarette butt in a way familiar from a thousand French films, the pinched digits and trail of exhaled white smoke giving him the allure of a suave gangster. If it had been any other morning, she would have filled her nostrils with the scents of baking and her eyes with these pale versions of Alain Delon, relishing being awake in a half-asleep city. On this morning, she just focused on the speed of her walk.

* * *

Magda was pulling her robe around her as she opened the door. "What?"

"I need to talk to Benoît."

"Then maybe you should phone his office." Her face was virtuous.

"Do I look that naïve?" Rachel put out a hand and opened the door wider, stepping into the apartment's small kitchen. "Please would you wake him up?"

Magda opened her mouth to protest but shut it when a voice behind her said, "He is already awake." Benoît stood in the archway behind her. "What is it you need, Rachel?" His tone managed to suggest that it was all in a day's work for him to be called upon to give advice in boxers and an undershirt—and indeed, he looked as capable in those as he looked in his suit.

"Forgive me," Rachel said, nodding an apology, "I've come so early because the police will be arriving at your office first thing this morning. The thing is, I need to see David Bowen's will. That is, I'd like to."

Before Benoît could respond, Magda asked, "Why?"

"I think it could have information that's important to us."

"Like what?"

"I think it could bring us closer to discovering who killed David."

"But your elevator men killed David." Magda sounded confused. "The capitaine said so."

"No." Rachel shook her head. "The capitaine said the case was circumstantial and they were also looking at other options." She was surprised by the firmness of her voice. Somewhere on her Métro journey she'd become absolutely certain that if she could just see David's will, everything would be clear. She must talk Magda into it somehow.

"Listen," she said. "They probably did kill David. But what if they didn't? The only thing worth killing David for was his money. If Mediouri and Brabinet were getting that money in exchange for drugs, they had no reason to kill him. Unless they could get more money by killing him," she paused, "because they were in his will."

"Do you think David would actually will money to two drug dealers?" Magda looked incredulous.

"I don't know," Rachel said. "That's my point. If he did, then we can be all but certain that they killed him. And if they killed him, we could add them to the list of suspects for Edgar's murder too. The capitaine said David 'often made use of their services,'" she echoed Capitaine Boussicault's phrase.

"'Made *frequent* use of,'" Magda corrected.

"Even worse! We know he had no money, and we know Edgar had cut him off." She made her voice smooth. "It's not hard to imagine. David says, 'If only my father were dead, I could pay you off in full and give you even more.' Mediouri and Brabinet take it as a hint. David says, 'Oh no, I didn't mean that, but now that it's happened, I'll leave you a huge bequest to ensure your discretion and loyalty in the future.' And they think, 'Who cares about the future? We want the loot now!' So—"

"So they kill him," Magda finished breathlessly.

"Yes!" Rachel made her voice calm again. "Of course, we'll never be able to know if that's plausible if we don't see the will."

Magda knew she was being conned, Rachel could tell, but the blandishments of the con—that she could be right! That her belief that it had been drugs all along could explain everything!—had wormed their way under her skin. Rachel waited, holding her breath.

"Pardon." Benoît still stood in the archway. "I don't think it's Magda you must convince."

Rachel collected herself. "Quite right. Excuse me."

He nodded forgiveness.

"I would very much like to see David Bowen's will. You've now heard my reasons." She gestured at the space between her and Magda, as if the reasons stood there. "Would you be willing to help me?"

She held her breath, watching him think: she knew that whatever he said would be right. At last he took a deep breath, then let it out. "First," he said, "let me dress."

* * *

"So here we are again." Benoît sat at his desk, frowning. Rachel imagined that he was remembering the rubbery croissants they'd bought from the *boulangerie* next door to Magda's building. Remembering them herself, she made a mental note that delicious scents do not necessarily equal delicious tastes. Benoît exhaled, straightened into professional posture, and began a familiar recitation. "This will is not out of probate. I can only read it and tell you what it says in a paraphrase." He spoke the last sentence very slowly and clearly. Then a strange look crossed his face. He put a hand on his stomach. "Ah," he said again, cocking his head as if listening. "Pardon. Perhaps I should not breakfast so early." He paused. Putting the open folder down on the desk, he stared hard at Rachel, then rose. "Would you excuse me for a moment?" He glanced at the folder, then at her again. "I will be back shortly." Letting himself out of the office, he closed the door behind him.

"Oh no!" Magda half-rose from her seat. "Is he all right, do you think? Should we go after him?" Her face was a mask of concern.

"No, you fool!" Rachel hissed. "He's left so we can look at the will!"

"What? No, he's feeling sick from those awful croissants. You heard him." She remained in her strange posture, knees bent, hovering a few inches above the chair seat.

"He's not sick! Didn't you see the way he looked at us? Then looked at the folder before telling us he wouldn't be gone long? He's faking so we can have a look!" Rachel spoke so low and so quickly that she nearly spat on Magda. Then, not wanting to waste time, she half-rose too and snatched the will across the desktop.

It consisted of only a single sheet. As in Edgar's case, the paper was thick, off-white, and printed on a computer. David's signature crossed the bottom. She swallowed hard, deliberately not thinking of him splayed out against the desktop and forcing herself to focus on the black print of the document. Here again was the same legalese that began her own will, but after that there was nearly nothing. David left an amount to be used for the upkeep of Edgar's grave in perpetuity, and all the rest he gave to his mother.

"No Mediouri and Brabinet," Magda pointed out.

"No." Rachel shook her head. She was thinking that Mathilde had Edgar's estate at last.

Magda seemed to read her mind, for she said, "You don't think . . ."

"No." Rachel shook her head more firmly. Already she was ashamed of her spitefulness. "I can't think it. She isn't Medea. She didn't kill her own child. She couldn't."

"You might," Magda said slowly, "if you thought he would end up giving it all away to drug dealers."

Rachel gave a short laugh. "Don't you worry. Those men will get their money. They'll collect it from the beneficiary." She tapped a finger on Mathilde's name. "She'll pay it too. It's a small price to stay safe and clear her son's honor. No," Rachel said, resting her hands on the desk, her head lowered, "Mathilde didn't do this. And Matthieu Mediouri and Laurent Brabinet aren't here at all, so they have no reason to kill David. They'd be better off with him alive. So again it's back to the start, only with three murders now." She sighed. She was so tired of rethinking, of starting again. "Or maybe . . ." She gave up at last. "Probably Edgar did have a heart attack and drown in the soup. Probably the whole thing was just me subconsciously not wanting to let go of a part of my youth."

"Whoa." Magda held up a hand. "It was only a bit of detection, not an existential reckoning."

But Rachel remained as she was, looking at her thumb against the creamy paper. She dropped her eyes to the signature, taking in David's bold "D," his slightly smaller "B." The same initials as David Bowie, she thought inconsequentially. Except David Bowie hadn't died sprawled across his father's desk. Again the image began to swim up to her eyes, and again she shoved it aside by focusing elsewhere, this time on the lines that held the witnesses' signatures.

"Wait." She grabbed Magda's wrist.

"What?" Magda looked at the will again, but when she raised her eyes, her face was blank. "What am I supposed to see?"

"Oh God," Rachel said. "Of course! I can't believe it didn't occur to me. It's so—I can't believe it." She tugged at her friend's arm. "We have to go. We have to go *now.*" She rose from her seat. "Come *on.*"

As they passed into the hall, they encountered Benoît, making his way back to the office at a leisurely pace. Rachel stopped and clasped his hand, kissing him on both cheeks. "Thank you." She smiled at him. "Thank you so much for this."

"De rien." He made a face of exaggerated but sincere mystification. "I am glad to help. *À bientôt.*" He smiled, and Magda cast "I'll call you!" over her shoulder as she followed Rachel out the door.

* * *

"What are you doing?"

Rachel stood in the gutter waving her right arm. "What does it look like? I'm hailing a cab."

"No," said Magda, "I mean what just happened? I obviously missed something."

Over her shoulder Rachel made a dismissive gesture while keeping her other arm aloft. One taxi whizzed past with its light on, then another. "God *dammit*!" she roared.

"Calm down." Spotting a third cab approaching, Magda stepped into the middle of the street, forcing it to stop. "All right? Now get in."

"Quai des Orfèvres 67," Rachel said to the driver when they were both inside with the door shut. "And no scenic routes." Once again she had spoken in English in her excitement; she took a breath and snapped, *"Nous ne sommes pas des touristes."*

The offended driver took off as if it were the last lap of Le Mans, throwing both women back in their seats. Struggling to sit up, Magda said, "Now will you tell me what's going on? We run out of that office like a bat out of hell, and then you won't say anything. What did you see?"

"Bats out of hell." Rachel was fumbling in her bag. "There are two of us, so it's bats out of hell."

"Bats out of hell, then. What is going on?"

She continued digging. "It's Fulke."

"What?"

Rachel took her hand out of her bag and faced Magda, letting out an exasperated sigh. "It's Fulke! Fulke did it! First he witnessed their wills and then he killed them." She turned back to her bag, at last pulling out her phone.

"What?" Having just sat up, Magda sat back again. "But he couldn't have. I mean, Edgar hadn't just signed his will. You said Maître Bernard said he drew it up three months before he died!"

But Rachel was busy jabbing at her phone's screen, then putting it to her ear. "Capitaine Boussicault," she said. Then, "capitaine, it's Rachel Levis. I figured it out. At least"—she remembered that she was speaking to a policeman—"I'm pretty sure I figured it out. It was the maître d'hotel. Yes, him. Yes. We'll meet you there; we're on our way now." A pause. "Yes, I promise we'll wait outside."

Chapter Thirty-Four

They waited on the curb, Rachel alternatively squinting up at Edgar's windows and checking her watch. Five minutes. There was a limit to how long they could stand there. Fulke could look out of those windows at any moment—he could be looking out of them right now—and if he saw them, he'd know something was going on. Eight minutes. Was this case a matter of priority for the police or wasn't it? And it was freezing. Were she and Magda going to freeze in the street and a murderer be allowed to escape while the police moseyed their way over? Would this investigation never end? She stamped her feet. "I'm going up."

"But—"

She gripped her coat more tightly around her. "I know I said I'd wait. But I'm cold. And I'll be careful. And it's Fulke: we've known each other for years, and I'm no danger to him as far as he knows. You can stay here if you want."

Magda only hesitated for a moment before following her into the building. Neither spoke as they waited for the elevator, but once they were inside it, Rachel turned to her. "Listen. All we're going to do is talk to him until the police get here. We're just going to keep him from leaving."

"Okay." Magda's voice was small, but it was steady. The bell dinged and the doors opened; they crossed the landing in a few swift paces, stopping in front of Edgar's door.

"Shit," Rachel said. Then, hoping against hope, she grasped the knob and turned it softly, putting her weight against the door. It was locked. "Shit," she said again. "I can't believe I forgot." She pressed her knuckles against her mouth.

"Are we locked out?"

Rachel nodded.

"Did you bring your bobby pins?" Magda wasn't joking.

Rachel shook her head. "Wait." She looked at the motionless Magda and held up a forefinger. "Wait, wait." She slid her hand around the inside of the doorframe, then over the top of the lintel, then over the outside of the frame. "Ah!" she said suddenly, a mingled sound of surprise and satisfaction. She pressed her fingers down lightly on the wood, there was a small click, and she held up a front door key.

"Wow!" Magda's face was a mask of astonishment.

"He had one in the doorframe of his old place too." Rachel smiled. "If it ain't broke, don't fix it." She slid the key into the lock and, braced for the door's weight, opened it. Despite her earlier evaluation, it made surprisingly little noise.

Inside the appartement it was so quiet that they could hear their own breathing. Rachel reached out and took Magda's hand, gripping it as they crossed the cream-colored carpet. Magda squeezed back. "What are you going to do?"

If Rachel's heart hadn't been pounding and her adrenaline hadn't been pumping, she might have reflected on how odd it was that, even after more than twenty years of friendship, she still didn't want to lose face in front of her best friend. What would Magda think if she turned and fled?

"I'm going to see if Fulke's here. You should wait for me."

"No!" Magda gripped her hand even more tightly. "I'm not staying by myself. If you're going, I'm going."

Rachel tried to reassure herself. After all, it could be that Fulke wasn't even in the appartement; he could be out doing the shopping, at a café having a small coffee and planning his next move, or upstairs packing for his escape. Yes, any of those could be true. She led the way down the hall. Once they were through the back door, she would call the capitaine again.

They walked through the dining room to the door to the butler's pantry door and pushed it open. There at the sink stood Fulke, cloth in hand, apron around his waist. On the counter to his right lay a collection of silver: forks, knives, a carving set, even the one remaining candelabrum. He turned around when he heard the door thump against the wall.

"Madame Levis!" He put the cloth down. "This is a surprise."

"Is it, Fulke?" Rachel had the sense that she was in a play; her voice sounded melodramatic even to her own ears.

"Indeed." He smoothed his apron. "Are you here to work in the library? May I offer you and—I believe it's Madame Stevens?—something to drink?" His face was blank of every expression except vague inquiry.

Rachel didn't have the courage for a standoff; she broke. "Oh, Fulke." She shook her head. "I know. I know you did it." Behind her, Magda gasped. Rachel took a step into the room in some kind of instinctive attempt to claim the space, and she followed.

Fulke's tone remained level. "I assure you, Madame Levis, I've done nothing. I don't even know what you could mean." Indeed, as he stood with the cloth next to him, one hand resting on the counter where it had ceased its polishing, he looked the picture of innocent confusion.

Rachel stayed still. She could feel Magda beside her, blocking the door to the dining room. "Fulke," she said. She tried to remain calm, but it was hard to accuse someone of murder in a level tone. "You killed Edgar and David." She decided to leave Catherine Nadeau out of it for the moment. "You knew they hadn't named you in their wills, so you murdered them."

Fulke raised an eyebrow. "That seems implausible, madame. Surely the time to kill someone is when one knows one *is* in their will?"

Rachel's experience of golden-age detective fiction had led her to believe that when faced with the truth of their crimes, murderers instantly gave up. How to deal with one who not only continued to deny his guilt but also raised an excellent point against it? She really should have waited for the police. She tried desperately to ignore these thoughts. Again she had the sense that she was in a drama, and this meta-commentary was a running review of the action.

"You did it," she said again, as if repetition would force him into an admission. "They used you as a witness to their wills, so you knew neither had left you anything. Did that make you angry? Did you think you'd earned something and were being cheated?" Fulke's face remained blank. "I can understand. You worked hard for years, and you were going to get nothing."

"I would never kill over money." Fulke tone placed "money"

on the same level as a poorly folded napkin or black tights with a pale skirt: a distasteful detail to be ignored and risen above.

"But you did kill Edgar and David." She felt like murder's bulldozer, forging ahead no matter what obstacles were put in her way. "I know you did. And I understand."

Fulke gave a little laugh. "You understand? You could never understand, madame."

Rachel blinked. Had he just confessed? She desperately wanted to look at Magda for confirmation, but she didn't want to break eye contact with Fulke.

"You keep talking about money," he said. "About my *job*. It's true, I am good at my job. It seems I'm so good at it that you all forget there's a person doing it. For example, madame, you never realized I was watching you. Yes," he said, nodding at Rachel's start of surprise, "I heard you talking to Mademoiselle des Troyes and Monsieur David; I knew you were trying to be a little detective. And it was easy to make you believe my stories of arguments between Madame Bowen and Monsieur Bowen. Just as I had done for twenty years with Monsieur Bowen and Monsieur David, I gave you what you wanted. And none of you ever gave me a second thought. To you, my loyalty is the loyalty of a robot: programmed, automatic. This is why you will never understand why I killed them."

Rachel jumped at this unexpected clear admission. She felt a cold shiver branch through her and nausea rise in her throat: she was suddenly very afraid. She had brought herself and her best friend, unarmed and unprepared, face-to-face with a murderer because she was cold and didn't want to wait for the police to arrive. And now they were alone with him in a space he knew better than they did, and there was still no sound of sirens outside. She clenched her teeth to keep them from chattering.

With great control she suppressed her panic and forced herself to think. Perhaps, though, they could still get out of it. Perhaps she could soothe Fulke, reason with him, even talk him into surrendering. Television detectives always began with empathy; she could start there too. "Well, Fulke, why don't you explain? I want to understand, Fulke." On television they also repeated the criminal's name to soothe him; she'd always found it creepy, but now she was willing to give it a try. "Let me help you, Fulke. We've always been friends."

She took a step toward him, her hand outstretched, but she misjudged her position and her hip struck the corner of the counter. For a second she was distracted by pain, and in that instant Fulke moved like a flash—or like a man intimately familiar with the space around him. He snatched Magda with one hand; with the other he grabbed the carving fork and pressed it to her neck. Magda gave a yelp of surprise, then froze, clutching at his arm, too scared to move or speak.

"We've never been friends, madame." He was breathing hard, but he spoke just as coolly as he had before. "As I have recently learned more than once, there is no friendship between servant and served."

"Fulke." She tried to think. How did you talk down a homicidal butler? "I've always admired . . ." the way you arrange muffins? your artistry with the duster? *Shut up, shut up,* she told her brain. "I've always admired you. I was just singing your praises to Magda yesterday." She pointed at her as she stressed her name—naming the victim humanized him or her to the criminal, wasn't that right? God, why was law enforcement so obsessed with names? "I was saying to Magda how good you are at your job, and how loyal."

The fork's sharp tines pressed into Magda's neck; Rachel could see blood pulsing beneath them. Where *were* the police?

"But Fulke," she said, holding up both hands in a gesture of submission, "please don't hurt Magda. The police are on their way. They'll understand what you did to Edgar and David. You were treated badly by your employers! This is France—everyone will be on your side! But if you kill an innocent woman? They won't be sympathetic to that."

Fulke smiled again. "Except that you assume the police will stop me. But this"—he pressed the tines more deeply into Magda's neck, and her breathing quickened—"this ensures that they won't, and you won't either. You'll let me leave this place, or I will spit your friend like roasted meat." Even on the last sentence, his tone stayed level. Rachel marveled at his self-control. No wonder she'd never suspected him.

Her eyes darted around the pantry. She had no weapon. Even if she had, she couldn't have surprised Fulke with an unexpected attack in such a small area, and with him and Magda taking up so much of it. She would have to let him go. "The police are on their way," she said again, pointlessly. She looked at Magda.

"Please," Magda said. Her pupils were huge. "Please."

"Okay." Rachel lifted her hands even further, into a position of surrender. She stepped closer to the counter, leaving space for Fulke and Magda's bulk to pass. Fulke, his butler-dom perhaps too ingrained ever to leave him, nodded his thanks. He turned slightly toward the dining room, moving awkwardly to hustle Magda through the door in front of him.

In the split-second that his back was turned, Rachel hit him over the head with the candelabrum she snatched from the counter.

Fulke jerked forward and grabbed the back of his skull. But although he dropped the carving fork to do this, his other arm kept its grip on Magda. Shaking his head as if to clear it, he swung both himself and Magda around to face Rachel again. For a moment she stood frozen, unsure what to do now that her villain had not been felled by a single blow in appropriate mystery fashion.

In fact, Fulke seemed entirely unfazed by her attack. "No," he said in the tone an adult might use with a naughty child. "No." He backed himself and his terrified guarantee of safety into the dining room, his right arm stretched out behind him. Rachel understood: he was looking for another weapon. And because he was familiar with the dining room and its contents, it probably wouldn't take him long to find one. Yet she could see his hand twitching slightly, and she bet he was distracted by an instinct to rub the back of his skull again. If she could build on that distraction, manage to keep him off-balance, she might be able to gain some advantage, however slight.

"Fulke!" She advanced but stayed just out of his reach, the candelabrum forgotten in her hand. "Don't do this. Don't do it, Fulke. Don't do it. Fulke, don't do it." She kept up this irritating repetition as she moved around him, trying to throw him off. "Don't do this, Fulke. Fulke, don't."

But Fulke was not thrown off. Quite the reverse. When his outstretched hand met the short edge of the dining table, he gripped it and steadied himself, and when he spoke, his voice was firm. "Madame Levis, you should try not to upset me. I don't need a weapon to kill your friend." As if to prove his point, he tightened his arm across Magda's throat, bearing down on her windpipe.

Rachel focused on that hard forearm and the face above it, on Magda's pale mouth gasping for air. If Fulke couldn't be shaken, her only option was to try to overpower him again. With a force born of fear and desperation, she took a long step toward him and swung her right arm wide. With one arm around Magda and the other holding the table behind him, Fulke couldn't move swiftly enough to block the blow. The candelabrum hit him in the temple, and this time he crumpled to the floor, unconscious.

Released, Magda took a great gasp of air, then let it out in a sob. She took one step forward before her legs gave out and she slumped onto the dining room rug. "Oh my God," she said, repeating it like a litany, or a charm, "OhmyGod, ohmyGod, ohmyGod. He was going to kill me. He was really going to kill me. You saved my life." She gave a little laugh, tight with hysteria. "You said you would, and you actually did." She stared up at Rachel with grateful amazement.

This was it, Rachel thought. She would never be more selfless or seem more noble in her life. She had felled a killer; she had saved a human being from certain death. Still feeling as if she were in a play, she was determined to perform the moment with panache. Keeping her hands steady, she put the candelabrum carefully on the table, then turned to look at Magda. Abruptly, the sense that they were onstage vanished. She had just solved a crime the police had dismissed as fantasy, knocked out a triple murderer, saved her dearest friend from someone who wouldn't have hesitated to kill her.

She wanted her mother.

She sat down hard beside Magda and hugged her, feeling her warm living weight in her arms. Staying there for a few seconds, she listened to her breathe. Then she stood up, smoothed the front of her shirt, took a deep breath, and said, "Where the hell are the police?"

Chapter Thirty-Five

"I can't believe the butler did it," Alan said. He, Magda, and Rachel were clustered around a table at the back of Bistrot Vivienne that evening. Alan gazed dejectedly at the tabletop as he spoke. "I didn't want to say, but I thought it would be Mathilde. After those arguments about money."

Rachel shook her head. "There were no arguments."

"But—"

"Fulke made them up."

"He made them up?"

"Isn't that terrible?" Magda was still outraged by this, as if being a murderer came a distant second to being a liar.

"I gave him an opening to steer me in the wrong direction, and he took it. There were no arguments with Edgar about money, and she wasn't cruel to Elisabeth." Rachel self-corrected, "Well, she was, but no more than usual. Fulke just made it up so we wouldn't consider him."

Magda's fingers strayed to the side of her neck. She said grimly, "When he was pushed, he had what it took."

"But pushed how?" Alan shrugged. "That's the part I still don't get."

"I don't blame you." Magda had heard the explanation already. "It's weird."

"It's not weird!" Rachel thought of Fulke as she had last seen him, sitting grayly across from her under the fluorescent light of an interview room. The police, delayed by a student demonstration on the Boulevard Saint Michel, had finally shown up and taken them all to the commissariat, where, after his interview, Fulke had asked to see her. He said he wanted to apologize. "It's not weird," she repeated. "It's sad. He killed them because he wasn't in their wills."

Alan stared at her blankly. "What?"

Magda said, "I told you it was weird."

Rachel sighed. "They didn't leave him anything. Remember, I told you that early on Magda and I thought Mathilde might have killed Edgar because she knew he'd reduced the amount of her bequest?" Alan nodded. "Well, we overlooked the effect of being left nothing at all." She leaned forward. "Fulke worked for Edgar for *decades*, with absolute devotion, but Edgar didn't care. When it came to it, he didn't make any provision for him. He included Elisabeth des Troyes, whom he'd used for his embezzlement, and he included his ex-wife who'd divorced him, but he didn't include the man who'd overseen his life for more than twenty years. And then, after Fulke stayed to do the same for David, the same thing happened! He was good enough to witness wills, but not to be in them." She paused. "So he did it because he felt"—she chose her words carefully—"taken for granted."

Silence. Then Alan said, "Are you serious?"

She nodded.

"But, I mean, it's counterproductive. If you're going to kill somebody over a will, surely you want it to be a will you're in?"

"That's exactly what Fulke said when he was trying to put me off the scent! And of course it's the logical way to look at it. But jilted lovers aren't logical. And effectively that's what Fulke was." She gave a sorrowful shake of her head. "He lived with Edgar for more than twenty years, cooked for him, anticipated his needs. And then all of a sudden he found out that he didn't feature as a person in Edgar's mind." She thought for a second. "That's the problem with anticipating needs, I guess. If you do it well, the other person doesn't realize they ever had them, so they can't be grateful that you've anticipated them."

"You know, I've been thinking about that." Magda's voice was speculative. "I suppose it does make a strange kind of sense for Edgar. But David had only just inherited—there hadn't been any time to create expectation."

Rachel remembered Fulke's shoulders slumped over the aluminum police table, his eyes wide as he looked at her: "Monsieur David knew Monsieur Bowen had left me nothing. And if I had been working for Monsieur Bowen for over twenty-five years, I had been working for Monsieur David his whole life." His voice trembled. "I helped him tie his shoes!"

Rachel had longed to take his hand, but she knew the young gardien on duty would tell her there was no touching.

"I'm sorry, Fulke," she said, then reflected that it must be the first time someone had apologized to a murderer for his motive.

"Thank you, Madame Levis." He would remain formal to the last.

"Constancy creates its own bond," she said to Magda, refocusing. "Or it can. It had in Fulke. He'd been a constant in David's life, a loving and devoted helper. But for David, that constancy just made him part of the furniture. Like father, like son. And so," she grimaced, "like father, like son."

"Well, not *exactly* like," Alan pointed out. "David's murder was much more violent. Why such different methods?"

Rachel shrugged. "Different circumstances. With Edgar, he had more time to plan, to brood on his injury and eat his revenge cold. Whereas with David . . ."

"I was so angry. I was overcome," Fulke had said. "Otherwise, I would never have used the candelabrum." He looked regretful.

"And when he realized that there was no way to cover up such a violent crime," Rachel continued, "he told a story about the men in the elevator coming around. That wasn't true either; they were just plausible suspects. But with Edgar he wanted something that would look natural, so there would be no suspicion and he could stay to help David. So he waited until a night when Edgar decided to have soup, and he made some extra. Then he . . . well, he . . ." She took a breath. "He drowned him in it. He told me that he stood where he would stand to serve, as if he were waiting for Edgar to taste the soup, and just as he picked up his spoon, Fulke pushed his head down." Alan looked shocked.

"Of course, everything went everywhere," said Magda, who had heard this part of the story in the taxi from the commissariat. "But he knew where replacements were. A new tablecloth, napkins, and he'd made extra soup, so he could fill a new bowl and make it look as if Edgar had just fainted into it. And then he hid the table linens to take them to the pressing when he went out the next day."

"And that's where Catherine comes in," Rachel cut in. "Because she came to pick up her things from the appartement before he'd taken the linens to the pressing. He didn't say how, but she found the original tablecloth where he'd hidden it—"

"She did seem like the type to snoop," Magda interjected

"Talking about snooping," Rachel said, "the receipt for them was still in the pile I saw, buried in there. If only I'd had the sense to look at each one closely."

"Beginner's mistake." Magda patted her hand.

"Anyway, she found them, and she took a picture of them with her phone before she left. Then she blackmailed him with the photo."

"Madame Nadeau was a very foolish woman." Fulke had shaken his head under the harsh light. "One would never have thought she'd make the connection. Perhaps her need for money sharpened her powers of reasoning." He didn't seem particularly sorry that he'd killed her, and he confirmed this impression by adding, "But it didn't sharpen them enough. I offered to bring her payments to her apartment, and I made two visits before I did anything, to accustom the neighbors to seeing me. The third time, when I got there, it was easy to back her out of the window and then wait and slip out in the hubbub over the body." He looked thoughtful for a moment. "I always found her very vulgar."

"And leaving the tablecloth to be discovered wasn't his only stumble." Magda's interjection brought her back to the present. "In the heat of the moment, he made a mistake with the wine too." She and Rachel exchanged a glance of vindication.

"He was nervous," Rachel said to Alan. "You can see how it might happen."

"Oh yes." He nodded. "I'm always nervous after I drown someone in a bowl of soup I've spent all day preparing."

She ignored him. "He was nervous, and Edgar had knocked over the original bottle while he was . . . um . . . struggling in the soup. But Fulke wanted it to look like a simple faint, nothing disturbed. And after he'd changed Edgar into new clothes—"

Alan gave a small twitch.

"I know, but I suppose he was used to at least *helping* Edgar dress, and fully dressing him was just one more step. And after he'd done that, and changed the linens, and the bowl, the nearest bottle to hand was the one he'd been planning to have with his own veal." She looked down. "I never considered that Fulke might like rosé." She felt ashamed. Fulke was right: she'd never really granted him any more humanity than the others had.

"Wait, the *butler* was having veal?" Alan raised his eyebrows. "It sounds to me like he was doing just fine. He didn't need to be included in anybody's will."

"Oh, Alan!" Rachel laughed, but then she sobered. "That's not the point, and you know it. Loyalty is the point. He'd been loyal to them, and he thought they should be loyal to him."

"And quite right." Alan put his hand over hers. "Loyalty deserves loyalty in return." Then he straightened up. "So, 'Amateur Investigatresses Solve Unnoticed Murder.'"

"Investigatrices," Rachel corrected automatically.

He let it go. "Very well done, ladies. Allow me to buy you a bottle of ruinously expensive champagne in admiration." He raised a hand to catch the waiter's eye. "I'll tell you this, though," he said over his shoulder to Rachel.

"What?" She smiled at him.

"You can cross 'butler' off that list of servants you should have. We're never hiring one."

"Wait," said Magda, who wasn't quite done. "I have one more question."

"What?"

"Edgar said you could choose a book for yourself when you'd finished. Now you're finished. So, which one are you going to pick?"

"Oh, that." Rachel saw the waiter coming toward them. "I'll tell you next time."

Glossary of French Words and Phrases

à bientôt—until another time
à deux—for two
ah bon?—really?
aide de bureau—office assistant or Girl Friday
'Allo—hello
alors—a word with many meanings. It is often used at the beginning of a sentence in the way English uses "Well . . ." or "So . . ."
ami—friend/boyfriend
amoureux—lover
apéro—apertif
appartement—a very large apartment
ascenseur—elevator
avocat—lawyer
les bagues—braces
bateau mouche—river boat
bien—all right
bien etablis—old families
bienvenue—welcome
bon—good or okay

bonjour—good day
bonsoir—good evening
boulangerie—bakery
bouilloire—electric kettle
boules—A French game in which small balls are thrown at another ball
bureau—study
un cabinet—a lawyer's office
les cabinets—a polite and slightly old-fashioned word for the bathroom
ça suffit—that's enough
café americain—black coffee
cahier—notebook
carte bancaire—ATM card
ça va—it's okay
cave/caviste—wine stop/wine salesman
C'est finis—that's finished
chambres des bonnes—small single room originally used for servants
citron—lemon
citoyen—citizen
comme tu veux—as you wish
commissariat—police station
le culture pop—pop culture
d'acc—okay
Dans sa soupe?—In his soup?
de rien—it's nothing
désagréable—disagreeable
désintox—rehab

distributeur—cash machine
enchanté—pleased to meet you
enfin—at last
excusez-moi—excuse me
frigo—refrigerator
fruit vert—literally, "green fruit," but also a name for a girl much younger than her lover
funérarium—mortuary
gardien de la paix—low-level police officer
hein—eh? or, right?
Infogreffe—register of businesses
jeune fille—young girl
hôtel particulier—townhouse
macaron—macaroon
Madame—Mrs. or madam
maître d'hôtel—butler
mais bien sûr—of course
mais oui—literally, "but yes," but used to mean, "of course" or "I swear!"
mesdames—ladies
mon Dieu—my God!
Monsieur—Mr. or sir
mouchard—snitch
nécrologie—obituaries
n'est-ce pas?—right?
notaire—a type of lawyer, roughly equivalent to a notary public
nous ne sommes pas des touristes—we are not tourists
nouveau riche—the newly rich

objets—objects
oeufs en cocotte—coddled eggs cooked in cream and butter
oh là là —oh dear!
pardon—pardon me
pas de vente au détail—no retail sales
père—father
petite souper—little supper
petite amie—girlfriend
pinces à cheveux—bobbypins
portable—cell phone
porte d'entrée—the public door opening from the courtyard onto the street. Most Paris buildings have a large outer door that leads to an interior courtyard; the actual buildings open off this courtyard.
pressing—the dry cleaners
ravissante—lovely (literally, ravishing)
résidence—a grand house
rue—street
salon—a grand or rather grand reception room/living room
séjour—a living room
secrétaire de direction—personal assistant
s'il vous plait—please
soigné—dignified
tarte tatin—apple tart
terrasse—paved or enclosed area outside a restaurant
université—university
vichyssoise—a cold leek and potato soup
vieilles fortunes—old money

Legal World and Police Ranks

The French legal system is very much like the American one, although also different in some significant respects. In this book, all that matters is that there are notaires, who are essentially notary publics and who deal with wills (legalizing them and reading them), and avocats, who act as lawyers.

Regarding the police, the ranks are as follows:

gardien de la paix—roughly equivalent to a police officer
brigadier—roughly equivalent to a sergeant
capitaine—roughly equivalent to the US detective
lieutenant—the same as in the United States

Acknowledgments

On September 30, 1628, Fulke Greville, Lord Brooke, was murdered by a servant. The servant was enraged that Brooke hadn't put him in his will. That counterintuitive crime was the inspiration for this mystery, so the first person I'd like to thank is Fulke Greville. Thank you, Lord Brooke, for laying down your life so that detective fiction might flourish: I thought naming a murderer after you might redress the balance somewhat. (And, awkward as it is, I suppose I also must thank Brooke's murderer, whose name was Ralph Haywood.)

In the world of the present day, my greatest gratitude goes to my agent, Laura Macdougall. She saw something worthwhile in a very early manuscript and stuck with me until I produced a mystery I could be proud of. She has quite literally changed my life. I also thank my editor, Chelsey Emmelhainz, who made this book the best it could be. She's patient, she's fair, she's canny—and I am lucky to have her. I also owe a debt of gratitude to Jenny Chen, who copy-edited this not-very-detail-oriented woman to perfection.

I'm also grateful to Mikhail Xifaras, who introduced me to the real Paris and who welcomed me into his home and family.

Acknowledgments

I give enormous thanks to my lovely friend Ruth Mattock for repeatedly putting me up in her tiny Paris room (later repurposed as Rachel's first flat) without flinch or complaint, including once when I was unexpectedly turned back by British immigration. I want to apologize again to her sister, whose weekend was ruined as a result of that.

I'm grateful as well to all the AirBnB hosts in whose apartments I stayed while doing research and whose floor plans I used to make some of the homes in this book. In the same vein, I give huge thanks to and for Google Satellite, which made up for the fact that I have no sense of geography by allowing me to rewalk the streets of Paris even when I wasn't there. In fact, I should give thanks to the internet generally, as it taught me how to pick a lock, how to knock someone out with a single blow, how to say "the bathroom" politely in French, as well as countless other small facts that influence this mystery.

Closer to home, I want to thank Sinéad Moynihan, who suggested I write this in the first place, and Kirsty Martin, who was always interested in its progression. Richard and Caroline Fox earned my eternal gratitude by reading a first draft thoroughly and thoughtfully, giving feedback that made all the difference—and, in Richard's case, supplying the names of the wine. Thank you. Ronald and Sara Piddington hosted my first reading, and I thank them for that—and for imbuing me with the Piddington love of a theme.

My father, Thomas H. Jackson, will never know this and wouldn't agree with it if he did, but whatever good writing this book possesses is down to him. Thank you, Daddy. And my mother let me read the whole manuscript aloud to her, a sacrifice so mom-ish that all on its own it would put her in the top tier of moms—had she not already acquired a place there because of the support and applause she consistently gave me as I wrote, rewrote, and rewrote again.

I also want to apologize to any and every person I didn't respond to, didn't get feedback to swiftly, or just plain neglected while I was writing and revising. And I want to thank the friends who let me behave that way without ever taking me to task for it, and who cheered me on even as I did so, particularly Ashley Bruce, Ryan Ammar, John Bolin, Jeremy Burns, Lydia Burton, Christine Dymond, Jemmelia Jameson, Katina Laoutaris, Stephen Markman, Hélène Martin, Sam North, Mercedes Okumura, Henry Power, Andrew Rudd, and Valentina Todino. And how could I not thank Dr. Marren, friend, cheerleader, and serene elegance personified?

As for Jennifer Piddington, not only does she know what I do, but she also knew what I could do. And that is much more important.